Bad Boy
BENEFITS

Bad Boy BENEFITS

J.D. HAWKINS

Copyright © 2021 by JD Hawkins

All rights reserved.

No part of this book may be reproduced in any form or by any electronic or mechanical means, including information storage and retrieval systems, without written permission from the author, except for the use of brief quotations in a book review.

Paige Press
Leander, TX 78641

Ebook:
ISBN: 978-1-953520-72-2

Print:
ISBN: 978-1-953520-73-9

ALSO BY JD HAWKINS

Behaving Badly Series

Playing Doctor

Bad Boy Benefits

BS Boyfriend

Cocky Men Series

Cocky Chef

Flawless

All In

Bad Boys Series

Confessions of a Bad Boy

Love and Ink

Unprofessional

Temptation

Insatiable Series

Insatiable

Booty Call

The Bet

ABOUT THIS BOOK

She's my sister's best friend...

The night we hooked up was definitely the best in my life. But you know sisters—they make things complicated.

So Maeve and I called it one and done, and for the sake of their friendship, we pretended it never happened.

It's pretty easy to develop a routine. We joke around, make fun of each other. And I never let on that I know what Maeve looks like without her clothes—or how often I think about it.

I'm starting to think we pulled it off when out-of-the-blue she sashays back into my jewelry store. The visit starts like normal. The banter. The teasing.

But then she invites me to a party. And what kind of gentleman would I be if I didn't walk her home after?

Let's be real—I'm no gentleman. And Maeve is no lady.

The kind of teasing we're doing now is dangerous. This is fast becoming a frenemies-with-benefits situation. It's complicated enough before my sister decides to set us up... with other people.

We can only keep our secret for so long.

I'm starting to think there might be a diamond in all this rough.

But Maeve never lets me have the last word...

1

TOBY

"Show me your woman."

"Huh?"

The guy looks at me over the glass jewelry counter like I just spoke an alien language. It's a beautiful Saturday morning, the clean L.A. sun exploding through the windows and dancing across the precious stones and metals I sell in my shop; shimmering and sparkling like there's magic in here. There is, in a way.

"Your *fiancée*," I tell the guy. "The woman you're about to propose to? The love of your life, the whole reason you came into my shop looking for an engagement ring in the first place. You don't have pictures of her on your phone?"

"Uh...yeah. Sure," he says, reaching into the pocket of his expensive-but-poorly-fitting suit to pull out his phone.

As I'm waiting, I glance over at the other counter to my assistant, Sharon, and give her a quick wink while she tends to a young Japanese couple. Five years ago she was an awkward, mousey college student who only applied for an internship at my shop as work experience for some management course she was taking. At the time, my jewelry business was one slow weekend away from failing, but she was desperate enough to risk it. Now Miracle Isle has become the hottest jewelry shop in the city—and Sharon isn't too far behind.

"Hold on a sec," the guy says, still fumbling with his phone.

"Sure, buddy."

I take a good look at him, though I sized him up the second he parked his Mustang Mach 1 outside and walked in. Mid-thirties but with a boyish face that's losing its handsomeness by the minute. Inoffensive haircut that he probably hasn't changed since the two-thousands. A slight beer belly he's given up on, though he still makes an effort with his clothes. An unremarkable guy. Probably came from a nice family, easy job, never had any big challenges in life, and maybe—more revealingly—never felt the need for one.

"Here," he says, holding the phone out. "That's her."

Though he intends to show me at a distance, I take the phone from him and check out the hot blonde in the picture. I let out a high whistle, and start scrolling through some of the other pictures too confidently for him to protest.

"Goddamn," I mutter, peeling my eyes away for a second to nod at him briefly. "She's a dime."

"Yeah. She is," he says with slightly embarrassed pride.

She's way out of his league, but she doesn't have the resting scowl-face of a gold digger. My guess is she's either a childhood sweetheart or just plain down-to-earth. Which makes me lean away from the kind of ring I call the "basic bitch": a big, round, brilliant cut stone in a classic prong setting. In platinum, of course. Maybe with a halo of small diamonds.

This girl will want something low-set that she can wear to the gym, something that won't snag on her sweatshirt when she's camping. A ring that's not so glitzy it'll draw tons of attention, but still unique enough to stand out. All of this flashes through my mind in a second, and I hand the guy his phone back with a nod.

"Very nice. So what were you thinking about putting on this fine young woman's finger?"

The guy peers over the counter and points at a ring.

"I think I'm gonna go for this one," he says.

I glance down and raise a brow. Platinum, prong setting, brilliant cut. "What's that?"

"This one? The one-point-oh-six carat?"

I look up at him but he's still studying the ring until I let out a little chuckle and draw his sudden attention.

"What?" he says.

"Come on, friend. I know you're not really that cheap."

"*Cheap?*" he says, too stunned to be completely offended. "It's five figures!"

"Barely," I say, still amused.

"That's a lot of money."

"Pfft. Who cares about the money? A ring is an investment. It's going to stay in the... What's your name?"

"Greg Miller."

"The 'Miller' dynasty for generations."

The guy laughs.

"I'm not sure about that."

"Sure it is. Tell you what, I'll cut you a deal," I say. "I'll give you the ring for that nice little Mustang you pulled up in."

"You kidding?"

"I'm deadly serious."

He twists his boyish face up into a look of confusion. "Why would I do that?"

"'*Why would you do that*' –exactly," I say, relishing the

feeling that I'm getting him on the hook now. "That Mustang's worth at least five times as much as this ring."

"Yeah but... I mean... That's my *car*. My pride and joy. I practically *live* in that thing."

I open my arms wide and shrug at him emphatically. "And what's your wife gonna do with her engagement ring? Only put it on in the shower?"

The guy squirms a little and I take the opportunity to round the counter so I can put an arm around his shoulder, both of us facing the array of shining jewels behind the glass.

"What kind of car could you get for the price of that ring you just pointed out, huh?" I say in a friendly tone. "A nice used Corolla? A beat-up 80s Corvette?"

"It's not really the same thing..."

"Damn straight it's not the same thing. A car gets less valuable the longer you own it. Takes money just to run a car. You can change a car whenever you want, but the only way your wife gets to change her engagement ring is by ditching you."

He shoots me a look that's meant to be offended but he can't hide the flash of concern in his eyes.

"How would you feel," I continue, "if your wife bought you a twenty-ten Honda Acura as a *symbol* of your love."

"I mean, it's not a bad car..."

"It's a great car. Sure," I say. "As a symbol it says that she thinks you're a *great* guy. But five years down the line... ten years...you're gonna be in that Acura and you're gonna think, *is that all I am?*" I let that sink in a while and the guy sighs, slowly starting to get it. I lean toward him as if whispering a secret. *"Why not the nine-eleven? Why not the Jag? She had one shot and she went for the Acura."*

He stares at the ring intently, his lips twisting a little.

Suddenly he laughs and looks up at me like he's just understood a punchline. He points at me.

"You're just trying to upsell me," he says. "Just trying to squeeze some more money out of me. I get it."

I look at him with a deadpan smile, then gently turn him around to face away from the counter, at the rest of my shop.

"Take a look, friend," I say. "It's nine-thirty in the morning and I've already got eight people in here. At least four of them are buyers. The old guy in the pinstripe and Cuban heels? That's drug money. He'll probably tip me more than that ring you want is worth. That guy in the khakis who didn't even comb his hair? That's Colorado millionaire money. Odds are he'll buy a necklace worth thirty k for his twenty-five-year-old girlfriend and still feel like he got a deal because it's half as much as he pays in alimony. In two hours I've got a backroom meeting with a Bollywood star who never spends less than six figures here."

I turn to face him and he's so enraptured he mirrors me.

"I'm trying to upsell you," I say firmly, "but it's not about the money, friend."

"What's it about then?"

I tap the back of my hand against his chest as I speak.

"It's about your wife. It's about *love*, man."

The guy starts to laugh but doesn't finish it once he sees the seriousness in my face.

"Huh?"

I take the phone from him again and say, "Look at her. *Really* look at your wife. As if you've never seen her before."

He looks from the phone to me then back again.

"She's beautiful," he says, though he sounds uncertain, as if giving the answer to a test question.

"She's a dime," I say, flicking through the pictures until I get to one of her in a bikini.

"Hey!" he says, when I settle on the bikini pic.

"Look at that body," I say, ignoring his protest. "You know how much work goes into a body like that? We got the best restaurants in Los Angeles... *Dunkin' Donuts* exists and your wife has a body like *that*—come on!" I flick through the photos. "Look at this makeup."

"What makeup?"

"Exactly. You can't tell. This woman's an artist. She can shade better than most art majors. And her hair... Not a strand out of place in any of these pics. I don't blame you for not noticing—she makes it look effortless. Good dresser, too. Most Hollywood actors need a team of stylists to pick clothes this well, this consistently. Look, even her pajamas are stylish enough for a red carpet."

"Hey," he says again when I settle on the pajama pic, and this time I let him grab the phone from me and put an arm around his shoulder conspiratorially.

"My point is," I continue, "your wife puts a lot of effort into how she looks, into what she wears on her body. And this ring... It's going to be something she wears all the time. Maybe the most important thing. She's gonna have to match it with every outfit. It's gonna have a lot of meaning to her. You get where I'm coming from?"

The guy sighs and twists his lips a little, then nods reluctantly.

"Sure, I get it...but...well, what do you suggest?"

"Have you heard of 'the four Cs'?"

He nods. "Of course. That first ring checked all the boxes. Cut, clarity, carat weight, color—"

"Forget all about 'em. You need a stone with a soul, not just one that looks good on paper." I move away from him, clapping my hands as I move back around the counter. "Now let's see," I say, looking over my merchandise with fresh eyes. "Lot of clues in the pics. Your wife's favorite color is green, clearly—"

"I knew that," he says quickly.

I glance up at him with a little smile.

"Of course you did... So something that'll make green pop. Maybe a red or pink stone accent? A gold band? Now...she's active, so you'll want a low setting. And she's not the flashy type, either, so the stone shouldn't be too big..."

"Yeah, yeah," the guy says eagerly. "Absolutely."

"But more than one carat for sure...maybe a trilogy... Hold up," I say, holding out a finger as I move away, "stay right there. I'm gonna make you make your wife happier than any other man on this planet could."

I wheel around the counter, past Sharon, to a storage compartment tucked away beneath one of the displays and grab what I'm looking for, then return holding the box as delicately as a ticking bomb. I lay it on the counter in front of the guy, and then gesture for him to open it.

"This is it, my friend. This is the one."

He looks at me a little nervously, then carefully opens the box. Inside is any woman's wet dream of a ring: a 1.5 carat center diamond, bezel set, with two flawless, pear shaped, deep red ruby side stones, all done in 18k. I make an explosion sound with my mouth. The guy whistles.

"Holy shit..." he says.

"Right?" I say, with a big grin. "It's perfect, huh?"

"That price..." the guy says, and I realize his whistle had nothing to do with aesthetics.

I let out a sigh and put a hand to my face.

"Okay, okay, okay," I say, defeated. I reach under the

counter and pull out the original ring he was looking at and place it beside the spectacular one. "You win. You like this one, customer's choice. It's *your* engagement."

Sensing that he's won, the guy says, "I get that you're trying to help. But it's just a ring. And my wife—*fiancée*—she understands we don't have that much money to burn on it."

I look at him with a mixture of incredulity and pity.

"She'll understand?"

"Yeah, she will. We love each other, that's what matters," he says.

I nod.

"Kinda sounds like the money matters a little more."

The guy laughs, incredulous at me now.

"Dude," he says, "I understand. You're trying to sell me on the other ring. It's your job. But I just can't spend that much. We're still paying off the house. And when we get married there's gonna be a whole lotta things I got to spend money on."

I look back at the guy and he looks back at me with an empty-headed grin. I don't know why I'm so set on trying to get him to buy the better ring, but something about the whole thing has just gotten under my skin. Maybe it's that this clueless, unremarkable man doesn't seem to realize that he's landed an extraordinary woman well out of his league. Maybe it's that he doesn't seem to respect the two things I love more than anything in this world: jewelry and women. Maybe I just like a challenge after my morning coffee.

"You know why I like jewelry?" I say wistfully, changing the tone between us completely. "Why I got into the business?" The guy looks a little stunned, but raises a curious eyebrow. "Because it's *permanent*. It lasts. Clothes, hair, fashions—they all change. The way people talk. The

Chapter 1

way they act. Even the way they think. It changes. But a quality, well-cut diamond was beautiful a hundred years ago, it's beautiful now, and it will be beautiful long after we're gone. Not even art lasts as long."

"Um... I'm not sure where you're going with this, dude."

"That's why we give diamonds to our partners," I say, feeling like I'm just thinking out loud rather than telling him anything, "because the other thing that lasts forever is *love*. Because it's a symbol of how tough and beautiful and long-lasting love is."

The guy looks at me like I'm a street corner evangelist he'd like to hurry away from. I gesture around me.

"Every piece of jewelry in here is a story. Sometimes the story ain't that interesting. A Colorado millionaire who's been burned too many times trying to find a piece beautiful enough to win something more than mercenary affection from his mistress. An aspiring rapper looking for a rock so loud and expensive that it can manifest the destiny he wants." I pick up the cheaper ring and hold it aloft between us, at eye-level. "I've worked with jewelry long enough that I can almost see the stories right there in the rocks... You know what story I see between this ring and you?"

The guy shakes his head and shrugs impatiently.

"I dunno. What?"

"Five, maybe ten years from now... Maybe you have kids... Neither of you have looked at the wedding photos for a long time. You've let yourself go, she's still trying to look her best but she's succumbed to the family budget and the fact that the kids come first... And you have an argument, except by now arguments are as common as conversations—maybe even a little more. And then a little later she's thinking about whether it was all worth it.

"She's thinking about all the guys—and there's for sure a

lot of them—that hit on her, that wanted her... All those other potential futures... And maybe she's eating her dinner, or washing her hands, or driving with her hand on the top of the wheel, and this ring... *This* ring...draws her eye... And she'll know exactly what you were thinking when you bought it—your wife knows about these kinds of things... And she's gonna think..." I take a moment, pause for dramatic effect. *"That cheap motherfucker. Even at his best he came up short."*

I snap the ring box shut in one hand with a loud clap, and put it behind the counter.

"I'm not selling you the ring," I announce in a firm tone, as if that little reverie was shut away with the ring.

"Excuse me?"

I look at him as if offended that he would make me repeat myself.

"I'm not selling you the ring."

"You can't do that," he says, sounding as confused as he is surprised.

"I told you: it's not about the money to me. *You're* the one thinking in dollar signs."

"Are you for real?" he asks.

"Do I look like I'm joking?"

"I'm just buying a ring, dude—"

"Then find another jewelry store—one that 'just sells rings.' I don't. I sell symbols. Stories. Manifestations of people's desires and feelings. You want to 'just buy a ring' for a cheap price, then find a gumball machine."

The guy shuffles on his feet and looks around him for support, but the store's so busy nobody's got time to notice the strange look on his face. He looks back at me and laughs awkwardly, stuck halfway between disorientation and anger.

Chapter 1

"What the hell's going on here?" he says. "I come in to buy an engagement ring and the next thing I know you're telling me about arguing with my wife and insulting me. What the hell, man?"

"Insulting *you*? Let me tell you something. I'm a romantic—I play the field plenty, but I'm a romantic at heart. Maybe I always want what I can't have, maybe I'm too picky, maybe I just can't give up the field—that's for *me* to worry about. Point is, I believe in love. Then a guy like you walks in here—one of the best jewelry shops in southern California, maybe even the whole state—a guy who bagged himself a dime against all odds. And you want me to sell you a ring like you're shopping for groceries—checking the price first.

"You don't even care what you walk out of this shop with. I'll bet if I went out there and scratched your car, you'd show more emotion than you have buying the symbol of your love for this woman. You talk about insults—that's an *insult to me*. That's an insult to me as a jewelry shop owner, and more importantly, an insult to me as a *romantic*. Do you get what I'm saying?"

Greg Miller stares at me like a fish, then gives me that awkward laugh again—a laugh I've grown to dislike immensely, and which I'm sure his future wife will one day hate.

"I just wanted to buy a ring, dude."

Just then, over his shoulder, I catch sight of somebody a million times more interesting, and even more beautiful than his wife. It makes me suddenly aware of how much time I've wasted on the guy, so I decide to get it over with.

"I'm gonna do two things for you, okay?" I say with an air of finality. "I'm going to knock twenty percent off the price of this—" I tap the glass behind the ruby trilogy ring on the counter. "And I'm going to give you the rest of the weekend to think about it—because you seem like a guy who needs time to figure things out. Now if you'll excuse me, I've got some other business to attend to. I don't wanna see you back here again unless you've made the right choice. Okay, buddy?"

I don't give him time to respond, and move around the counter instead to get a good look at who just walked in before I approach her.

She's alone, but she has the presence of an entire crowd. Maybe it's because she's impossible not to notice, so everyone around her becomes engulfed by her aura, lending her their energy via looks and awareness. She's taller than the average woman, aided by a pair of red heels that she walks on as if she was born in them. A light summer dress over her body, white and patterned with tropical flowers that seem to come alive with her movement. The dress clings and hangs over every curve—her hips, back, breasts...accentuating every elegant, swinging step she takes. A small, blue, leather handbag bouncing against her hip in a way I can't be the only guy to think is erotic.

She's more than a sexy body, though. She's a pretty face as well. Eyes so exquisite they could turn you to stone, and lips so sensual they could kiss life back into you. A platinum blonde pixie cut that reveals every delicate contour of her cheekbones. A neck so soft it's as much a turn-on as any other part of her. High and haughty, her shoulders pinned back confidently, chin high, back hard and straight and just begging to be pressed against... Bent over... Everything on her draws the eye.

Those pretty feet in those high heels, her slender calves, the asymmetry of her hair to that mouthwatering neck, the knowing eyes. The silver bracelets pulling my attention to the graceful movement of her hands.

Even though I know her, every time I see her it feels like the first time.

Maeve.

She's my sister Mia's best friend, which is why she's completely off limits...but we've got history. Not enough to fill a textbook, but a weekend hot and crazy enough that it stuck in my mind all these six years later—even though I don't remember much of it.

Maeve likes to party, just like me. She also knows that the best kind of fun is the kind you have in private...just like me. But in the end, when it came down to it, she knew anything more, anything longer than a weekend, would have probably put Mia in the middle when it blew up, and Maeve cares about Mia more than any quick thrill. Just like me.

I watch her glide through the store, perusing the merchandise, her powerful presence causing people to move out of her way even though her gaze is toward the displays. When she bends a little to look at something more closely, I have to bite my lip to stop myself growling like an animal.

She knows she's hot—there's no "innocent little beauty" act with Maeve—but it wouldn't surprise me if she knew I was watching her right now. Nothing gets past her. I've heard a lot of women complain about men playing games with them. Maeve loves it, because the guys who try always end up losing more than their shirts.

Somehow, I manage to peel my eyes from the way that summer dress falls and sways over her ass to check on what piece has grabbed her attention. I find something better than anything I own: a pair of hard brown jewels gazing back at me in the reflection of the display.

I laugh gently to myself, then stick out my tongue to show that I've found her out. She doesn't show an inch of guilt as she stands up straight and glances back at me over her shoulder, pushing a strand of perfect hair behind her ear and smiling as if she wanted me to catch her looking. She probably did.

I round the counter and make a beeline for her.

"Toby," Sharon calls but I wave her away, my full attention reserved for Maeve now.

2

MAEVE

"Of all the jewelry shops in all of L.A..." he murmurs in that unmistakably mischievous tone.

I don't move away from the display, but turn my head and allow him a brief smile before turning back to look at the pieces. He's not looking too bad these days. Either he's been hitting the gym or pulling back on the drinking—the smart money would be on the former.

Wavy auburn hair that's a few shades darker than his sister Mia's coppery red, with just enough product to tame it while looking natural. Green, palm tree-patterned short sleeve Hawaiian shirt over a white tee, aviators hanging from its collar. Tattoo sleeve on his muscled right arm, Rolex on his left. And underneath it all, the kind of body that you rarely see outside of an underwear ad. Despite his many other faults, Toby's always had that thing rare among men—the ability to look like what he really is: a flashy, roguish party animal who rarely thinks more than ten minutes into the future.

"Yours is the only one with a parking spot," I finish for

him as I move away from the display and saunter over to the counter on the other side of the shop.

He laughs as he follows me closely. His assistant calls him but he doesn't break step, and remains by my shoulder while I peruse the bracelets below the counter.

"Ah come on, Maeve," he says through a smile. "Don't pretend you didn't come in here for the *personal* attention I can give you."

"Well, you do have to deal with the rough to get to the good diamonds."

"Seriously," he says. "This is the first time I've ever seen you in here. Were you just in the neighborhood and realized you need a gem-studded whip? A gold-encrusted ball-crushing device, perhaps?"

I stand up straight and turn to project my smile at him finally.

"I'm definitely *not* interested in the silver-tongued lothario."

"Oof," he says mockingly, slapping his hand to his chest. "*Lothario? Me?* You of all people know I'm actually a romantic, Maeve. Unlike you I actually believe in lo—"

"Oh honey, don't tell me you're still using that line," I say, turning back to the jewelry. "It's too depressing to think there might still be a woman out there naïve enough to believe it."

"You know, I've got a piece in the back that would look great on you," he says.

"Let me guess—it's in a discreet spot behind some boxes and the entryway is so tight I'll have to remove my clothes to get in there."

I glance at him and enjoy the half second of hesitation in his smile. His eyes trail an imaginary hand up my bare legs, into the curve of my waist, over my cleavage.

"Of course not," he says. "You're hardly wearing anything as it is."

I let loose an eye roll and a sigh, turn back to the pieces, and move along the counter, past where he's standing, my side brushing slightly against his leg. I know exactly what I'm doing. The little game we play.

"No thanks. I'm not in the mood for disappointment."

To others it might seem like an odd thing, our semi-insulting flirtations with each other. But it's an odd relationship. We're just about acquaintances—friends only via our connection to Mia. Familiar enough because of that lapse of judgment so many years ago, but otherwise strangers in all aspects of our lives.

I'm not shy when it comes to men. Not afraid to take what I want from them, and experienced enough to be able to tell if they even have anything I want at first glance. Without Mia, without the messiness and risk involved in getting in deeper with my best friend's brother, I would have had my fill of Toby in a week and been done with him —maybe two if he was lucky and I was particularly bored.

He would have been a nice little plaything. Good in bed, often funny, potentially able to spring a few amusing surprises, and able to carry his own as a plus one. Any other man, and any other situation, I would have ended it as suddenly as I started it, leaving him wanting more (I always get bored before they do). In another lifetime, Toby would be begging me to let us "try one more time," and I'd be avoiding him because of it. Luckily, we both came to our senses and agreed our little frisson would end the same weekend it started, before our mistake turned into a problem.

But because we finished where we started, our relationship is forever stuck in that night so many years ago. An eternity of flirting that we both know can go nowhere, that we've already *agreed* will go nowhere. I'm fine with that, and judging by all the reports I hear of Toby screwing his way through every hot, unavailable woman in Los Angeles, I guess he is too. It's better for both of us if we remain as we are—frenemies.

"How's Mia?" I ask, ditching the flirtiness for a moment and turning to face him head-on.

"You probably see her more than I do these days." He shrugs. "I spoke to her on the phone yesterday. She sounded good. Baby Alison is keeping them both plenty busy. But she and Colin are still staying in his apartment while they're looking for a house."

"Well, you know Mia—if there's a wall one inch from where she wants it, she won't settle. She's probably done a degree's worth of research into building materials already."

Toby laughs and nods.

"At least she was smart enough to marry a guy who could put up with her overanalyzing," he says. "She did say something about dinner at her place this week. I guess you'll be going?"

"I guess I might," I say nonchalantly, then turn back to the jewels. "To answer your original question, yes, I *was* in the neighborhood. I'm attending a very lavish birthday party this evening and I need a fabulous gift, and given your history of unseemly bragging about the shop, I hoped you'd have just the right thing. My friend wears necklaces a lot—shorter ones, she's all cleavage—but I don't want anything too flashy. Something classic, minimalist. Like the one you gave to Mia."

"Stay right there," he tells me as he starts to move away. "I wasn't joking when I said I had some great stuff in the back."

Chapter 2

A few minutes later he emerges on the other side of the counter and lays out a cloth spread with several glimmering necklaces, the dancing light on them drawing me in for a closer look.

"These are lovely..." I murmur as I pick out one with a hammered O-shaped pendant and hold it up.

"So your friend with the cleavage," Toby asks with a half-smile I can see through the necklace. "Do I know her?"

"I don't think so," I say, turning the necklace in the light. "She's too sweet to move in your circles."

"Is she single?"

I turn my eyes from the necklace to him.

"Aren't you still chasing that married pop singer from Texas?"

"I wasn't *chasing* her," he says indignantly. "I'm not that kind of guy. Not a homewrecker. I was just...infatuated. In love. The heart wants what it wants."

"She was very hot. You sure it was your heart that wanted her and not another part of you?"

He groans a little, losing his smile at my undermining of his emotions. I place the necklace carefully back down again and peruse the others.

"You wouldn't understand, Maeve. You're incapable of love."

"I wouldn't say that. I'm currently having a tempestuous, on-off relationship with a Margiela dress. And I've got a pair of Louboutins I've been in a loving, loyal union with for nearly a decade."

He says nothing for a while, and it's only when I pick up another necklace with aquamarine beads and hold it to the light that I can see he's watching me keenly, studying my face with an expression of deep, intense thought on his brow.

"You can't really think that," he says, in an almost intimately sincere tone. "I find it hard to believe a woman can be that cold all the time. So...opposed to the idea of romance."

I smile and lower the necklace, but keep my eyes fixed on his, so he can see the sincerity in them.

"It frightens you, doesn't it? That a woman might actually *not* be besotted with the idea of 'soulmates' and 'relationships' and 'everlasting love.' It *terrifies* you to think a woman might actually be perfectly satisfied with a complex, diverse wardrobe and only need men for the occasional distraction."

Toby laughs but I can sense the lack of confidence in it. The assistant calls his name again but he ignores it once again.

"Why would that frighten me?"

"Because you've been using the 'dashing romantic' line to pick up women for years now," I reply easily. "Talk about finding something hard to believe..."

"It's not a 'line,'" Toby says, trying to sound cool but there's a quickness in his tone which indicates I've touched that nerve again. "I mean, I like to have fun—sure. But I'm not dumb enough to think I can keep doing that forever. *You* aren't either, Maeve."

"No... You're right," I sigh, as if giving in to his incredible logic. I give him a moment to feel as if he might have cracked me, then say, "I suppose at some point I'll have to get a dog." Toby shakes his head and smiles, and I hand over the necklace. "I'll take this one. With your most generous friends and family discount, if you please."

He gives it a quick polish with a cloth and tucks it into a nice velvet box. I watch him as he gift wraps it.

Chapter 2

"So tell me more about this party tonight," he says casually. "What's the venue?"

"It's at her place," I say, then sigh. "She's old money, so it'll probably be full of boring stiffs and their obnoxious offspring. But it's just next door to me, so I'll be able to escape easily enough."

"Old money, huh?" he says as he ties a ribbon around the box with a dexterity that's almost arousing. "I love rich girls."

"Of course you do—they tend to lean a little on the gullible side."

He shrugs. "I am getting a little bored of sweaty nightclubs and dive bars..."

I grin. "Are you angling for an invite?"

Toby finishes the wrapping, then slides the box across the counter to me.

"Depends whether you're angling for a date. A platonic one, of course."

Cocking a brow at him, I give it a think. Being within a ten foot radius of Toby is like playing with fire, especially when Mia isn't around to keep us on our best behavior...but he's on the rebound, per usual, and there will be plenty of single women for him to choose from tonight. Women who aren't me.

In fact, that must be the whole reason he wants to go to the party—to pick up his latest victim. It has nothing to do with me. Which is why it's completely safe for us to be there together. Completely.

"All right," I reply, looking him up and down. "It's a date. A not-date. As long as you wear that gray Tom Ford suit you have—and *anything* but black shoes with it."

Toby grins as he takes my card from me and charges it.

"I forgot how much you like to give orders."

"And I remember how ghastly some of your sartorial choices are," I say as I take my card back, already stepping away. "Nine p.m. The house just to the south of mine."

His assistant calls his name again and Toby finally rushes away. I take a few steps to the door but then turn and move to the other side of the shop to appreciate a pair of earrings that catch my eye. Toby's obscured by the growing crowd at the counters now, but I can hear his confidently loud voice cut through the hubbub.

"Ah! Greg Miller—that was quick... Good decision. I knew you'd see sense, buddy... *Her?* Ha ha! No...not my wife—never will be anyone's wife, buddy. That one's not marriage material...she's a tiger."

I smile to myself, holding back a laugh, and then move toward the exit feeling inexplicably fantastic.

3

TOBY

It's been a while since I wore that gray suit, but when I dig it out and put it on, I remember how good it looks, how good I *feel* in it. No surprise Maeve remembered and gave the advice—she works in fashion. A designer... Or no, was it a buyer? Something in management? I don't remember. Strangely, or perhaps not, my immediate instinct is to wear black shoes with it, but her words echo in my mind like a warning and I resist. Going for brown leather just as instructed.

I wasn't lying when I said I hadn't been anywhere fancy for a while, and she wasn't wrong about me falling for that pop star five minutes away from becoming famous. Tara—an all-American blonde singer-songwriter from Texas. How could I not, when I saw her in those cut-off jean shorts and cowboy boots? At a gig in a dive bar, I spent the whole evening working my magic on her as she worked some kinda magic on me, but as usual, just before I made a move she told me she was taken. Story of my life. It's happened so many times to me that my first reaction was to laugh.

Mia once told me that it's not bad luck. She said a part

of me enjoys falling for women I can't have. Like I enjoy being some kind of lovesick loser, or I'm so used to getting what I want I've become obsessed with the things I can't have. I told her she was being overanalytical again; being complicated when it's actually pretty simple—the best girls are all taken.

I'm just about getting Tara out of my system now, thanks to about fifty nights out at the hottest events, about a dozen one-night stands, and a couple of girls who are still sending me nudes and asking for another round. Even the fact that Tara's been getting progressively more famous isn't fazing me much anymore.

The last time I saw her, I was turning the TV on to some morning show she was being interviewed on. A pang of painful regret in my chest made me have to click it off immediately, though those jean shorts made it a little tough. I guess I'm still healing. But surely someone at the party tonight will catch my eye. Give me the distraction I so desperately need. Though it's Maeve that's got me distracted, if I'm honest with myself. Still, I'll be on my best behavior. As my sister's best friend, Maeve is firmly in the no-fly-zone.

The suit's got me feeling classy for the first time in such a long time that I decide to drive my classic Ferrari to the party. Only five hundred were ever made, and the only way to one-up a rich dude is find something he can't buy even if he wanted to. But first I need to get it back from a film director who's been desperate to buy it from me for years now.

He's a quiet guy, obsessed with his craft, but when I get to his home I find it full of glamorous stars and their entourages, all taking a break from a script reading, enjoying the sunset by the pool. I manage to turn down his insistence

Chapter 3

on having a drink with them, but not the introductions. I take a few numbers, leave a few cards (including one to a Spanish actress whose incredibly erotic eyes seemed to already be looking at me whenever I turned to her) and manage to get out with the car despite the director insisting we make a deal right there and then for it.

I take a quick detour into the hills to drop off a pair of earrings to one of my oldest clients, spend the next twenty minutes politely declining the offer of dinner, and then get back to my car. When I check my phone, it's filled with the usual Saturday night offers to come to this rave or go to that bar or check out this gig. I ignore them all apart from the girl who sends me a hot selfie of her in the bathroom somewhere, her name a mystery to me, though I have her down as "the all-nighter" in my phone.

What time did Maeve say again? Ten? Eleven? Either way, I'm late by the time I'm done with all that, and I still have to make a stop since the director gave me the car with hardly any gas in it.

Pumping gas at the quiet, empty gas station, I suddenly feel reflective and content. The smell of the fuel mixes with my cologne. Far off in the distance there are sirens, the occasional sound of drunk laughter. Lit-up billboards reflecting across the Ferrari's feminine contours. From the open space of the gas station you can look off far into the streets beyond, catch the dark silhouettes of the mountains, and it feels like the city of L.A. goes on forever, that the joy of its million parties is somehow being carried on the air. Nights out always give you these strange moments of quiet in the midst of the madness. Or maybe I've just been smelling too much gas...

A laugh from somewhere behind me breaks my mood and makes me realize the gas station isn't as empty as I thought. I turn around to see two women by an SUV—both of them looking at me. They laugh again and it sounds like the sparkle of champagne.

Both of them are tall brunettes in minidresses so tight you can count their ribs, high heels they probably needed stepladders to wear. I smile back at them as the pump clicks and I put it back into place. I keep my eyes on them as I move toward them, grabbing the receipt that's printing out.

"Nice car," one of them says through a pouted smile.

"It's as fast as it looks," I reply without breaking stride.

The girls seem to find this hilarious, hands to their mouths as they laugh, leaning on each other so they don't topple off those heels. It brings a smile to my face as I step inside the station to get an energy drink.

I find myself behind a blonde just as tall as the other girls—no minidress, but her leather pants leave even less to the imagination, and the white blouse above them accentuates a rack I feel like I should be paying to see. Just beyond her, the attendants are changing shifts, counting out the register, and the blonde's looking wistfully outside. She glances at me. A hard, serious face; I'd guess Scandinavian. A flash of green eyes that catch the light like a cat's. A glance is all she needs to imprint the memory of them on me.

As I thumb my wallet counting bills I say, "So you're the designated driver, huh?"

She flashes those emeralds at me again, her hard lips in a tiny smile.

"I don't drink anyway."

I look out of the window to see the minidresses throw another champagne laugh into the sky.

"Looks like they're not letting your share go to waste," I say.

That thin smile again, green eyes lingering on me a little longer. She turns back to look at her friends, and after a little too long says, "To tell you the truth, I'd rather be at home with a book."

I forget counting dollars and consider her a little more thoughtfully now.

"You're in the wrong city for that."

That thin smile again. "Maybe," she says.

"No," I say, a little more loudly, as if we've gone beyond idle chitchat to a proper conversation. "You know what I think? I think you just need a different kind of Saturday night."

Now she lets those green eyes rest on me.

"Is that so?"

I nod and look out at her friends, who are still staggering just to stay upright.

"Yeah. I'm guessing your friends drag you out regularly, right? They like the bars where it's too loud to talk, and the guys are too dumb to say anything interesting anyway."

The blonde breaks into a small laugh, looking down at her chest as if feeling guilty for it.

"They seem like nice girls," I continue, "but they can't resist getting smashed while you have to watch from the bar with your orange juice, fending off guys while you make sure they don't do anything they'll regret *too* much."

"Something like that," she says, looking away again.

"And there's no chance of you convincing them to spend an evening at the theatre—you're outvoted two-to-one." Those eyes soften a little on me now. "But that's no reason to make the weekend as boring as a weekday."

She lets out a gentle sigh. Eyes not quite rolling, but her expression says it all. She knows I'm hitting on her, and I'm probably the twelfth guy to do so this night.

"And you're the guy who can show me how to, I suppose?"

"Something like that," I say, mimicking her words and her tone. "An hours-long drive across the coast, at night with the windows down, neither of us saying a word until I drop you off and you tell me what a good time you had."

That thin smile again, but the eyes are squinting at me a little, half confused at the idea of me taking her out and saying nothing, doing nothing.

"Ma'am," the attendant calls, snapping her away from scrutinizing me. I wait behind her as she pays and a minute later she turns back to me.

"Annika," she says, holding out her hand.

I take it and say, "Toby," then reach into my pocket and give her my card.

She looks at it for a moment.

"A jeweler..." she murmurs.

"I'm all about beautiful things," I say. I step closer to her, intimately close, as I move past her to the attendant. "Any time you want something different."

I move past her to the counter and pay for my drink, pretending to be done with Annika as I pull out my wallet and pay, though I look back out the gas station window when she leaves. Legs incredible in those leather pants, a posture as gracefully composed as her expression. When she pushes my business card into her bra, I can't help smiling. I turn back to the attendant to see that he's as impressed as I am pleased.

"How the hell did you do that, man?"

I laugh when he says it.

"Is it the clothes? The car?" he asks, his curiosity intense.

Chapter 3

I look at him with a smile—a slightly chubby guy in his early twenties.

"You just got to offer women what they don't have."

He screws up his face, glancing outside where the girls are bundling into the car, then back at me. "What? A silent drive?"

"She's the quiet type," I say, nodding outside to where the SUV is pulling out. "Likes to keep her thoughts to herself. But unfortunately she was born in the body of a goddess. Imagine looking like that. Every day guys from eighteen to eighty try to get inside her head and inside her pants. She probably can't look outside the window without getting hit on. And then on the weekend she has to be the responsible one while her friends have a good time.

"So yeah...a silent drive—the chance to spend time with a man who isn't trying to get her to 'open up' or 'give in' is the one thing she doesn't have."

I tap the counter to say goodbye, then turn and leave the station, checking the time and wincing a little when I realize how late I'm going to be to the party.

Maeve lives in Beverly Grove, a pretty upscale part of L.A. that's south of the Sunset Strip in Hollywood and north of all the businesses on Wilshire in Miracle Mile. A big house on a street of big houses. The kind of place where you could knock on any door and be answered by a household name. There's a lot of money in fashion, but it helps when there's a line of men begging to buy you dinners and fund any side projects you come up with.

Finding the place is easy—I just follow the trail of expensive cars. At this time of night, the party's already spilling out onto the street. Luckily, finding a parking spot isn't too hard either. Most guests are probably neighbors, or too determined to drink not to Uber.

I guide the Ferrari through the wrought iron gates, past the appreciative gazes of a few stragglers, then swing it into a gap under a manicured oak tree, right beside a Rolls Royce. I get out and take everything in with a low whistle. The place is twice as big as Maeve's, and I take my time moving toward the Tudor-style house, soaking in the vibe and getting a good look at the people there.

It's old money, for sure. The men look pampered and the women look bored. Tuxedos and gowns. The music not too loud. Laughter that sounds restrained. I pass a waiter carrying a tray of drinks and grab myself a glass of champagne, then decide to round the building and head for the heart of the party at the pool to the back.

It takes me about five minutes of strolling around the pool area to get the lay of the land, and eventually I remember why I haven't been to this kind of party in a while. Nearly midnight and nobody's been shoved into the pool. Nobody dancing, as if their greatest fear is creasing their clothes. Most of the people here already know each other—hence the bored looks. Worst of all, there are about five guys to every girl.

This doesn't look like it'll be a night to remember, but still, I might be able to find a few potentially big clients for the shop. I continue stalking the crowds, throwing out a few smiles, standing around to listen in on a few dull conversations about property and politics. Eventually a young guy whose easygoing manner looks out of place comes up to me to talk about the Ferrari. We chat a while and I eventually ask him if he knows where Maeve is.

"Maeve?" he says, looking around the pool. "You might wanna ask Chad there. He works with her."

The kid points out a tall guy with tanned skin that's so deep it looks like he uses furniture polish on it. Hair with so much product, he could probably take it off like a hat. He looks like a knock-off Ken doll. He's talking to a woman and clearly not doing a good job of it. I catch a slightly repulsed look on her face as she walks away.

"Thanks," I say, handing the kid my card and setting off to engage the waxwork.

"Chad?" I say holding my hand out. "Toby. You work with Maeve, right? Any idea where she is?"

He grabs my hand and smiles like he's up to no good.

"She's probably in the bathroom getting railed by the third guy this night." He laughs too much at his own joke, and I find myself mimicking the same look as the girl he repelled. "How do you know her?"

"I'm an old friend," I say, already looking around to extricate myself from him.

"There's a lie," he says, laughing again. "She might have friends, but not old ones. They turn into enemies pretty quick."

I frown at the guy, but he's so dense he doesn't pick up on any of my irritation with him. "You sound like you don't like her."

"Oh, I like her," he says, lowering his voice like a schoolboy about to tell a secret. "I'd like her to sit on my—"

"You sure you don't know where she is?" I interrupt, before the guy angers me enough to make a scene.

He shrugs and takes a long sip of his drink. "Try inside. The birthday girl's been in the living room all night. Maeve's probably with her."

"Here, hold this a second," I say, handing him my empty champagne glass and heading into the crowd.

The house seems almost bigger on the inside, but after weaving through partygoers like one of the waiters, I find myself in the living room. It's furnished with the over-exuberance you would expect. All old antiques and a huge stone fireplace that probably never gets used, a bunch of framed large paintings alongside a gigantic TV, and speakers big enough for a block party. The anxiety of old money trying to distinguish itself from the new.

And then I see Maeve. I didn't need to look for her—she attracts the eye anyway. In a little purple dress, not tight enough to kill any mystery, but hugging her waist enough to beg the question. Short blonde hair slicked back, a few strands loose, framing her face. She's in a group of about four men and two women, all of them looking at her even when she doesn't speak. Even money can't change the fact that she looks a cut above.

I sidle toward a wall and lean against it so I can look at her a little while. The party might be disappointing, but Maeve never is. Maybe it's the lingering lust from Annika at the gas station, maybe it's the drabness of everyone else here, or maybe it's the way those strands of hair dance and touch her face in a manner so tender, I forget for half a second all the reasons nothing can happen between us.

She looks like a prize. Like a mountain to conquer. More than a woman. The kind of challenge that ancient Greek men would have fallen to in droves. Untamable but irresistible with it. Enough to make a married man doubt his life choices, and a single man wonder why the hell he'd chase anyone else.

I shake the thoughts out of my mind just as she catches my eye across the room and uses me as an excuse to push her way out of the group she's in. The way she walks making the men in the room feel guilty about looking.

"I'm flattered," she says, glancing at a grandfather clock beside me, "only three hours late."

Chapter 3

"I had to stop for gas," I say innocently. "Anyway, I'm here now."

She smiles and places her long, feminine fingers on my shoulder. "And *I'm* just leaving."

"Already?"

"I've got plenty I need to do tomorrow."

"But tomorrow's Sunday."

"No reason to waste it. Besides, we both know you didn't come here for me. Why not mix and mingle? There are plenty of sweet young things to go around."

I know there are, but she's drawn me in like a magnet already, and now it's as if something inside me can't bear to let her out of my sight.

"I'll walk you home," I offer, and with those four words, I feel a sudden crackle of electricity spark between us.

Our eyes lock, and Maeve smiles slowly.

"That's really not necessary, Toby," she says, her voice gone sultry and teasing. "I live right next door."

"Predators only need a second to strike."

"Oh, I know—I think one's striking right now."

I laugh and look around me.

"You got a lemon at your place?" I ask.

She narrows those cat eyes at me. "A lemon?"

"Yeah."

"I might," she says. "Am I going to regret telling you that?"

"This party's a bore."

"You did *ask* for an invite."

I nod. "Sure. But if I'm going to salvage anything of my Saturday night, I'm going to need to drive my car somewhere more exciting—and I've had a glass of champagne. I'm not drunk, but just to be on the safe side, eating a lemon overrides the effects of the alcohol."

She says nothing, but her expression articulates more than words. A slightly incredulous gaze precedes a full eye-roll that then relaxes into a look of indulging someone.

Without another word, she turns away and starts to walk. I follow her closely as she scythes through the crowd, which parts almost magically for her vibrant presence. A pause every now and then for her to say a goodbye and politely decline staying a little longer.

Soon we're outside, moving toward the front gates, and then stepping out onto the sidewalk. After the stuffiness of the party it feels like coming up for air. The sound now a muffled, mixed hum behind us. Maeve's heels a loud click, mingling with the cicadas. The air aromatic with neighborhood's carefully chosen citrus trees, blooming jasmine bushes, and gardener-maintained flowers.

Without turning to look at me, her head high and elegant, she says, "That Ferrari back there was yours, wasn't it?"

"How did you know?"

"You always were a show-off."

"No more than you."

As soon as I say it she stops and turns to me, offering me a wry smile. The sudden break in her clicking heels feels dramatic, intensifying the already-buzzing atmosphere.

"Excuse me?" she says.

I smile at her, enjoying the fact that I've drawn a reaction from her. With Maeve, that's a hell of an achievement.

"Maybe not a show-off…" I shrug. "But you can't deny you like attention. Being talked about."

"There's a world of difference between the two, honey," she says, quickly walking again so I have to jog a little to catch up with her leggy strides.

We turn to enter her gate, the trees around her Italian

villa-esque home muffling the sounds of the party even further. It's dark, but in the slivers of light from the street I catch the curve of her calf, her hair, the silky fabric of her waist-hugging dress, and I hang back a little so I can look at her. When she takes the couple of steps up to her door, her dress rides a little high up her thigh, and I start to feel like I've had a bottle rather than a glass of champagne.

She unlocks the door and steps inside, as if I wasn't there. I move into her house behind her and close the door as she hits the lights, tosses her heels away casually, and twists her neck as she moves toward the kitchen. It feels almost voyeuristic seeing her do that in the quietness of her house—her typical coming home routine. Strangely intimate to see that Maeve doesn't spend *every* second of the day with diva-ish poise.

It's been years since I've been in Maeve's house, and though the paintings, furnishings, and even the color of the walls are different, the vibe is the same. Sophisticated and individual. Fashion photography on the walls, presented with as much attention as a gallery. Paper bags with designer labels neatly arranged in the hallway, presumably for her job. Dim mood lighting, arched doorways, and exposed beams. Only a few ornaments, but each one of them interesting. It's a place like Maeve herself, meticulously put together and guarded—it makes you work to find its secrets, but you know they exist.

"A lemon," she announces as I enter the large kitchen. She places it in the center of the island, beside the dangerous-looking knives, puts her hands on the counter, and leans over it like a bartender.

I step to the other side of the counter, meeting her mildly amused gaze. Oddly, there are some dirty cups over by the sink, a few plates and cutlery. Just a few, but even the smallest mess seems a large one in such a perfect home.

"You want me to peel it for you? Cut it?" she offers.

"I'm okay," I say, pulling out the sharpest-looking knife with a loud, metallic sound. Maeve doesn't even flinch.

Within a few seconds, I've sliced the lemon and set the knife down beside it, Maeve watching me with an entertained interest. I look at her as I brace myself, then put the first slice into my mouth. I wince at the acidic sharpness, and for a second Maeve mimics my expression sympathetically, before shaking her head and laughing. I chew a little and swallow, then grab the next piece. Maeve only stops laughing for a second to look in disbelieving horror, then puts her hand over her mouth as she giggles, doubling over a little.

I work my way through the rest, my whole head exploding with the acerbic citrus and Maeve finding each new contortion of my face hilarious, until the whole lemon is gone and only the rinds on the table remain. I step away from the counter, shaking my head and blinking my eyes. She scoops the rinds and throws them away.

"That's the most interesting thing I've seen you do in a while," she says, turning to the sink to start washing dishes.

"Hoo! Like a drug," I say, still pacing, feeling ready for whatever party's coming next. "You should try it some time. Hell of a wake-up."

I stop at the counter again and look at her back as she washes those last few cups and plates. Her movements causing the hem of her dress to jog gently up her thighs. The curve of her back impossible not to stop and stare at.

"Oh, I'll watch you do that any time, honey," she coos, nonchalantly looking back at me over her shoulder, a strand of hair falling across her cat-like eyes, neck twisting beautifully before she returns to the dishes.

Maybe it's the lemon stinging my eyes, but the moment doesn't feel quite real. Quiet on a Saturday night, nothing but the sound of the tap and the cicadas outside. Glamorous, unimpeachable Maeve leaning over a sink. Everything so out of place, and yet making such a strange kind of sense that it could be a dream. And the second I start to feel like this could be a dream—her dress still shaking against her thigh, her back still arched forward, ass out toward me—I let my imagination get carried away with me...

I look down, trying to snap out of it. My hands are still wet with lemon juice, and Maeve left the knife on the counter. I take it and round the island to move beside her, a little behind her at the sink.

"Careful," I say.

It's a simple, innocent warning, as I bring the knife in front of her to put it in the sink, but it seems loaded, metaphorical, about something else entirely. As if I couldn't help revealing my inner thoughts, my inner fantasy, even in those two syllables.

She freezes, and I'm not sure if she's just waiting for me to put the knife down, or whether my closeness to her is catching her off guard. As if being this close she can suddenly read my mind. I drop the knife with a metallic clatter and she continues to wipe the inside of a glass.

"I guess I'll see you at Mia's," she says, and maybe my mind's working in overdrive now, but there isn't her typical sassiness in her tone.

I bring my hand under the stream of water to rinse it, and she moves to rinse out the cup at the same time, our hands accidentally touching. It feels like a static shock, but instead of moving away we both freeze instead. My fingers on the back of her hand beneath the running water and neither of us is doing anything is the most intense thing we've done all night.

I glance sideways at her, my head over her shoulder, my chest an inch from her back, and I see her eyes are closed. I push my fingers over her knuckles, then trail the warm soap suds back over the inside of her wrist. She drops the cup and starts to sway in front of me, shoulder brushing against my chest, head tilting, eyes still closed as I play tenderly with her fingers beneath the tap.

"This is a bad idea..." she murmurs.

"I know..." I reply, locking fingers with her and then drawing them up her forearm as she turns her palm to mine, my breathing getting heavier.

She's right. It's a bad idea. We've already gone too far. But we're just touching fingers and we could still make excuses...

Except my need for her is bigger than me now, overwhelming. My lust gathering too much momentum to turn away. Her soft, purring breaths turning me on too much, too fast.

My other hand behind her lifts the hem of her dress. She jumps a little when I bring my fingers to the back of her soft thighs, to her inner thighs, up to the curve of her tight ass. A finger between her panties and skin, down again as she squeezes her thighs together, a soft touch turning into a firm press, a desperate pull at her flesh. My nose is at the nape of her neck now, breathing heavily against her skin as her head lolls. Close enough to smell the champagne on her breath, the warm rush of her blood.

"We shouldn't..." she purrs.

"Then tell me to stop," I whisper back.

She says nothing, and instead pushes her ass further

back onto my hand, winding herself over it so my fingers slide between her ass cheeks, towards her wetness, her thighs squeezing my hand as if to pull them inside. Her hand teasing and twisting her fingers with mine while she braces herself against the sink with her other hand.

She catches her breath enough to say something else, but it only comes out as a soft moan. Her head leans toward me, her temple touching mine, that strand of hair tickling my face, and something clicks. It feels suddenly too intimate. A gesture too tender to write off as simply physical satisfaction. A feeling too profoundly gratifying to dismiss as a simple carnal urge.

As hard as it is, I manage to pull back from her, unwinding my fingers from hers, my hand from between her legs, and step back.

4

MAEVE

There's nothing crueler than a tease. People get used to pain, they can even draw a perverse pleasure from the nobility of suffering. But to show someone something they want, to *make* them want it, and then not give it to them? It's the ultimate punishment. I should know—I've built my entire personality around it.

And I'm not used to having it done to me. Which is why when Toby pulls away, I turn to glare at him almost angrily, and not just a little impressed. A man with restraint is a hell of a turn-on.

He stares back at me blankly, breathing slowly but deeply. I reach behind me to turn the tap off and the silence that follows seems to close the world until there's nothing but both of our excited bodies and the intense space between them.

"Why did you stop?" I say.

Toby smolders at me like we're in a Mexican stand-off. His only movement the rise and fall of his chest in that sexy suit, which frames his muscular, broad body beautifully. A shift in his jaw, a dimple, as if he's clenching down to hold himself back. His eyes dart away from mine, down across my body, to my legs and back, sending a little shiver through me. He looks like a mind bottling up something immense. A man one nudge from exploding. How can I resist that?

I reach forward and roughly grab the lapel of his suit, then say, "I didn't tell you to," as I pull him toward me.

It's just a tug, but it's all he needs, and he crashes into me like a freight train.

A mouth that tastes like lemon meeting mine hungrily, tongue a citrus sting. He slams me back into the counter with the force of his kiss. Hard chest squeezing my breasts, the bulge beneath his belt pressing me into place. I suck his tongue into my mouth until the acid makes my eyes water. My arms around his neck, clinging to him as we devour each other.

His rough fingers grab aggressively at the hem of my dress, lifting it roughly over my waist. They grasp and pinch at my ass, my hips, my thighs, until he takes a hold and lifts my legs, pulls them around him, feet off the ground.

My body is throbbing and soft for him now. The little buzz I was on from the party, the excited tingles from his game with the fingers at the tap, it's all deepened into a craving I can't hold back. The need for something hard and forceful to fill me up. For something big and determined to crush this heat out of me. And right now Toby is exactly that.

As soon as he sets my ass down on the counter, cold marble against my thighs, I tear my lips from his and nuzzle against the side of his face, biting his earlobe as he licks my neck. I reach down to his pants and start to unbuckle his belt.

"That's it, honey," I hiss into his ear. "Give it to me."

"Oh, I'm going to give it to you," he growls as his hand

Chapter 4

works its way up my thigh and inside to my pussy. "I'm gonna tear you apart."

The sex in his voice, hard and flinty, a primal sound that could only emanate from a man's lust, makes me smile. A half laugh, half purr emerging from my wet lips as I push my tongue into his ear. His fingers massage more wetness out of me as I unzip his fly and stroke the dangerous bulge in his boxers. The two of us intertwined now, arms grabbing and pulling as he pulls a condom from his back pocket and puts it on blind.

He brings his hand back to my panties, pulling them aside, and it feels so good I can't help biting a little harder on his earlobe. He recoils with the pain, hand at the back of my head, grabbing my hair to pull me away so we're both looking at each other. I give him a sultry smile and a tiny smirk appears in his expression of stern lust.

"Fuck, you're sexy," he snarls at me before smashing his citrus lips against mine again in a ravenous kiss.

I twist away, still enjoying the tease, and say, "Don't tell me. *Show* me."

He glares at me like it's a challenge, and a second later I hear the sound of smashed glasses as he sweeps them into the sink and dives into me. His teeth at my neck, hot breath like steam against my skin, fingers digging into my ass cheeks as he pulls my center against his, right onto him. I have to reach backwards to steady myself on the counter, squeeze my thighs against his sides, wind my feet around him like I'm taming a wild bull.

His cock presses against my pussy, hard and unyielding, our movements too desperate and instinctual to be anything but inelegant, and his head ends up pushing against my clit, shaft against my lips, though even this draws a gasp from me.

I grab his cock and guide him inside, and it's the last time I'm able to control myself, because Toby fucks me like he's taking revenge. As if the years of flirtatious teasing were just the longest foreplay he's ever had. As if he's aware that once this moment is over we'll have a whole lot to deal with, so he's damn sure going to make the most of it.

He's got me off the counter now, slamming the small of my back, my ass, against it for purchase. He claws at me almost viciously. Pounds his cock into me like he's trying to break me. Lifts my dress higher so he can squeeze and pinch at my breasts as if he wants to rip me into pieces. His mouth on my shoulders sucking and biting as if he wants to swallow me whole. Toby the fun-loving romantic's dirty secret is how rough he likes it—a fact I learned years ago and which I'm glad hasn't changed.

I let out the kind of moan I haven't been able to make in years, my voice vibrating to the rhythm of his lust.

"You like that, huh?" he mutters through gritted teeth like it's a threat.

Somehow, even in the throes of sensation, with one hand having to grab the tailored collar of his suit to keep steady, I gain enough control of myself to bring my head down and our eyes catch, lock, and we stare at each other like combatants. The animal desire in his eyes fascinating me. The unhinged lust in them making me feel divine. Until I lose our little game of chicken and have to toss my head back, his surging cock hitting the spot and sending an earthquake through me.

I forget where I am, what I'm doing. As if my soul is spinning in a bliss so rich and deep it's beyond time. Unable to think, my body only reacting instinctively to his, everything gone but this sensation of drowning in absolute pleasure. Spinning and flying weightlessly...

Chapter 4

It's only when he slams me back up against the refrigerator, its cold, hard metal against my back, that I realize he's carried me off the counter. The shock snaps me back into the present with a gasp, and I open my eyes to find his face close to mine. Tiptoes of my left leg down on the floor as he squeezes me into the cold surface, uses it to steady me as he pulls my thigh up against his side and continues to press a hand under my dress.

"You sexy bitch..." he growls in between lip-biting kisses. "You've been driving me wild for too long..."

A throaty laugh turns into a hissing breath in my mouth, suffocating slightly between his heavy chest and hammering cock. Squeezed and pressed by his hardened muscles until the sensation of blissful elation is compressed into a warm glow in the center of my body that pulsates with every thrust he makes and threatens to explode.

He kisses and bites, pinches and pulls, and when I open my eyes, I see him looking at me once again like I'm the biggest turn-on he's ever had. It only lasts a second, but it's like pulling a trigger for both of us.

He groans and I feel him come inside, hot and deep, the muscles of his body tightening into stone. As he spills into me, a shuddering inside sends embers through my limbs, and I use the last of my strength to cling to his shoulders. I squeal with my head back, letting the waves engulf me, until a cold, satisfying relief floods every inch of my body.

It's a slow, almost tender unclenching. The tight grip he has on my thigh softening, but gently holding my weight until I let my other foot onto the floor. I feel his breath slow against my neck, and I relax the life-saver tightness of my arms around him.

As slow as foreplay, we part. He turns away to pull the

condom off and discard it as I pull my dress down my waist and straighten it—though it's probably ruined.

"That's one way to sober up," I say, grabbing a half-full wine bottle from my rack and pouring a glass for myself.

He looks at me with a little cute bashfulness and shrugs. "I honestly feel a little more intoxicated after that."

I smile at him as I take a sip, then start to walk over to the living room.

"Guess I'll get going then?" he calls behind me.

I stop and turn to smile at him, taking another sip and dangling the glass between my fingers playfully.

"Got someplace to be? Another party, maybe?" I say with a smirk.

He frowns a little, confused. "Maybe..."

Another sip, another look.

"Who said this one was over?"

The moment the words leave my lips I cut a path toward my bedroom, knowing he'll be right behind me.

Because tonight, we're more than just frenemies.

We're frenemies with benefits.

5

TOBY

I've always been an early riser, never needing much sleep. It runs in the family, but while Mia used the extra time to study hard and overthink her life, I just used it to make the good nights last longer and leave before the mornings ruined it.

At Maeve's, I got up before the sun did, beside her naked body—as silky and luxurious as the white sheets. She didn't even stir as I pulled myself out of bed and got dressed, in the kind of peaceful and deep sleep only a night as exhaustive as the one we shared could induce.

That was half an hour ago. Now the sun is halfway up and I'm heading back up the stairs to her bedroom, carrying a tray loaded with croissants and coffee I just bought from a French boulangerie a few blocks away.

I had planned to leave; not even a plan, a routine at this point. I had meant to go next door, get in my Ferrari, and head home for a shower before I hit up some errands. But before I had even turned the engine on, I had changed my mind. Maeve isn't some casual, forgettably fuckable hookup whose name I'd have to put some effort in to remember—

she's my sister's best friend, and we've just broken a years-long promise we made to each other. Sooner or later we're gonna have to talk and make that promise all over again. Why not sooner? Or better yet, why not break things a little more before we fix them?

It didn't help that I woke up to the sight of her smooth back turned to me in the bed and couldn't get it out of my mind even in the sober light of day. My appetite for her completely renewed, as if the multiple times last night had never even happened.

When I step back into the room holding the tray, she's still on her side. The sheets twisted around her, clutched to her front, one leg and her back exposed like they're an avant-garde gown. Even in sleep she possesses some kind of intense elegance, a reposed, effortless, feminine sensuality.

I set the tray down on the nightstand and move back to where I was asleep on the bed behind her. Once again stunned, appreciating her all over again. When I run fingers down her thigh she groans and squirms as if melting into the mattress. My hand on her waist and she purrs. My mouth on her shoulder, the night's stubble tickling, the tip of my tongue tasting, and she sighs as beautiful as she looks.

She rolls onto her back in front of me, a dreamy smile on her face. Groggily, she opens her eyes, finds me in the mist of the morning, and immediately awakens fully.

"What the—" she yelps as she rolls away from me and onto her feet beside the bed.

"Morning, gorgeous," I say as I sit back on the bed to appreciate her nakedness.

She stares at me as if I just sprouted horns for a few seconds, her wide eyes and open mouth extremely arousing, then I grab a croissant to appreciate the novelty of seeing Maeve lost for words. And still naked. Only for a few seconds, and then she composes herself and moves to a dresser to grab a pair of panties.

"This isn't funny," she scolds with a growing composure. "You know the rules." She pulls out a pair of leggings next and slides her long legs into them in a hurry, but still with the grace of a ballet dancer. "If it's *their* bed, it's *your* duty to leave before morning."

"But I brought you croissants," I say, grabbing one and taking a bite as if to prove it. Immediately I hum at their still-warm buttery softness. "They're delicious," I say, muffled through the food. "You gotta try them."

She stops on the way from her dresser to her wardrobe and turns once more to glare at me. In nothing but her yoga pants she looks even more mouthwatering than the breakfast. Despite her naked breasts she still looks more proud and tough than other women can when they're clothed.

She frowns at me then says, "You woke up...went out...bought breakfast...and came back here?"

I smile and don't hide the fact that I'm looking at her breasts.

"How could I leave?"

Maeve turns, marches to the wardrobe, pulls out a workout tank, puts it on, and then strides toward me. Just as I'm putting the croissant to my mouth for a second bite she snatches it from my hand and dumps it on the tray, which she grabs and walks out with. I'm caught off guard for a moment, then bounce to my feet and follow her.

"What's the big problem, Maeve?" I say, following her down the steps into her kitchen. "I was just trying to be nice."

She turns in the kitchen to look at me and smiles so warmly I'm almost convinced she's not acting.

"That's very nice of you," she says, before scooping the

croissants into the trash can and grabbing the coffee cups to dump into the sink. "Thank you."

"Hey! You're wasting good food there."

"I'm on a carb hiatus—and I like to make my own coffee," she says with her back to me, as she busies herself doing just that in the kitchen.

I watch her for a few seconds, but she's so busy filling her coffee maker and cutting up some fruit that I could almost believe she's already forgotten about me.

"Fruit's a carb," I point out.

"Don't get cheeky," she snaps.

"You know..." I say. "I'm starting to feel a little unwanted."

"Trust your gut, that's what I always say."

I stare at her tight ass in those yoga pants as she makes her breakfast, except now my desire feels tainted, tougher. Less the exciting, eager prelude to something and more the uncomfortable yearning for something I can't have. It's mixed with guilt and confusion now, and there's something unpleasant about the mixture.

Maeve acting cold isn't rare, or much of a surprise, but here, now, it wasn't the reaction I expected. This is nothing like it was years ago, when we first hooked up. Back then there was a little mutual agreement, communication. This feels like something's up. I quickly search my memories of last night, looking for something I said or did that might have made Maeve act this way, but I can't find it.

"I know exactly what you're thinking," she says, bringing her fruit bowl to the island where she drizzles rose water on it. I'm on the other side and can see the nonchalant ease in her expression now. The sound of her Italian coffee pot steaming rises in volume behind her.

"What?"

"Firstly, you were staring at my ass."

"No shit, detective."

The tiniest, delicate smile appears in the corners of her lips. I only notice it because I'm looking at her so intently.

"Secondly," she continues, setting the dressing down and spearing a banana slice with her fork, "you're wondering if something happened, if something's wrong, if you did something to annoy me, etcetera, etcetera..."

She puts the banana in her mouth and I watch her chew it for a few seconds.

"Well, did I?"

She swallows and laughs, casually waving the fork now as if playing with me.

"Toby...honey...*bringing me breakfast?* What are you thinking?"

I shrug and look about me innocently, suddenly feeling like I'm on a witness stand for a crime I had no idea had even been committed.

"What's the big deal? I thought you'd appreciate something to eat when you got up... What's the rush? I thought we could hang out a little—"

"You thought we'd spend the rest of the day fucking," Maeve says bluntly, smiling broadly now. "Don't play the gentleman. Last night was last night. When have we ever 'hung out'?" she asks, looking at me keenly. "That's not what we do. We flirt. We ridicule each other. We cross paths, push each other's buttons a little, have our fun, and leave it at that."

"Yeah, but..." I trail off.

Maeve puts her fork down and moves to the refrigerator. I get a flashback to last night.

"But what?" she asks.

"But last night was different. You know... We actually made the mistake of—"

"No," she interrupts, pulling out a bottle of water and slamming the fridge shut. She opens it as she moves back to her salad. "Not 'we'—*I* made the mistake last night."

"What do you mean?"

She eats a few bites before answering. "You know exactly what I mean. I finally caved in."

"Whoa!" I suddenly call out loudly, holding my palms up and having to take two steps away from her then two steps back. I even laugh before I can continue. "You're not gonna paint this like *I* came onto *you*, are you?"

She stops chewing and looks at me with a raised eyebrow and a smile like I'm trying to sell her something fake.

"Is there any other way to paint it, sweetie?" she says, words dripping in sarcasm. "Begging me for an invite to the party? That whole thing with the lemon? I don't know where you learned that routine, but full points for originality."

I'm so filled with incredulity at the gall of this woman, I smack the table and facepalm as I walk away from her, then back into the kitchen, laughing.

"You *know* I ate that lemon so I could get the hell out of here—and don't even try—damn, Maeve! Come on. You're too smart to pretend to be dumb," I say, still laughing in disbelief. "You *know* what you're doing—what you *did*. That whole little ass routine."

"Ass routine?" she says, looking at me like I'm crazy.

"Yeah! Ass routine!" I say. "At Miracle Isle yesterday, bending over to look at the sapphires—since when are you into sapphires? You were just trying to get a discount! And then again, last night, turning around to wash those cups while I'm still here. As if 'Her Majesty Maeve of the shopaholics' does her own dishes! In your evening dress, even. Gimme a break."

"Ha!" Maeve laughs, head back and loud. "Listen to yourself. You're so cocky you think any woman turning her back on you is an invitation!"

I point at her accusingly. "You know asses are my weakness."

"Everything's a weakness when you're as horny as a feral animal."

Scowling, I shoot back, "Nothing's a weakness when you can't admit it though, right?"

"Admit it?" Maeve says, pretending to choke on a piece of orange. She clears her throat and smiles to the side as if an imaginary audience is there. "Do you honestly believe that I'm *so* short on male attention I'm reduced to enticing a man who has to be told not to dress in Hawaiian shirts?"

I put my palms on the counter and lean toward her.

"Yeah—when that man can fuck you better than every empty-headed poser and clean-shaven dullard you've been with in the past year put together."

She stares back at me, eyes narrowing slightly, our smiles for show, a challenge between us. For a moment there's a spark, a tension. But it's not like the tension of last night, the kind that threatens to erupt into something real, dangerous, and physical. It's the tension we've had for six years, of two people pushing the 'just friends' line as far as we can but not overstepping it. The tension of a boundary we formed all that time ago—a mutual agreement—and relishing the love-hate relationship we have with it. A flirtation more like competitiveness. A competitiveness too respectful to turn sour, and a flirtation too sexual to take seriously.

We break at the same time. Maeve dropping her head to her fruit salad, me sighing and turning away from the counter, both of us laughing. Not with sarcasm-drenched humor, but with relief now. In that instant, the weight of the whole night, what we did, and the consequences of it, disappear as easily as the sound of our amusement.

"I guess it wasn't that hard to slip back into the old rhythm."

"Of course," Maeve says, spearing another piece of fruit. "Business as usual."

I tap the counter as I turn to leave.

"See you around, Your Majesty," I call over my shoulder.

"Already dreading it," I hear her say as I make for the door.

6

MAEVE

I tend to wear skirts on Mondays. Today a leather one with heeled combat boots. Anything more comfortable or relaxed and I might succumb to the typical "back-at-work" fatigue. Midweek, I mix things up depending on my tasks. Fridays I dress most formally. As the head of buying for a fashionable department store chain, it's my job to be seen as much as it is to see. The younger men and women at work might be able to take the safe route of tasteful, classic compositions, but I have to uphold a higher standard. Not that I don't relish it.

Last month I told a national magazine that fashion was how I understood the world—I'm sure the interviewer thought I was pretentious, but it's the simple truth. It's a language. A collection of symbols we use to tell the world—and ourselves—who we are and who we want to be. Our aspirations and our desires. It's an art, and only disregarded as one because it is interwoven into life. To me, that makes it one of the highest arts of all.

A red button-up shirt, enough product in my swept-back hair to match the matte sheen of my skirt, a few chunky solid gold bracelets (vintage, thanks for asking), and a perfume as stark and cold as my appearance, and I'm ready to get to work.

Harrold's department stores have existed for nearly a hundred years, and the head office still bears the art deco fundamentals and sense of calm, sophisticated tradition, despite the tastefully chosen glass walls and modern desks. Heavy oakwood and structural detailing in the ceilings and doorways enclose spacious open-plan work areas and conference rooms with gigantic arched windows that people would probably complain break all manner of health and safety regulations were they not so beautiful.

It spans three floors of a building that also houses established legal firms and businesses equally as old and as respectful of their histories. Even the elevators possess the sort of old-world elegance that instills a sense of glamour to all who ride them.

I make my way through the lobby, past the tweed-suited gentlemen and intensely focused women there, my boot heels clicking loudly on the marble floor, echoing off the vaulted ceilings and across the professionally low-voiced crowd.

An older man, a familiar face from the bureau below, holds an elevator open for me and I step inside.

"Thank you," I say.

He conveys his warmth with a smile and a nod and by pressing the button to my floor.

The doors are inches from closing entirely before a desperate, youthful hand shoots inside and clutches at it desperately. I dart forward but the gentleman beats me to it as he stops the door from closing and pushes it open for the young woman to get inside.

Chapter 6

"Thank you!" she gasps, out of breath and agitated from running some distance.

"Morning, Harriet," I say as the elevator starts moving.

She's wearing a knitted, oversized crop-top with black jeans and black heels. Button-cute face framed with big, curly, eighties-style hair. She's one of my better protégés.

"Oh, Maeve," the girl says, "I wanted to show you my floor plan idea for the new rollout in the men's section of the shop in Bel Air."

She clumsily pulls away a few folders she's clutching to her chest, finds the right one, and opens it up to present to me. Harrold's is not just old in name—it's old in practices. So much of its internal documentation is still done via paper documents, which are filed via an inscrutable and archaic system. Honestly, I love it.

"You weren't working over the weekend, were you?" I ask her.

She looks at me guiltily, which with her big, expressive, dark eyes looks very puppy-like.

"I *really* wanted to do this well," she explains, as the doors open and the older gentleman nods to me before leaving.

"Then you should have had a little fun," I tell Harriet. "Inspiration finds you when you're not looking for it. I did visual merchandising for over a decade—I would know."

I take the folder from her and start to scan her work.

"Uh, I know," Harriet says, with the tiredness of a conversation we've had many times. "I just thought... Well, since the data team was really pushing for—"

"Screw the data, sweetie," I say, still staring at the folder as the elevator opens again on our floor and I start to walk with it. "They'd fill the stores with poorly made versions of last year's trends if we let them."

I stride past reception, between desks, and toward my corner office, never taking my eyes from Harriet's design strategy, but still receiving and handing out hellos to all the usual suspects. I know the office and its people like the back of my hand, like intimate family. I could find my way around in the dark and tell who's present by the smell of a particular cologne or the breeze from a certain window.

At the door to my office, I snap the folder shut and hand it back to Harriet.

"This is good. We'll talk about it more in the morning meeting."

She smiles and says, "Would you like anything with your coffee?"

"Whatever fruit's lying around would be fine, thanks," I say, waving her away as I turn to my door.

My office isn't the largest, but it's by far the most beautiful. Its gigantic windows offer a panoramic view of both the Verdugo mountains and the modest skyline of Downtown in the distance, the accumulations of my work—vendor samples, clothing racks, bolts of fabric, piles of fashion and architectural magazines and paper—lending it the atmosphere of an artisanal tailor's. A mahogany desk weighs it down, but the scarcity and beauty of the objects on it makes it more welcoming.

Walls of art and photography, a corkboard that's always cluttered in the most stimulating manner, a mannequin in the corner wearing some of our latest products—mostly decorative but occasionally useful. The office is beautiful enough that the magazine I did a piece with last month decided to take several pictures of me here, using the natural light from the breathtaking windows to create some rather nice images.

As always, I stand before the stunning view of the

sunrise over the city for a few moments to center myself and slow my mind down a little, then I get down to work on the pile of paperwork, catalogs, and printed requests that have been placed on my desk.

Three coffees and two hours later I've got a handle on things and I'm ready to attend the typical Monday morning meeting that I have with Harriet and Brent—the two assistants I'm working most closely with these days. It's held in a small, more modern, glass-walled meeting room on the other side of the floor, so I grab a few things as well as my half cup of coffee and leave my office.

I'm the first there, and take a seat at the head of the long table before bringing out some papers. Brent and Harriet arrive at the same time, carrying their laptops and coffees, both of them sitting to my left.

"So," I say, spreading out Harriet's folder, "let's get started. We can begin with Harriet's merchandising plan, which—"

"Actually," Brent interrupts, and I stop talking to glare at him. He shares a look with Harriet that's almost conspiratorial, then looks back at me. He's a boyish-looking beach-blond with a preppy style and an energetic way of moving his hands when he talks. "We wanted to..."

"Present something to you," Harriet finishes.

"Yeah," Brent continues. "It's like...our own idea."

"A presentation."

"No. More like a proposal."

"Right," Harriet agrees.

I fold my arms, swing my legs to the side to cross those too, and lean back in the chair.

"I'm all ears," I say.

"Well..."

"We were thinking of a...sort of..."

"A jewelry line, basically."

"Yeah."

I smile at them and their nervousness for a moment, then shrug.

"Good idea," I say. "I think it was inevitable anyway that we'd have to do something new with that. We sell well in the accessories department and we've got the capacity to increase it, but the problem is finding lines which are as high quality, well priced, and on trend as our clothing. Is that what you were so anxious about telling me?"

Again they look at each other like they're sharing a secret.

"Not exactly..." Brent says.

Harriet leans forward. "Well, there's more to it."

He nods. "Yeah."

"You see, we were thinking of doing our *own* line—"

"Under the house brand."

I lift a brow, but gesture for them to continue.

"I know we already have stuff under our house brand, but we were thinking more..."

"A brand *within* that brand..." Harriet puts in.

"Yeah, or, like, its own brand totally."

"Which we might even be able to sell elsewhere."

"Right."

I look at them both, Brent biting his lip, Harriet giving the puppy-dog eyes, and immediately realize there's more to what they're saying than just collaborating with a vendor on a new jewelry line—something which isn't remarkable or adventurous enough to warrant the nerves, even from assistants.

"Go on," I say, my tone making it clear I'm anticipating the tough part.

"Well..." Brent says, twisting his fingers together.

"Brent and I were throwing around ideas—"
"For the brand."
"And the marketing."
"We had one idea that just sort of..."
"It makes sense."
"Maybe not at first."
"But the more we thought about it, the more we loved it."
"It *really* would work."

My assistants have become an adorable, excitable, manipulative two-headed monster. I let out a deep sigh, getting a little impatient.

"So? What's the idea?" I ask.
"It's..." Brent starts.
"*You*," Harriet confirms.

Moments pass in which I feel like I know exactly what they're getting at, though it's so ridiculous I want them to confirm it themselves.

"Me?" I say.

They nod eagerly.

"The thing is," Harriet says, "all our jewelry lines are already affordable, fun, and cool, but according to the data, what we really need is something more..."

"Glamorous."
"Expensive. Investment piece-expensive."
"Exclusive."
"Avant-garde."
"High fashion."
"Bold."
"Yeah, bold."
"Adventurous but..."
"In a classic way."
"And that's...well, that's..."

"You."

"So..." I say blankly, knowing this is not what they mean, "you want me to choose the designs for the pieces in this new range?"

"We want you to be the face of it!" Harriet says, smiling triumphantly at being able to deliver the final blow.

I unfold my arms and rest on the table, tapping my fingers on the surface.

"I can see why you might think that's a good idea," I say carefully. "But there's a big problem: I'm not a celebrity."

"Oh, but you are!" Brent says with glee.

"You're the *perfect* celebrity!"

"Ever since you did that magazine piece people have been talking about you."

"And how stylish you are."

"And funny."

"Smart."

"On forums you're getting a sort of cult status."

"Photos of you at premieres and parties are popping up all over online in people's fashion idea blogs."

"And that documentary you participated in two years ago about that Italian designer."

"You were the best part of it."

"Even though you were only in it for a little bit."

"Somebody clipped your part and put it online—it's still getting a decent amount of views."

"We're getting more and more requests for interviews with you."

"Podcasts...documentaries..."

"Aspiring fashion critics who just want to work with you."

"You're *perfect*."

They stop on this note, and I have to admit they're

certainly passionate. Enough to flatter me, even though they know I hate it. At least at work. I let the silence go on a little before speaking—though I don't need to think about the idea much, it's just a question of letting them down gently.

"I really like that you're both thinking creatively," I say, "and looking for innovative, fresh ways to do things. But a few fashion obsessives posting on obscure forums isn't really enough to launch an endeavor as challenging as this."

"It's not just a few obsessives though," Harriet says, pushing another folder toward me.

"It's pretty influential people," Brent adds. "Last week a girl with two million subscribers did a video on your look at the premiere you went to in June."

"The magazine you did that piece in did a follow-up piece the month after with items you'd worn at the photoshoot."

"All these stories about you are circulating."

"*Good* stories," Brent emphasizes.

"About how you're always at the hottest parties, how you're so empowered."

"*Always* with a hot guy."

"Incredibly talented."

"How you don't take shit from anyone."

Harriet nods. "People want to *be* you."

"Or at least dress like you."

"You're becoming a style icon, Maeve."

"Whether you want to, or not," Brent concludes, looking a little afraid to say it.

This time I don't take so much time to answer.

"Even if that's all true," I begin, "it's not really something we can do—you know that. You'll have to run it by the data department to get a proper industry analysis and a P&L forecast—"

"Already did," Brent says.

"They say the online analytics of your name are all really great."

"Certainly good enough to act on."

I'm suddenly feeling like I'm losing power in this exchange.

"Okay. There's still the question," I say, "of the marketing department—"

"They love it," Harriet interrupts.

"It's not just publicity for the jewelry, but for the brand as a whole."

"They see it as purely additive."

"The accounting people like it too, you know, since they don't have to set aside cash for a celebrity."

Now I'm starting to realize I never had power in this discussion from the start.

Carefully, I say, "Home office has the final say, though. They'll want to see a full presentation, and the executives still need to give their approval for something as big as a new—"

"They're up for it if you are," Brent said.

Finally, I'm stunned. "What?"

"I bumped into Mr. Greer three weeks ago and just mentioned it casually."

"He's very friendly."

"*So* nice."

I uncross my legs and lean forward over the table, staring down at the folders before me as I consider an idea I would have laughed at half an hour ago.

"It's totally up to you, Maeve," Harriet says. "If you're not up for it, then that's that."

"Right. It's all up to you. It's just... It would work."

I take my time turning it over in my mind. It's not that

the idea of me having my own line, of essentially becoming a public celebrity, is strange, intimidating, or even challenging. The reality is that I'm already well-known on the L.A. circuit of lush parties and trendy events. I'm already a name that people talk about more to each other than me, I already have interested parties investigating who I'm fucking and where I'm going—I already have most of my style ideas stolen.

If anything, Brent and Harriet's idea makes almost *too* much sense. It's *too* easy and obvious. If I have any hesitation, it's in knowing that nothing is ever that simple. There's also the fact that it would make my status somewhat "official." I enjoy the fact that I'm talked about, but also the fact I can claim innocence of it. This would be like I'm finally acknowledging something which I enjoyed pretending didn't exist. I suppose it was only a matter of time, however.

I look back at them and smile.

"All right," I say, and they immediately squeal and jog in their seats at each other. "I'm up for it. But this is something that will need a *lot* of forethought."

"Of course," Harriet says, grabbing the largest folder yet.

"We've already worked a lot of things out."

Harriet drops the folder in front of me and it makes a loud slap, several photos slipping out. She turns to Brent.

"Should I start or you?"

Our Monday morning meeting ended up becoming a lunch one, and it's only by putting my foot down that I can finally stop Brent and Harriet from assaulting me with a never-ending stream of mood boards, logo ideas, advertising concepts, and taglines.

Once I break free of the terrible twins I head back to my office to make some calls. Brent and Harriet had the foresight (or perhaps deviousness is a better word) to clear my schedule of meetings before their kidnapping, but I still need to speak to a few people before they leave their own workplaces.

I'm halfway to my office when I hear my name called in a distinctly quiet but flinty tone.

"Maeve?"

I turn to the blonde girl who's getting up from her desk to come toward me. She's a quiet girl with a tortured, icy beauty that would have made her a film star in the sixties—though she'd probably have turned down every offer.

"Yes, Annika," I say. "Everything all right?"

"I wanted to ask you something..." she says, with atypical cautiousness.

I turn my body to dedicate my attention to her fully.

"Of course. What is it?"

She hesitates a moment and looks a little uncomfortable.

"It's kind of silly. It's not really about work."

Her careful tone is enough for me to dismiss my previous urgency.

"Come on," I say, nodding toward my office.

She follows me there and shuts the door behind her as I lean back against my desk to face her.

"Tell me, sweetie," I say in a more compassionate tone I reserve only for the most sensitive of people.

She stands there, probably feeling a little nervous but struggling not to look utterly beautiful.

"As I said, it's sort of silly."

"Nothing's silly if it's making you look like that. Go on, get it off your chest. You know you can trust me."

She looks at me, her face as still as her beauty, only her eyes darting about a little revealing her nerves.

"I met a guy—well, he hit on me. I guess," she says, taking a step toward me. "It was weird, but..."

"Weird?"

She reaches into the breast pocket of her loose, blue-striped linen shirt and pulls out a small card.

"He gave me his card and... Anyway, I probably wasn't going to... But I was sort of thinking about calling him. I don't know. I guess I was just bored..."

I nod sympathetically. It wouldn't be the first time someone had come to me for advice on romance, and I know that despite Annika's beauty she's fairly inexperienced. There's such a thing as too beautiful, and Annika probably intimidates all but the biggest assholes from approaching her.

"Okay," I say. "Well, tell me about him. Take your time."

"That's the thing," she says, looking down at the card. "I checked his name online and... I found a picture of him at some of the events you've been to. I thought you might know him..."

She hands me the card and I have to pretend to clear my throat to maintain any kind of poker face. *Toby Taylor. MIRACLE ISLE. Owner, Full Service Fine Jeweler, GIA Certified AJP + Gemologist. Bespoke design, stone setting, jewelry + watch repairs.*

There's a sudden knocking at the door and I instinctively yell, "Not now!" in my sternest voice. Then I look back at the card as if to double-check.

"I don't know..." Annika says. "You weren't even

standing together in the pic... I just wondered if you might have met him before."

"Yeah, I know him," I say, smiling up at Annika.

"Really?"

"Yeah. Pretty well, actually," I say, pushing away sudden memories of being slammed against my refrigerator. "When did you meet him?"

"Saturday evening," she says. *So right before he arrived in my neighborhood.* "So... What do you think of him?"

I take a deep breath, then sigh it out. That knocking at the door again.

"Get lost!" I yell, then relax my attention back on Annika. "Honestly?" I say, handing her the card back. "I don't think you should call him."

"Oh... I see... How come? He's not as nice as he seems?"

"No. Actually, he's a really nice guy. He's generous... funny...charming... He's a good guy."

Annika almost frowns at the card—as close to expressive as she gets.

"I don't understand. So what's wrong with him?"

"He's..." It takes more than a few seconds before I can figure out how to say it. "When it comes to women, Toby's somewhat...reckless."

"He cheats?"

"No... He doesn't do that. He just sort of...believes his own bullshit. He's incapable of thinking long term. He enjoys the chase more than what comes after. He plays the field quite a bit, but every once in a while he'll convince himself that he's 'in love.' But he's not really, he's just...a hopeless romantic."

"I see..."

"And in a way," I continue, "that's even worse. He'll end

up hurting you, and you won't even be able to hold it against him."

She nods, and then there's that irritating knocking at the door again.

"I'm gonna fire whoever I see out there!" I shout out.

"It's all right," Annika says, pocketing the card and turning to go. "I don't wanna take up more of your time, Maeve. Thanks a lot."

"If you're interested in dating, I could—"

"No, I'm fine. Really," Annika says, looking back to smile at me so I know she genuinely means it. She puts her hand on the doorknob. "Thanks."

I smile back and she leaves, her effortlessly striking presence replaced by the insidiously annoying figure of the man who was knocking.

Chad plays a painfully fake game of "accidentally" side-stepping and blocking Annika's path a few times, all the while beaming his big ivory teeth at her, then checking out her ass as she moves past him. He steps inside my office still smiling and shuts the door. I move around to my desk to get started on my work—partly to show him that I don't care much for his presence, and partly because looking at him is enough to make my skin crawl.

He's head of market analysis—the so-called "data guys," though the department is half women—but that's only the beginning of my problems with him. He's a creep with a terrible personality that not even his male-model good looks can redeem. For the past year he's been affecting a slight European accent, and been rejected by every woman in the building.

Fortunately, the slimeball works on a different floor, so having to see him wear white pants so tight I can see that he's circumcised, or overhearing him improvise a story about his prior night's "conquest" is a rare occurrence. Rare, but still too often.

He seems particularly happy today, which is making me depressed.

"So," he says in a cheerful tone, "you're gonna be a star, are you?"

"I already am one, sweetie."

He laughs but I can tell it's a little forced, that my lack of interest in his mockery has taken the wind out of his sails.

"I just figured it would be a sex tape that made you famous," he says. "Not a jewelry line." I say nothing, instead writing a few notes on Harriet's merchandising plan while he drones on. You get good at blocking people out when you work with someone like Chad.

"You know, I kept telling people it was only a matter of time," he says, casually checking out the mannequin and probably considering hitting on it, "until your ego grew too big for the company."

"Did anyone accidentally pay attention?"

He drops a folder on my desk and I glance up just long enough to see that his smile looks rather bitter now, his eyes glaring at me with a sense of defeated anger.

"The analysis for your new career," he says. "But if you want my advice—"

"I don't."

"—You'll ditch the idea before you make a fool of yourself."

"If you want *my* advice, Chad, you'll change your cologne. I'm going to have to get Harriet to make a copy of that report so my office doesn't smell like a slaughterhouse."

I continue to keep my eyes on my desk but I can sense his frustration from the way he dashes to the door. He opens it and stops, turning back for one final attempt at rattling me.

"You know, Maeve, it's only a matter of time before we hook up. It's inevitable."

I look up at him and laugh, genuinely amused.

"Oh, honey, even if I genocided a small country, I would still regard that as an unfair punishment."

Chad's face twists into a bizarre expression as he tries to look anything other than petulantly upset. He settles for pointing a finger-gun at me, winking, and leaving. I shiver the cringe away and get back down to work.

7

TOBY

"Be here at seven sharp, Toby."

"Sure thing," I tell my sister, gesturing across the shop to show Sharon that one of her regular and best customers just entered.

"I *mean* it. This isn't some all-night party we're having. We're gonna have the food ready for that time and we've got to think about the baby. If you turn up at nine we'll all have eaten and the food will be cold and we'll have probably put the baby to sleep already but you'll want to see her and probably end up just waking her up and—"

"Mia, relax. I'll be on my way as soon as I close up shop today. Straight there."

"Okay, good."

There's a brief silence on the phone and I decide it's the most natural time to ask. I walk into the back as I do so, not hiding anything, but feeling like I should.

"So... Who else is gonna be there?" I ask as innocently as I can.

"Ah... We've got a few people coming," Mia says, unable to hide a sense of mischief in her voice.

"Who?"

"You'll find out when you come."

That same tone, except now it's making me a little anxious. What's with the games? Is she talking about Maeve? Does she know what happened between us? Would Maeve tell her? Even if Maeve told her what happened, why would Mia sound almost excited at the prospect of us meeting there?

"Come on. Tell me."

"I'm not saying a thing. Just come on time, okay?"

"Sure, I will, but—"

She's hung up before I can think of a way to word my curiosity without revealing anything, and I stare at my phone for a second in confusion. I pace a little in the back, trying to figure out what the hell might be going on, then head out purposefully.

"Hey Sharon," I call as I grab my coat and round the counter, "I'm heading out for a while. Gotta get a present for my niece. If I'm not back, just close up yourself."

She nods and turns back to the customer. I head out in a hurry. Mia's right about one thing—curiosity will get me there on time tonight.

I'm not the kind of guy to dwell on hookups, but my night with Maeve last weekend has been playing in my mind like a movie stuck on repeat. I've even been checking out a few of her socials to "jog" my memory. No surprise, it took a year before I stopped jerking off to her last time we hooked up.

Maeve's the kind of woman who always leaves quicker than you'd like, but the kind you can't get out of your head quite that quickly. I even went cool on an Eastern European supermodel who was giving me an easy in today at the store because it felt like a downgrade. It feels almost like with-

Chapter 7

drawal, like I've got to recover from Maeve before I can fully get into my rhythm again.

But that doesn't mean I'm a fool. Not this time at least. I might have wasted a lot of time (and a lot of opportunities) falling for women I can't have, but even I am not self-torturing and idealistic enough to consider making Maeve mine for longer than a night. No. She's a pinup. A femme fatale. A vamp. The kind of woman you want more than any other—but only for one thing. I pity any man who ends up desiring something longer with Maeve, because he'll never get it. If a man ever does, I'll probably pity him even more.

I make a few stops around town, clearing up some business before it can threaten to make me late, go home to get changed, then buy some flowers and spend an hour scouring a department store for a nice gift for the kid.

My sister knows me all too well—I'm terrible with time. While I'm still browsing the aisles deciding between a teddy bear or a mobile, I check my watch, believing I've still got hours to go, and find that I've got just enough time to make it to the dinner if I leave immediately. I grab the bear like I'm rescuing it, pay for it, then jump in my car and drive there—wishing I hadn't returned the Ferrari and left myself with just the comfortable but slow BMW.

Their place is a large apartment in a condo. It used to be Colin's bachelor pad, and it's a little small for a family, but Mia's not going to buy a house unless it's perfect, and Colin's been busy starting up his new solo practice. I take the elevator up to their floor, still wondering what the hell Mia was hinting at on the phone.

As I make my way through the corridor to Mia's door, I start to hear the music. A muffled burst of laughter emerges from the apartment. Sounds like more than a couple of people. I ring the doorbell.

Five seconds later Maeve opens it. Though for the past week I've been building her up in my mind as an ultra-sexy, perfectly beautiful, larger-than-life goddess, her hotness exceeds even my fantasies.

It's just a tight black long-sleeved top but her angular face, short blonde hair, and incredible torso make it the sleekest thing I've ever seen. On her it looks like the fur of a puma prowling. Cream trouser pants hide her incredible legs, and a pair of sparkling chandelier earrings draw attention to her striking face.

"I think it's Toby," she calls back over her shoulder with a smile, "but it's seven o'clock so I'm not sure."

"Hey, Maeve," I say, smiling as I lean in to kiss her cheek and try not to get so turned on I end up pulling her out of the apartment and far away from prying eyes. I smell her and feel the brush of her lips on my face. For a second, time seems to slow, and then I realize she's lingering there. In a half second, I get my hopes up, start to wonder if this is a sign she's been as unable to forget our night together as I have.

Then she whispers, "Remember: It never happened."

She pulls back, still wearing her innocent dinner-party smile, and I nod before she turns back to join the others. I follow inside.

"I'm shocked," Mia says, coming to greet me with a kiss. I hand her the flowers and she appreciates them for a moment. "But I appreciate you coming on time."

Colin calls from over by the couch where he's tending to little Alison and I make a beeline for the kid.

"There she is!" I call as I approach with the bear. "How's my little niece doing?"

Chapter 7

"Not *another* gift!" Mia says as she moves back to the kitchen. "You've bought her more toys than *we* have!"

"That's what Uncle Toby does," I say, making the bear dance in front of her cute, wide-eyed expression. "He brings gifts."

Maeve comes over and hands me a beer. I look up to thank her, and our eyes linger a little too long. She clutches her wineglass a little too sensuously, stands with her hip out a little too arousingly. Or maybe it's my imagination. Everything Maeve does is aesthetically charged—but it's hard not to think it's all explicitly for me now.

"How's things?" Colin asks, but before I can answer Mia calls from the kitchen.

"Toby. Come help me."

I shrug and hand Colin the bear, then carry my beer over to the kitchen. On the way I catch sight of a guy out on the balcony, through the large glass windows of the apartment. He's on the phone, pacing and talking.

"Chop some cilantro for the curry," she orders, pointing at the sprigs and chopping board. "I like it fresh."

"I thought you said you were gonna have dinner ready by seven," I say, as I take up the knife. "'On schedule' you said."

"Yeah, well, Alison decided to have a cranky moment while I was preparing things. I suppose it's better she had it then—she'll probably crash out soon. Anyway, we're still waiting for someone to arrive."

"Who?" I say, stopping and turning to Mia, who's stirring and jiggling a pan of curried chicken. "Jake? Colin's friend from last time?"

"No," Mia says, and I see her try to hide her smile. "Nobody you know. *Yet*."

"Who's the guy out on the balcony?"

"That's Asher," Mia says, moving past me to check something in the refrigerator. "One of Colin's soccer buddies."

I glance back at the balcony again and see him finish his call and come back inside. He's noticeably good-looking. A rock star face and a rock star haircut. Stylish, too. He's got a loose red shirt and a pair of seventies-style pants that could only work on a guy that attractive and swaggeringly confident. I watch him move back inside and join Colin and Maeve around the baby. He sits on the floor in front of the couch and smiles easily as he jokes with them. A brief, bitter surge of envy rises up in me.

Mia leans in to me as she circles behind me.

"He's perfect, right?" she says.

I frown a little at her, thinking that it's a strange way for Mia to describe a guy—then I realize what she meant.

"Wait a minute," I say, leaning toward her now as she starts dressing some rice. "You invited him for *Maeve*?"

That mischievous smile again and she winks at me, expecting (why wouldn't she?) that I'll be as happy about it as she is.

"He's a movie producer, but he's really into fashion and design. Studied architecture. He's quite a hot name in the business. They're practically the mirror image of each other."

As if to confirm her point, there's a sudden outburst of laughter from the gathering around the baby, Maeve's sparkling laugh and Colin's gruff chuckle the loudest, so it's clear Asher told the joke. Mia looks at me and raises her eyebrows as if she just won a victory. I start cutting the cilantro like it did me wrong.

Eventually my thoughts get the better of me and I blurt out something I wouldn't if I was a man any less reckless.

Chapter 7

"Why the hell would you try to set up Maeve with someone?"

"Shh!" Mia whispers back, glancing over to the others to check they didn't hear, then coming closer to me.

In a lower voice I continue, "She's the last person to be up for that. It's not like she can't find a guy herself. She's just not interested in long-term stuff. You're her best friend, you know that." Mia looks at me intently for a second, and I realize I've shown a little too much interest. I smile and shrug as if I just find it all amusing and then continue to cut the cilantro—which by now is turning into mush.

"That's enough," Mia says, talking about the cilantro, and I set down the knife. She grabs some and starts tossing it into the curry. I grab my beer and hang around, pretending not to be as interested in what's going on across the apartment as I am.

"We just thought they were too good of a match not to invite him," she says. "Sure, Maeve is Maeve, but you should see her with Alison. She's softening up a little these days. I mean, I know she meets plenty of men, and has her fun—but it's not like she meets guys like Asher that often. It's always playboys and lotharios. Guys with big personalities and flashy lifestyles. Guys who 'live for the moment' and can't see past how sexy she is."

I sip my beer and wonder if Mia realizes she's basically describing me. "Asher's different. He's more... I dunno. Intellectual. Smart. Sweet. The kind of guy who's about more than the next five minutes."

I feel the urge to protest that I can be smart and sweet too, but I manage to swallow it down with another gulp of beer instead.

Then it hits me.

"Hey, hold up," I say, as Mia gets increasingly busy, darting from one end of the kitchen to the other.

"Would you help set the table, Toby?"

"This other person we're waiting for—"

"Use the bamboo mats—and don't forget the chopsticks, they're in the back of the cutlery drawer."

"It wouldn't happen to be a woman, would it?"

Mia glances at me as she busies herself. Again with that "I did it" smile. She shrugs, and immediately I know.

"Yeah..." she says.

"You're setting *me* up too!"

"No! Toby..." she says, stopping what she's doing to look at me, but she can't hold it long, and immediately has to look away and smile. "Okay. I mean...not *exactly*."

"Oh fuck..."

"She's a friend of mine, and she's really cool..."

"Come on, Mia..."

"You don't have to *marry* her! We just wanted to see if you'd hit it off."

"We were supposed to just be having a casual dinner, catch up, spend some time with the kid—"

"It *will* be casual."

"Now you got a whole singles night going on!"

"We've invited friends over for dinner before—"

"Of all the people to set up—me and Maeve...the last people who need it. If anything I need *fewer* women in my life, not more..."

"You'll like her, I promise."

At that moment the doorbell rings and I close my eyes to sigh heavily.

"Why would you do this to me, Mia?" I say, opening my eyes.

Chapter 7

She looks like she's having more fun than she's had in a long time.

"Go answer the door and find out," she says, grabbing me and turning me around to face it. "Go on."

She gives me a gentle shove and I head toward the door, glancing over at the others as I go and noticing that they're still so engrossed in their conversation they didn't even seem to notice the doorbell. I get to the door feeling like a kid being forced to spend time at a dull relative's. My hopes of spending the evening chilling out with the newest member of the family, maybe flirting a little with Maeve, now feels like work. More work than my real job. Now I get to watch some hot shot with Mick Jagger hair get his way with the woman I've spent a week fantasizing about, and my only consolation is...

I open the door and find all my expectations leaving through it.

"Hi," the girl says, holding out her hand. "I'm Hazel. This is Mia's place, right?"

She's hot. Hair tinted a silvery purple softly falling about a tanned face with a perky nose and blood red lips. Two perfect, narrow, sleeping-cat eyes that are alive with humor and secrets. Blue jeans hug a pair of hips that conjure all kinds of dirty thoughts, and a gray crop top reveals a midriff of soft skin that makes me want to wrap my hands around it.

"It sure is." I smile at her. I take her hand softly. "I'm Toby, Mia's brother."

"Oh, ha ha!" she says, laughing easily and happily. "She told me so much about you."

"Don't believe a word she said," I say as she steps inside past me. Hazel laughs again and her happiness is infectious.

She swaps a quick greeting with Mia and I move back to the kitchen to continue setting the table.

"Forget that. I'll do the table," Mia says quietly and quickly, shooing me away. "Go talk to Hazel, she only just got here. Get her a drink."

I look back at Hazel. "What do you like to drink, Hazel?"

She pouts as she thinks about it awhile, either too nervous or too unaccustomed to dinner parties to come up with something.

"You know what," I say, "I'll make you a cocktail. I guarantee you'll like it."

"Oh, all right. Thank you!"

She laughs again and seems to find the idea more exciting than a simple drink should be. She follows me to the drink cabinet and I start mixing. Every few seconds she looks at me and laughs like she's already having the best time of her life.

Mia was right, she's a nice girl. My kind of girl. Hot and fun.

But the best part is that whenever I look over at Maeve, she's pretending not to look over at us, pretending not to look just a little bit jealous.

Maybe this evening won't be so bad after all.

8

MAEVE

"...But what Alessandro Michele is doing at Gucci is pretty great so far, and I think you're going to see a lot of other houses have to be more innovative too."

"It's great, no doubt," I tell the tall, dark, handsome Asher beside me, "but I'm not too sure it's that innovative. Inevitable, perhaps."

He's leaning over his plate, chopsticks in hand, but facing me beside him, his head and shoulders directed at me with an intensity that could make a woman forget there are several other people at the table. Everything about him has a sensual intensity—his lively dark eyes, his shaggy black hair, his broad lips—so that even though he's talkative and animated, there's a sense of mystery and allure about him.

"Oh come on, have you seen his shows?"

"I've attended several of them," I reply with a smile. "Florid patterns, seventies color palettes in modern shapes. He does it well. Very cohesive and just the right side of striking."

"Right, exactly..." he says, nodding and looking even deeper into me, as if appreciating my insight.

"But I'm just saying that we were always going to get somebody like him. There's only so long we could go down the 'stark classical' route, and recent attempts to revive a distressed looseness have all felt more like a dead end than an opportunity."

That look gets even deeper, his eyes even more focused, his smile even more appreciative.

After a few moments he says, "You're pretty incredible," in a tone like he's telling me a secret, and I have to laugh.

As I return my attention to the food I notice Mia across the table, looking at me the same way she'll probably look at Alison when she takes her first step.

What an idea! Setting me up with someone? To think not that long ago Mia was coming to me for advice as she muddled her way through a turbulent relationship with Colin. I suppose this is her attempt at returning the favor. She's been so loved-up and happy for a year that she probably wants to share it. And then Asher certainly is something special…

Mia knows me well, but this is her optimism getting the better of that. Introducing me to Asher and hoping we'll hit it off is like bringing a parakeet to a cat and hoping they'll become friends. The cat will enjoy it, but not for the reasons you hoped.

Hazel explodes into another giggling fit down the other end of the table, each one louder than the last, and we all turn to see Toby still saying something into her ear. They seem to be getting on well—of course they would. Hazel's cute, and Toby's good at getting along with cute girls regardless of what they're like.

For some reason, though, I find Hazel's laughter immediately irritating. Unjustifiably. I barely know her, and she seems nice, but every time I hear her explode with joy at something Toby told her it gives me a slight frazzled feeling under my skin. And despite having my own devilishly handsome and deeply interesting partner at the table, every sign of Toby and Hazel getting along wonderfully makes a part of me feel like something's wrong, rather than right.

"...that the problem with European fashion is that it's so attached to their broader sense of aesthetics that only parts of it catch on in the US, don't you think?"

"What? Sorry," I say, only just realizing that Asher's been talking to me. "This curry is sensational," I tell him, turning and repeating myself to Mia, who's still watching us proudly.

"It really is," Colin agrees, looking lovingly at Mia.

"Well, I wanted to do something special." She shrugs. Suddenly she looks surprised. "Oh! Maeve, tell everyone about your new thing. I totally forgot."

"My thing?"

"Yeah! You know, your work thing."

Even Toby and Hazel have stopped talking because of Mia's excitedness now. Everyone's attention patiently waiting on me now.

"Right," I say, putting down my fork and dabbing my mouth a little. "Well, it's early stages still—and it wasn't even my idea—but I'm launching a new jewelry line. Actually, *my* new jewelry line."

There are smiles and interested noises around the table, and I pretend to scan everyone to return their interest, though the face I'm most interested in is Toby's.

"Your own jewelry?" Toby says, playing with his food so he can pretend to only be half interested. "Your name on it and everything?"

"That's right," I say, looking straight at him with a smile. "My name on it and everything."

Toby looks amused as he twirls some noodles around a fork.

"So..." he says, like he's starting to tell a joke, "the whole world is going to finally find out who Maeve is."

"Enough of the world already does," I reply. "That's why we're doing it."

Toby chuckles gently, the rest of the table quiet enough to hear it.

"Heh, well you've got the ego for it."

"Ego is the easy part—backing it up is what people struggle with. *You* know that, darling."

Toby holds his fork with noodles up but doesn't do anything with it.

"So what's the *Maeve brand* going to be about? Women who are never satisfied?"

"I think we'll go for 'women who don't take any shit.'"

Mia and Colin laugh, shaping the strange tension into nothing but a little amusing play, while reminding both me and Toby that we're not alone.

"Ignore these two," Mia says, looking at Asher and then Hazel. Colin nods and murmurs his support of his wife. "They're always at each other's throats."

As we turn to our meals, something about the phrase "at each other's throats" sticks with me, as if it were more than a saying, and actually literal. A memory of his teeth on my neck, my tongue in his ear, faces close and bodies twisting against each other. I push the memory away, sighing as I do so, then quickly checking that nobody notices it.

"That's really cool," Asher says, turning his wolf-like intensity toward me again as he grabs another dumpling. "Your own jewelry—I'm sure it's gonna be incredible. You've got great taste."

I look at him and allow him a smile and the kind of eyes

I reserve only for guys I'm genuinely intrigued by. Then a thought strikes me. A half realization. One that I'm not ready to face, to think about. Probably ever, but certainly not at the dinner table in a situation like this.

"Asher, would you mind mixing me another martini?"

"Of course," he says, seeming to relish the opportunity to satisfy my request. He starts to get up from the table, and takes my glass. At the other end Hazel lets off another firecracker laugh. Toby glances in my direction, revealing nothing, but I smile over my irritation.

"Oh," I say, loud enough for Toby to hear, putting a hand on Asher's arm as he stands beside me about to go. Looking right back at Toby, I say, "And put a lemon in it."

Toby holds my gaze, confusion in his eyes but a knowing smile spreading across his lips. I look at him like I'm challenging him, holding it a second longer than I should, then turn back to my food.

When Mia's dessert comes to the table—fried bananas and coconut ice cream—it's so good that a heavy silence, as delicious as the food, sets around the table. Colin goes off to put Alison to sleep, and the sound of spoons scraping the last of ice cream-drenched banana is low and careful. Even Hazel seems to mellow a little, her voluptuous body sinking into her seat.

Mia looks around and says, "There's more if anyone wants it."

We all murmur our satisfied refusals and appreciation for the food and spend the next half hour digesting. When the conversation starts up again, it's more mellow and easy. The warmth of full bellies and cautiousness of the sleeping baby coming through on our hushed voices and slightly less excitable chatter.

We move to the couches, Asher sitting up close, and still

dedicating his full attention to me. I let my third martini turn my senses a little sweet, and enjoy the cozy burn of his dark eyes on me.

"Hey, you know what?" Mia says, seeming suddenly surprised. She's sitting cross-legged on the rug and looking up at us. "I just realized something obvious. *You're* doing a jewelry line, and Toby... Well, Toby could help you, couldn't he?"

Toby's sitting on the armchair, Hazel on the armrest—not quite in his lap, but close enough you could mistake them for an old couple.

I look at him and he looks back at me, as if waiting for me to make the first move.

"Makes perfect sense," Colin adds, from his position on the other armchair. "Not that I know how this stuff works, but surely you could help Maeve out with the designs, or the right connections. Get her a deal maybe. After all, you don't want it to fail when it's your own name on the thing."

Almost apologetically, I say, "They're different markets. Toby deals with high-end stuff. Bespoke one-offs. Exclusives. Very expensive. We're doing a department store line. It'll be a little pricier, sure, gold vermeil and real gems, but not quite the same league. Demi-fine, it's called."

"Ah, right," Colin says, nodding his comprehension.

"No, no. I can help," Toby says, staring right at me. I search his face for a clue, wondering if he's playing some kind of game, acting for the sake of the others, or challenging me. "I mean, sure you can get a third-party supplier to make the stuff, but finding the good ones is something I can help you with. Materials are almost more important with the lower-end stuff. You can get lower-end pieces that are as well made as the real thing, *or* you can get lower-end stuff that's as bad as you'd imagine. I've seen it all in the shop. You'd be surprised what kind of stuff people try to trade in... I can help. Put you in with the right people, tell you what to watch out for."

Mia smiles broadly and looks at both of us, surprised at this positive turn of events—though not as surprised as I am.

"That's great! Oh my God, that's so exciting. Maeve! Your name's going to become synonymous with the *best* jewelry—I can *so* imagine it already."

"As long as you guys can stop fighting for long enough," Colin adds, and Mia playfully slaps his shoulder.

It's not the fighting I'm worried about when it comes to Toby, I think to myself, smiling at the inner joke and passing it off as being pleased about the offer to the others. When they return to talking about something else, I look at Toby, and eventually he looks back. In expressions so subtle that only years of knowing someone could decipher them, I show him my confusion, and all he shows me is a mischievous wink.

I turn back to Asher and try to lose myself in his compelling, rich voice and beautiful face again, but this time I can't seem to forget where I am, to shake off Toby's presence across the room. It's obvious to me this has become a game now. Except I'm not quite sure what the rules are, or even who's winning.

Perhaps if we keep playing this recklessly, we'll both lose.

9

TOBY

I don't get it. None of it makes sense. I'm starting to feel like an alien in my own body.

Hazel is hot. Ridiculously, insanely, absorbingly hot. She's cool too. Easygoing, kind, and likeable. She hasn't stopped smiling since I opened the door to her. Sympathized when I told her about my struggles learning French, and laughed *with* me rather than *at* me when Mia told that story about me getting stuck in the couch as a kid. She's sweet as sugar, but flirts just enough to let me knows how to be the opposite when needed. Apparently, she's a new nurse at Mia's work—and who doesn't like a nurse?

So why the hell do I feel like I'm going against the flow rather than with it? Why do I feel like I'm only pretending to be into her? Why haven't I grabbed her by the hand and snuck her out of here yet? She clearly wants me to...

The evening is already winding down, it's almost midnight, and outside the night sky is pitch. The baby wails and Colin goes into the bedroom to bring her out so everyone can coo her into smiles one last time. I overhear the words *share* and *cab* come from Asher, and turn around just in time to see Maeve nodding her agreement.

"Would you..." Hazel starts her question in a slow, slightly different tone. She's got a great voice, musical and lively, but now she sounds a little shy, a little coy. It's incredibly sultry—or it would be if I wasn't ruining it by glancing over at the other side of the room constantly. "Mind driving me home? I only live a couple of blocks from here."

"Oh, sure. Well...actually, I'm a little too intoxicated to drive," I say, immediately thinking I'm too drunk even for my lemon trick—though I'll never do that again without thinking of Maeve. "But I'd be happy to walk you home."

"Even better," she says through a big smile. The light in her eyes dancing with possibilities.

"Toby," Mia says, coming near, "you want me to pack you a little food?"

"Oh absolutely," I say. "As much as you can. Those dumplings if you have any left."

Mia smiles and then heads into the kitchen. I look back to see Hazel heading toward Colin, who's holding Alison, so that she can make goo goo noises at the baby. Asher asks Colin something about soccer.

And then I see Maeve head into the bedroom where the coats are. I don't consider whether it's a bad idea to follow her in there—I don't have time, and I don't even think about it at all. All instinct. An opportunity to get Maeve alone.

I make sure everyone's too preoccupied packing food, pleasing babies, and talking about soccer to notice me as I slink casually after her and shut the door. The coats are on the bed, and she's leaning over it slightly as she carefully moves them aside to find hers, her back to me. She shows no signs of hearing me over the music and chatter next door,

Chapter 9

but then again, Maeve likes to pretend she knows less than she does.

I step toward her perfect ass, her sleek, irresistible back, suddenly feeling the full, uncensored version of what I only felt the tiniest hint of for Hazel. My body dirty with lust, my senses fogged by the blood rushing inside. I should say something, but I'm struck dumb now, my body leading me to a place where my mind can't function.

The curve of her back in that tight black top makes me feel dangerous, sets my muscles on edge. The curve of her waist like water in the desert. I put my hands on its perfect symmetry. Soundlessly, she whips around in my arms to face me. The fact that she doesn't yelp or make a sound makes me think she knew I was there all along, but she glares at me angrily, shocked—but only for a second. Lips parted, eyes wide, and what she meant as shock inevitably reveals that she feels this electrifying moment as much as I do.

Our faces are too close to be reasonable, but still it feels painfully far. This close to her I don't need to talk. She can probably hear my heart thumping a carnal rhythm, can feel the animal heat from my body, can see a reflection of how arousing I find her in my own eyes. My closeness becomes a question. A challenge. I stand there doing nothing but looking back at her with my desire written all over my face, waiting for her to make the next move. For her to shove me away, to resist me, to show me that she can uphold our agreement as much as she expects me to.

It turns out she can't.

Her lips collide with mine, her wet tongue curling in my mouth, her hands at the sides of my face, gripping and clawing into my neck like she's angry she wants me as much as I want her.

I squeeze her ass, pull it against me, the soft fabric of those pants almost as silken and inviting as her skin. Her chest presses into mine, and she arches her back as if desperate for every part of her body to be in contact with mine. She sucks on my tongue, hard breaths like hot steam across our faces, unable to come up for air. She grabs a fistful of my T-shirt and twists it so it feels like she's constricting me, her body winding around me while I drink the poison venom of her kiss. A death I would be happy for.

It tastes so good, feels so good, that we could almost believe this kiss is magic. A spell that could take us somewhere entirely different, so that we don't need to worry that there are a group of friends in the next room, any one of whom could enter at any moment. A lotus kiss, making us forget everything except the kiss itself.

Eventually, she does resist, tearing her lips from mine like it's a violent act, that fistful of T-shirt turning into a shoving palm. And it's the shock more than anything that makes me weak enough to oblige, to allow myself to be shoved a couple of feet from her. We glare at each other, like panting animals circling for round two.

"The *hell* do you think you're doing, Toby?" she hisses in a low voice, as if she wasn't just as into it as me. Maybe trying to convince herself of that. "What happened to our *agreement*?"

She touches her lips as if checking for blood, then I realize she's just checking her lipstick. I check mine too, licking away the taste of it and only getting turned on further. When she strides over to the mirror to check and smooth the wrinkles in the ass of her pants, I have to look away before I grab her for another bout.

"Fuck the agreement," I say bluntly. My thoughts still too primal and clouded to come up with anything smarter.

Chapter 9

"Do you *want* to get caught or something?" she says, glaring at me in the mirror as she moves to fix her hair. "Is that it? The fear of getting caught turns you on?"

"*You* turn me on," I growl, still in caveman mode, though with just enough sense now to straighten out my shirt.

She lets out a dismissive, haughty grunt, slipping back into her too-cool-for-this persona.

"What's your excuse?" I ask her.

She turns to look at me for real now, her blank expression a good act, but I know I've touched a nerve. She can't hold my gaze, even though she plays it off as she strides to the bed to grab her cream cashmere trench coat.

"I prefer not *making* stupid mistakes to excusing them," she says, as she slips into the coat.

She steps past me to the door but I take her arm and stop her. She glares daggers at my hand, then at me.

"If you're so into the 'agreement,'" I say, "what was all that with the lemon, huh? Don't act like you didn't know what you were doing. You're playing games."

"*Games?*" she replies, slipping into her typical semi-dismissive, mildly amused tone. "If you want to talk about games, let's talk about you telling everyone you can 'help' me with the jewelry line. You *know* Mia is going to be asking about that now, and *expecting* us to work together."

"I *can* help you," I say. "It makes sense."

"Oh, I'll bet it does, honey. I'll bet it makes sense to you. I'll bet you *love* the idea of getting me alone in your shop. Laying out a half-million dollars' worth of jewels and *fucking* me on them."

The way she says it is a little too emotive. If I wasn't so intoxicated from the kiss, I'd have detected how she likes that little fantasy as much as she presumes I do. As if to misdirect my attention from it, she clasps my hand and removes it from her arm like a dirty tissue.

"You know, Maeve, you keep acting like *I'm* the only one who wants this, but I know you too well to fall for the 'ice bitch' routine. You want it just as much as I do, and the only difference between us is that *I've* got the balls to go for what I want rather than pretend I don't."

"Balls, but no brain," she replies, tightening her coat and tying up the belt. "No capacity to think ahead into the future, or about anything beyond your own, rather simple desires. This is already messy. Taking it any further would make a mess big enough to involve *your* sister—*my* best friend."

As if that's the final word she steps to the door, but just as she puts her hand on the knob I say, "So, what then? You're just going to go home with Asher tonight, and fuck him instead, huh?"

She turns to look back at me over her shoulder, flashing that above-it-all smile.

"Aren't you walking little Hazel home? Am I supposed to believe you'll settle for a peck on the cheek?"

She doesn't move after she says it, as if it's a real question, and not a point-scoring retort. For a moment there's something between our gazes that is more than confrontational. A moment of vulnerability, a hesitation that could only reveal a mutual weakness.

I clear my throat and look down sheepishly, running a rough palm over my stubble noisily.

"No, I... I'm not gonna do anything with Hazel," I say, trying to make the admission sound as nonchalant as possible. "She's had a few drinks... Seems like a lightweight anyway... Wouldn't be right."

I glance back up at her and she nods, her smile gone, a pretense at civility.

"Well..." she begins, in the same forcibly casual tone I attempted. "F.Y.I. Asher's place is a mile closer than mine, so I'll be taking the Uber farther... I have an early, busy morning at work tomorrow anyway... Not that it's any of your business."

I glance up at her and nod, both of us struggling to meet each other's gaze now. The two of us looking guilty though there's nobody else around. I look away, rub the back of my neck, look over at the bed, and Maeve opens the door to rejoin the others.

Twenty seconds later I straighten my shirt and hair, grab my jacket, and go outside as well.

"Hey, Toby—there you are. I thought you were in the bathroom," Colin calls. He's standing with Asher, the baby now in Mia's arms being sung to by Hazel and Maeve.

"Uh...no," I say. "I was...just admiring the uh...your uh..." I laugh at myself as if embarrassed about admitting something. "I was looking at your shirts. You've got some good taste, man."

Colin laughs and shares a quick look with Mia before turning back to me.

"Listen, Mia told me you played soccer in high school. She said you were pretty good."

"He was brilliant," Mia calls out. "As unpredictable as he is in real life. Unfortunately, about as unreliable, too."

I step toward Colin and Asher, grateful for the change of topic.

"Yeah. I used to love playing. Why?"

Colin thumbs toward Asher and says, "We play every weekend, and we're getting a little short."

"Not 'short,' exactly," Asher adds. "We got a couple of

guys... They're getting pretty out of shape. Their hearts aren't really in it anymore."

"They only join us for the drinks afterwards," Colin clarifies.

"Hence being 'out of shape.'"

"We could really do with another player."

Asher nods. "Anyone who can kick a ball, really."

"Are you up for it?"

I hesitate before answering, but only because I catch a glimpse of Maeve on the other side of the room and my mind immediately returns to an entirely different subject.

"Sure, absolutely," I say, instinctively.

I'm always up for anything new. It's part of the reason I keep getting into trouble. And even tonight, with all that's happened setting a strange mood in me, I can't think of a single reason to say no.

"Fantastic," Asher says, looking pleased. He slaps my arm. "Look forward to seeing what you can do."

I smile back at him, starting to wonder if he's going to become a problem.

10

MAEVE

There are benefits to always being so busy that you barely have any time to think—such as not having any time to think.

So when Saturday rolls around and I wake up with no man to kick out of bed and no hangover to nurse, the day ahead seems vast, empty, and irritating.

During a long shower—water too hot to relax, scrubbing too thoroughly to think—I conduct an imaginary interview with myself about my jewelry line, already cultivating some interesting but briefly witty answers to questions. Everything in my line of work is preparation, and everything in my life I think of as work in some way.

After the shower, in my bathrobe and carrying my coffee, I wander around the house a little, checking plants, turning on the TV and then turning it off again, looking for something to eat and then realizing I'm not hungry. I put some music on but find it more of an annoying distraction than enjoyable. The right song not existing. Everything from classical to Katy Perry jarring against my own mood. There's a profound restlessness in me, a tetchy desire to do something, and an inability to focus on anything. Still, it feels like if I actually stop and ask myself why I feel this way, I might find something even tougher to deal with.

I open my laptop and try to get down to some work, but my mind feels like a wild animal. I need something physical, something to occupy my body. I check my planner for something to occupy me. An event or a meet-up perhaps. There's a book launch across town, an art exhibition at LACMA. The third day of a student fashion show at a local design college. But as soon as the opportunities present themselves, I realize that I'm not in the mood to be around other people, either.

Though I feel like I simply don't have the energy for it, I get dressed in my cycling shorts and sports bra, make sure my phone's charged, and head out for a run.

It's a hot day, and it isn't long before I break into a sweat —sooner than usual. I make my way through the neighborhood, eventually taking an uphill trail that's too much for me to handle right now. Calves aching, shoulders burning in the sun, face drenched in sweat. For a while it feels beautifully tiring, and I can almost believe I might rid my body of that restless tension I woke up with, but soon the tiredness only seems to make my mind as active. The restlessness leaves my body, and it turns out it was the only thing saving me from my thoughts.

Toby's kiss...

Despite the burning sun and the gravel I'm kicking up, I'm back there in the bedroom, cool and calm, until he arrives to mess up my perfectly composed outfit with his roving hands... I almost had him out of my system until he stirred it up again... Stirred it up and didn't settle it, letting it linger inside of me... That's why I'm restless... That's why I can't focus... That's why pounding my way up this hill while my muscles beg me to stop and my lungs feel like they're in overdrive isn't enough still... I'm fucking *horny* for him...

I stop running, almost collapsing to the dirt. Bent over double, hands on knees, I gasp and pant until my breath starts to slow. When I manage to stand up again, a guy with the body of an eighties action hero is jogging up toward me, smiling and getting ready to say something.

"Hot day for it. You look like the kind of girl who—"

"Not now, honey," I interrupt, in a tone that kills any thought of a second attempt. He looks at me for a second longer and then carries on running past. I watch him go a while and then start walking, needing to catch a little more breath before I can run again.

That mini-revelation I had at Mia's dinner table last night comes back to my mind, and I'm too tired to fight it this time. I'm too aware of it now. Toby turns me on because he's the only man I know who isn't afraid of me. The only man who'd *dare* to grab my ass like that when our friends were just a door away. The only man who'd make a fool of himself eating a lemon in front of me and not worry about my opinion of him. The only man who gave as good as he got...

Sure, a lot of men put on a good show of strength. I've had models who could go for three nights straight, Europeans who could talk you to multiple orgasms without even touching you, businessmen who could crush other guys with a look. But you scratch any of them under the chin and you discover that they're lapdogs underneath.

Whereas with Toby... He might dress like a drug dealer from Miami, and live with the spontaneity of a hedonistic teenager, but he's the only guy who doesn't flinch, who doesn't roll over. The only one who makes me feel like a woman somehow. With him, the softness is the pretense, and the toughness is what he's hiding.

Another difficult thought comes to mind, and instinctively I start running, as if to leave it behind. *Is that why I told Annika not to call him?*

No. I'd tell any woman I care about the same. Toby's not dating material—especially not for a bookish, inexperienced girl. He wouldn't hurt her, but she'd get hurt for sure.

I tell myself that, and I *know* it's true. But the day is turning weird, and the sun is becoming a torturer, and soon I find myself admitting that it's not the *whole truth*. When I saw his name on the card she handed me there *was* a pang of jealousy. A hint of defensiveness. Small, irrelevant...but there. But jealous of what? That Annika might get to enjoy him while I'm constrained by our agreement? By our complex relationship around Mia? Probably.

Probably.

It's not like I have actual feelings for him. Not even remotely. I just want to fuck him. I want him to fuck me. It's that simple.

I want to drain every last drop of pleasure from our bodies. I want to drink him up until there's nothing left, and I want to see how many ways he can slam me up against the wall and draw sounds from me I've never made before. But feelings...no. I'm Maeve. The fashion icon with her own line of jewelry. The first name on VIP guest lists to parties I don't even attend. The woman with a trail of broken hearts and fixated men behind her.

I don't *do* feelings.

As I reach the halfway point of the trail, a cliffside peak with a glorious view of the ocean, my phone rings. Mia. I answer it.

"Hey, sweetie," I say, slowing down to a walking pace.

Chapter 10

"Maeve? You sound out of breath..."

"Yeah," I say, still panting a little. "I am."

Mia pauses before speaking again, and as she does I can hear her smile.

"Are you with Asher?" she says in a whisper, as if anyone else would hear her over the phone. "Oh my God, did you two—"

"Sorry to burst your bubble, but no. I'm just out on a run. Working off that food you gave me and resenting you for making it so irresistible."

"It was a fun evening, wasn't it?"

"It was great."

"We'll do it again next week."

I hesitate to answer. The brief flash of hope at the prospect of seeing Toby again startling me more than anything.

"Sure," I say. "Any chance to see Alison."

"Yeah. So..." she says, shifting tones. "What did you think?"

I'm too hot and bothered to pretend I don't know what she's talking about.

"I think he's a sexy, smart guy, and the five dates we go on will be fabulous."

"Oh Maeve, come on! He's perfect for you!"

"He is. That's why it'll probably be five dates—the longest relationship I've had in years."

"*Maeve...*" Mia's voice sounds almost like she's pleading with me. "Give him a chance. A real chance. I promise you won't regret it."

"What's the big idea, anyway? Setting me up like that... I should punish you for it. Springing it like a surprise on me."

"I...well...it..." Mia stumbles over her words a little and I can tell she wants to lie, but won't be able to. "Honestly? I sort of noticed you'd been a bit...well...different lately."

"Different?" I ask, stepping off the trail to rest in the shade of a eucalyptus tree. A light breeze running across my sweat-drenched body, tingling and refreshing.

"Yeah... I don't know. Maybe it's just me. And having the baby and looking for a house..."

"Different how?"

I hear Mia sigh on the line as she searches for the right words.

"Like...as if...as if you're getting tired of..."

She trails off and I say, "Tired of what?" in a gentle tone to show her I won't be offended.

"Tired of being *you*," she says, then quickly follows up, "I mean, I've *always* wondered how you managed to be you, because you're so incredible. You know... It's silly... Playing all these guys and doing such a great job at work and just generally always being so cool and composed and dressing so well and...well...just being 'Maeve,' you know? I don't know. It's silly. Forget it."

"No...no...I think I understand," I say, trying to keep how shaken I am out of my voice. It feels like somebody's plucked a guitar string in the center of my gut and it's vibrating through me, and I'm not even sure why it feels like that.

"You do?" Maeve asks innocently. "I mean, I know you've always been confident in the idea of never settling with a guy and enjoying your life and focusing on your work and... You know, it's not like I'm one of those people who thinks all women have to have a guy to be happy—I mean, God knows I loved my career enough to forget about guys for most of my life. And it's what makes you *you*. I *always* loved that about you. It's just...

"The past couple of weeks...it seemed to me like you were sort of...perhaps...wanting something a little more permanent? Meaningful? Bah! Forget me, I'm talking a lot of nonsense. You know what it is? I'm just so in love and happy that I feel compelled to try to share it with everyone. To have them feel as good as I'm feeling. Even when they're completely different types of people. Like you."

I start walking again, smiling at Mia's flustered explanations, her endearing kindness shaking that strange vibe I had moments ago.

"Oh honey, I'm going to get diabetes if you act any sweeter."

Mia laughs, then says, "Well anyway, it's up to you. But he's a great guy. Even if you love him and leave him, I'm sure he won't have any complaints."

"The only problem I have these days is time. This jewelry line is like a second job. As if the creation, the packaging, and the distribution weren't enough, being the face of it will really pile on the workload. They'll probably send me to every event from here to New York in order to promote it."

"As if you don't attend everything anyway," Mia quips.

"Of course, but I like the luxury of pretending I don't have to," I reply.

"Well...I shouldn't say this, but Asher would probably make a nice companion to hit the red carpets with, you know? He actually dated a few pretty famous actresses—and even became a bit of a mini-celebrity in the gossip mags—I mean he's so hot, they picked up on him. But he's used to that life, and might even be able to help in your new career as an 'icon.' Not that I'm trying to convince you or anything."

"Are you suggesting I use his notoriety and power to help make my jewelry line a success?"

"Gosh, no!"

"Shame. It's a good idea. I thought I was rubbing off on you after all these years."

Mia laughs again and I hear Alison cry in the background.

"I'd better go."

"Sure. Give that little one a kiss from me."

"I will. Speak to you later, Maeve."

"Bye, sweetie."

We hang up and I stop walking to gaze out at the Pacific a while through the bushes lining the cliffside. The sea air seems to clear something out of me, finally a little of the restlessness gone, finally a little sense of peace. Maybe it's not the air, but simply having a good friend.

Mia might be a loved-up, obsessively generous, perpetually optimistic new mother—but she's right. I *have* been feeling a little different these days. She just admitted it before I did. Maybe it has nothing to do with Toby, or Asher, or jewelry, or even the warm happiness I feel when cradling Alison. Maybe I *am* just getting tired of being me.

But then...who else can I become?

11

TOBY

On Sunday morning, I wake up to a phone that's nearly vibrated off the table. Dozens of messages about errands I haven't yet run, about deals I haven't yet finalized, about places and parties I didn't go to. Stranger still, I slept late. A full ten hours. I haven't done that since I stayed up for three nights straight a couple of summers ago in Vegas.

It's no mystery to me. I've been so wrapped up in one thing that the rest of my life has faded a little into the background—become less important, less interesting. My work, my shop, my lifestyle, it's all become the distraction rather than the purpose. My purpose now, the thing I wasted an entire Saturday thinking about, is to finish what I started with Maeve.

It's not like I don't know what obsession is. I'm no stranger to getting fixated on a woman. But this is different. *Maeve* is different. She's no simple hottie with a nice personality. No quirky girl with a few nice attributes. She's the ice queen herself. Feminine strength incarnate. The femme fatale that was supposed to exist only in movies.

Maybe that's why the thrill of taking her is ten times that of any other woman I've had.

Mia says I always want what I can't have, and though I keep telling her she's wrong, I keep proving her right. Well, it doesn't get more forbidden than Maeve. Even without the messiness of ruining my sister's best-friend relationship with her, Maeve is an Everest kind of challenge.

For six years I kept a lid on it, suppressed my lust for her, forced to look but not touch. Only letting out my sexual frustration in our tense, mocking, flirtatious exchanges, the prospect of anything more seeming ridiculous. It took one little accident—brushed hands under a tap—to break us, and it turned out that six years of holding back makes for a hell of a climax.

The genie has to go back in the bottle at some point, though. This can only end one way—with us going back to the "agreement." With us as friendly, competitive acquaintances. The only question is if we can risk a little more.

Truthfully, I've always been a gambler.

I've been so horny for her since that night at her place that I'm even starting to think the unthinkable. So what if people find out? So what if we keep on doing it until it blows up between us? Sure, it would be hard for Mia if her brother and her best friend weren't on speaking terms. Uncle Toby and Auntie Maeve having to alternate between dinner parties, and a little care taken so they don't end up visiting at the same time. It sucks, but it's hardly the end of the world. I guess the problem is that there's no way we could end this prettily—which is why we never really ended it six years ago anyway.

It would end badly, we both know that. The first one to get bored would have to drop the bomb on the other, who would take a bruise to the ego which could be permanent. A

Chapter 11

game of Russian roulette where the stakes are our own identities. Maybe we'd end up getting under each other's skin so much that we wouldn't be able to stand the sight of one another. Maybe it would be so good that we'd spoil each other for future lovers...

But it's hard to think of the cons when the pros are so compelling...

The way her thighs quiver and her tongue twirls... The way she claws like she wants to tear you to pieces and the way those eyes harden when she comes... The way she walks, and talks, and stares, and moves like everything is foreplay... She's worth the risk.

And after all, it's not like we're going to catch legitimate feelings for each other. I'm just about smart enough to keep my heart out of things, and she's barely even capable of that to begin with. It's impossible to even imagine a connection anything deeper than sexual with Maeve. Impossible to envisage affectionate words coming from lips designed for put-downs, tenderness from a body that's dressed and sculpted to elicit lust and awe, sex that's more emotional than it is a selfish physical contest... I can't even imagine it...

But for some reason I'm trying...

I skim through the rest of the messages on my phone as I stretch out in bed, and make mental excuses for why and how I can delay responses a little longer. Then I see the one about the soccer match.

"Shit," I say, instantly awake.

It takes me half an hour to shower, get dressed, pack a sports bag with my shorts and shirts, and then another half hour to search for my old soccer cleats until I remember I gave them to Goodwill. I grab my things and get to my car, only then realizing that my phone is half dead and I left the charger upstairs. Regardless, I drive straight to the nearest strip mall, once again wishing I hadn't sold the Ferrari, and try to remember if I've forgotten anything else.

Once there, I park and probably look like a manic father-of-four on the last minute of opening hours on Christmas Eve as I race inside. I pick a pair of shoes based on color and buy them without trying them on, make a quick stop to get a charger, then another (slower) stop for some coffee and a donut, which I eat like a starving kid on the way to the location Colin had sent me earlier.

Eventually I reach the soccer fields, and park in a line of luxury and sports cars. Sugar sprinkled and high on the strongest coffee I could buy, I dash for the building. After checking in on the wrong locker room (probably the opposing team's) I find the right one and enter as everyone's just finished getting themselves ready and are in the middle of a team talk.

"*There* he is," Colin calls from the far side of the lockers, and I make a beeline for a free one. "Everyone, this is my brother-in-law, Toby."

"Hey…how you doing? What's up?" I say, returning everyone's confused but welcoming greetings. "Yes… Hello… Sorry I'm late, guys… Jake, is it? Hey there…"

"Thank God for that…" I hear a guy who looks red-faced from putting on his shoes say behind me.

I dump my sports bag and quickly start getting ready.

"Lucky you," I hear someone tell him.

"Lucky us," I hear someone else respond. "We get to play someone who does a little more than a lamp post."

"I told you," the red-faced guy says, "I got an injury."

The others laugh dismissively.

"Remind us of that when you get drunk afterwards and start dancing like you're at a wedding."

I'm down to my boxers, pulling my shirt over my head, when I hear a familiar voice right beside me.

"Hey, Toby. Glad you could make it."

I pull off my shirt and look toward the voice to see Asher there. Somehow I manage to hide the conflicting things that seeing him brings up, and force a smile. We clasp hands.

"Hey, man. Wouldn't miss it for anything."

"Okay everyone," Colin calls out across the locker room, commanding attention. I suddenly realize he's the captain. "We haven't played these guys before, but you'll know their best players from other teams. Best plan Jake and I have come up with is to stick to our strengths, that means the same back four as last time—Roddy on the left. The dual pivot..."

I concentrate on getting ready while Colin gives the team talk, pulling on my new cleats just in time for him to finish up and get around to me.

"Toby, you're on the wing so you won't have too many duties, other than making an attack happen whenever you can. That okay?"

I give him the a-ok sign and then finish off tying my laces.

"Perfect," Colin says, then claps his hands and shouts out some last-minute words of encouragement. The other guys join in, hollering and shouting, their energy levels up, before they follow Colin out onto the field.

For the first ten minutes of the match I realize just how much of a bad idea this was. The match moves at a pace far quicker than I can follow, and I find myself ball-watching, ball-chasing, and barely getting a touch. That donut and coffee combination in the morning not doing me any favors

—I feel just as bad at the game as the red-faced guy in the locker room looked, and I'm probably playing worse.

But I've never been one to get embarrassed, or derive my pride from others. And I certainly don't like giving up on anything. After we go a goal down, the ball comes to me out wide and I trap it well. I look up and see that I can pass it safely inside to Asher, who's in space, but decide to try to make something happen. Old muscle memories kick in, my body settling into a physical, swaggering cockiness. Now a little attuned to the pace of the game, I turn to an oncoming defender, send him the wrong way with a feint, and neatly skip past him with the ball.

I'm not the fastest on the field, but I weave between the last defenders like the cleverest, soon through on goal but too wide to shoot myself. I loft in a hard and fast cross that our striker sprints through to head past the goalie and the celebrations even take me by surprise.

"That's it," someone says, smacking the back of my head.

"More of that, Toby. More," Colin encourages as we move back to kick-off again.

For the rest of the first half, I only get better. The other team puts a man on me to stop me from getting the ball, and I enjoy myself spinning and feinting away from him. When I do have the ball, their defense holds back a little now—a little afraid of getting turned—and I make full use of the space. Still, they put up a hell of a fight, battles all over, and when we head in for halftime the score is still even.

In the locker room we catch our breath as everyone talks over what we should be doing. Asher hands me an energy drink and sits beside me as I tell myself that I should really ease up on the booze.

Chapter 11

"Great little get-together last Friday, huh?" he says in a friendly tone.

I look at him and nod.

"Yeah."

He laughs gently to himself for a second and then says, "I didn't even know Colin was setting me up. He told me he just wanted to show off how good his wife was at cooking Thai food."

Suddenly I'm interested.

"Really?"

"Yeah," Asher says, chuckling again. "I'm not complaining though. Maeve is...something special."

I cough, the drink sticking in my throat a little, then manage to clear my throat.

"You're into her then?" I ask him, trying not to sound too curious.

Asher shrugs and smiles.

"Who wouldn't be? She's crazy hot."

"Did you and her...?"

"Fuck?" Asher says, and I wince at the word like it's a hammer blow to the temple. Not the word itself, but the fact that someone's using it in regard to Maeve. Someone other than *me*. "No. I get the impression she's the type to play hard to get."

"Ha!" I blurt out, then straighten my face up a little and shrug as if that wasn't a personal reaction. "Yeah... Really? I mean... I get that impression too."

"Right?" Asher agrees. "Anyway, we're seeing each other again this week—"

"You are?" I interrupt, then pretend to be more interested in sipping my drink to hide how surprised I am.

"Some art exhibition. We were both going anyway, so she agreed to let me pick her up." Asher winks at me and smiles. "Second time lucky, right? I'll bet you didn't have that problem with Hazel, huh? She seemed pretty hot for you all evening."

I choke on the drink again and even splutter a bit of it over my dirtied sports gear. I thump my chest to clear my throat.

"Shit..." I say. "Never liked the taste of this stuff."

"Me neither. I always stick to water when I—"

"So you think you and her might get something going?" I ask, too interested to hide it anymore. "Do you think she's really into you?"

Asher seems to think about it for a moment, then says, "Who knows? All I can tell you is that I'm gonna have as much fun with her, and take it as far with her, as I can. She's a prize, even in L.A."

"Yeah, but I mean, are you like *into* her or do you just wanna—"

My words are drowned out by the sudden surge of hollering and noise in the locker room as the guys get up, start jumping and stretching as they begin making their way out, Asher included.

"Shit," I say, but nobody hears me over the sound of studs on hard floor and the cries of "come on!"

Now I'm back out on the field again, but the last thing on my mind is how to turn my defender or when to make my run. Now all I'm doing is repeating Asher's tone and words back in my mind and wondering what he means by it. *Have as much fun... And take it as far as I can with her...* What exactly does that even mean? Is he into her or what?

Obviously, he wants to fuck her—I didn't need to ask to find that out, any straight guy with blood above freezing would—but does he actually want something deeper with her? Is he trying to date her? Maybe women are right when they say men are just as confusing as they are…

Twenty minutes into the second half and I'm playing worse than I did at the start. Defenders taking the ball from me like I'm moving in slow motion, and the few times I try to pass forward, I end up misjudging. My head's somewhere else now, trying to figure out what Asher's all about—and realizing that I'm maybe not as casual about the whole thing as I thought I was.

And what the hell was Maeve doing arranging a date with the guy? I mean, sure, I swapped numbers with Hazel, but I didn't even think about when or how we might meet again. That moment in the bedroom, where we told each other we weren't going to fuck our respective "dates"—it wasn't a promise, of course. We never said it out loud. We couldn't. We didn't need to. It was understood. And now it turns out Maeve simply found a "loophole." A way of getting around it. Is she planning to fuck him after that art thing? Did Asher have to try hard to persuade her? Is she even planning to go?

I find myself glaring at Asher—who's playing as the number ten, so we're not too far apart—and I'm glaring at him so intently, trying to figure out if Maeve would be taken by him, that I completely miss a beautifully placed pass that Colin plays to me. A perfect ball that would have put even the red-faced guy I replaced in a dangerous position.

"Wake up, Toby!" the striker yells at me, and I raise a palm as apology.

We're getting close to the end of the match, and it's still even. Both teams desperate now, throwing more bodies forward, flying into tackles and taking more risks as we both chase a winning goal.

But I don't care. None of this shit matters anymore.

Maeve's about to go off and fuck some other guy and I'm supposed to just be cool with it when I'm not. When I *can't* be.

My surprise and confusion soon turns into a bristling anger, deep inside. A thorn in my side that makes me hyper-aware and itching to do something, to move, to act. The kind of focus you can only get from pain. And it's in this frame of mind that the ball comes to me once again, hurtling at a speed that I have no right to be able to control, sure to go out.

I kill the ball dead, bringing it down right in front of me with a touch so deft Picasso would admire it. I knock it past a defender while I run the other side, switch feet to dance past two more, then change direction to leave another sliding into nothing. Through once again, but once again too wide, I look inside to see who's there for the cross.

Asher. He's making a perfect run, and all I need to do is pass to him to give him a chance he could score with his eyes closed. But it's Asher—and I've already given him too much. I look at the goal, the angle impossibly tight, the keeper covering almost every space to shoot in. There's maybe seven inches of goal above him that I can score in, but I'd need to hit it razor-accurate, and even then with the force of a freight train to get it past the goalie. And I'll have to do it now.

I strike the ball guided by nothing but instinct, nothing but passion and reckless abandon behind my foot, not caring if it flies miles wide. A wild, aggressive, outrageous— and almost selfish—attempt.

Maybe it's the sheer audacity of it, the keeper himself expecting me to pass to Asher, or maybe it's that I'm so in the moment it's like time slows as I connect with the ball, but it heads straight for the top corner. The keeper gets fingertips to it but not enough to push it away. It slams against the underside of the crossbar with a satisfying thud and crashes down into the back of the goal.

I hit the ball so hard and at such an angle that it had left me on the ground, and before I can get up there are roaring bodies piling on top of me. Whacks on the head and an ear-busting chorus of joyous, primal victory screams.

"You fucking beautiful son of a bitch!"

"*That's* how you do it! *That's* how!"

"That was glorious, you bastard!"

The shouts ease up, but only a little, as the weight of the bodies on me do, and I find myself being pulled up to my feet. A victorious glare in my face as we make our way back for another kick-off, my new teammates continue to come in for fist bumps and shows of appreciation.

"That was some fucking goal!" Asher says, smacking me on the back. I turn to nod at him as he moves ahead, jogging backwards. He wags his finger as a joke. "And a good thing too, or I'd have been on you for not passing it!"

I smile back at him.

"I don't like giving things away that easily."

12

MAEVE

My Monday at work has been the busiest in a long time. Brent and Harriet are so enthused about the new jewelry line, bombarding me with ideas and proposals for it throughout the day, that you'd think *they* were the ones putting their names on it. Add to that a weekend spent with the dinner date at Mia's and roaming about the house taking care of myself, and it's no wonder I'm falling behind on the social engagements and event-attending that anyone in fashion needs to maintain in order to secure their connections and status. Time to focus. Get myself back on track. Show everyone what I'm made of.

I cram about twenty hours of work into the ten hours I'm on the clock. Half of it outside the offices, visiting a few of our stores to clear up some inventory issues, and meeting with a supplier whom I had to charm out of his disappointment at waiting so long to see me.

By the time I'm gathering my things to leave, the last person in the office, I'm ready for a long bath and a deep sleep, but instead I only touch base at home for a quick shower and change of outfits before heading out again. It's been too long since normality—and for me normality is other people, dressing up, and enjoying life.

It starts with drinks at a bar where I know the bartender well and the exclusive clientele even better. Before I'm halfway through my cosmopolitan, I'm chatting with a man I know from a fashion chain who is almost as interested in a lucrative deal for both our companies as he is in me. Then I get a call from a friend who writes for a European fashion magazine asking me if I'm free, and I turn down the first man's invitation to dinner to take up this writer's instead.

I agree to meet her at a restaurant so new it's not even open to the public yet, only available via a reservation process that's more like a secret society initiation. The writer invites a few of her European colleagues as well, and I invite Harriet—it's about time she started taking steps into the big leagues. The conversation is just about interesting enough to distract, but just about boring enough for me to evaluate the environment and the food, and wonder if it's worth inviting Mia here for one of our dinners.

The most interesting of our co-diners—a dangerous-looking young Frenchman—takes a shine to Harriet, and judging by the fact that she hasn't stopped playing with her hair since she sat down, I would guess the feeling's mutual. He invites her to a Latin dancing club and she asks me to come along, though I'm not sure if she wants me to protect her from the Frenchman, or her own impulses.

At the club, a floor filled with tango dancers and an atmosphere full of pheromones and music seem to loosen Harriet up a little. After half an hour of her necking with the Frenchman I let a handsome stranger invite me to the floor where I show off moves I learned during an incredible summer in South America years ago.

At midnight, once I realize Harriet texted me to tell me

that she's taking the Frenchman home with her, I leave the club, my handsome stranger knowing nothing more about me than my ability to move even in a tight skirt. But I don't make it home. The allure of an after-party for an indie film's premiere sounding too good to resist.

When I arrive at the bar of the small theatre, it seems that most of the cast were an extraordinarily beautiful assembly of Pasolini-esque men and women. One of the female leads compliments me on the piece she read about me in a fashion magazine, and we spend the rest of the evening talking shop, the young woman smarter than her years and without a doubt a star in the making. As we talk, one of the beautiful male actors makes eyes at me so crude and sexual they would be vulgar in any older man.

Though the night has been a return to the norm for me, a familiar rhythm full of familiar twists and turns, I diverge from the pattern at this point. The typical thing, the customary thing, the thing I would do as instinctively and as nonchalantly as sipping water after dinner, would be to take this young actor home and fuck his brains out. To take his dirty, debauched gaze and turn it into one of absolute, satisfied, reverent fatigue.

But I don't. Instead, after giving the fascinating young actress my number, I take advantage of a moment when he ducks into the restroom to leave the party and head home. I tell myself I've given up the opportunity for a night of hedonistic indulgence because it's nearly two a.m. and Tuesday promises to be as busy as Monday. It's a good enough excuse to not think about why any further.

I end up sharing an Uber home with a drunk dullard, but the trip is short enough for it not to sour my night too much. At home I feel the force of all my drinking, a heavy drowsiness setting in, but my assiduousness winning through still so that I diligently remove my makeup and shower thoroughly before putting on a face mask that I peel off just before I'm finally ready for bed.

Half drunk and fully tired, my head still dizzy and my limbs cool and stiff from fatigue, the softness of the bed and its sheets feel like a kind of drug themselves. I sigh with an intimacy I reserve only for myself as I lie back on the pillows, reaching over the nightstand one last time to turn off the light.

It's then, with perfectly imperfect timing, that my phone rings. No vibration or noise, but the screen alighting with the name of the caller. I grab it to turn it over but accidentally catch the name and pause.

Toby.

I stare at the name for several seconds, every sensible part of me in no doubt that I need to turn the phone over and get to sleep, but a part of me I've been trying to ignore for a long time too intensely curious to actually do it. It's the latter which wins. I press the green button and put the phone to my ear.

"What are you wearing?" his recognizably mischievous voice says.

"A clown suit. You?"

He laughs, seeming in a good mood, but I try to pretend that I don't find it infectious, hiding the sound of my smile.

"I'm just sitting on my couch looking really hot in nothing but boxers and one of those Hawaiian shirts you hate. Unbuttoned. Try to picture it."

"It's quarter to three, Toby. Why are you calling me?"

"The bigger question is: Why did you answer?"

There's a long silence. The sound of a car outside making it seem even heavier. I shift a little in the dark and the rustling of my bedsheets sounds like a cacophony. I wonder if he can hear my breath. Though I'm not too sure, I *feel* like I can hear his.

"I heard..." he begins, in a slower, less playful tone. "You were going to see Asher again."

The statement feels like a curveball, and I decide to hide how odd I find it.

"That's right."

"You like him?"

"I think I'm in love with him," I say. "I've been thinking of baby names ever since we met."

"Come on, Maeve. Be serious."

I laugh but it comes out a little too breathily.

"Isn't that something? Toby Taylor asking somebody else to be serious."

He says nothing and the silence once again seems too intimate, somehow the fact that I can't see him, can't read his face or look into his eyes making this moment even more intense than it should be. The quiet lasts too long, and I shift in my bed a little, the rustling covers sounding like brushed skin.

"What are you doing, Toby? Are you drunk?" I ask.

"So... Is it like a sexy clown outfit?"

I laugh too genuinely to pretend I'm irritated by his call now, so that it sounds insincere, like I'm only playing his game, when I say, "I have to sleep. I've got work tomorrow."

That long silence once again, and it's too comfortable now. Too easy. *Dangerously* so. Nothing we could say could possibly make us feel closer than the silence—the sound of each other's breathing. I should hang up. I *could* hang up, and it wouldn't even be rude or an insult... But I don't.

"I was just thinking," Toby starts again, "about that big garden party in Holmby Hills about four years ago. It was for some movie or something. You remember it?"

"Vaguely."

"You even invited Mia along—I think you were trying to set her up with someone."

I remember it vividly and smile. "Yeah."

There's a pause, but not long this time.

"I was surprised to see my sister there. Wasn't her sort of scene."

"Still isn't."

"And you…" Toby says, then leaves another pause. "You were with this guy. Some model."

"An actor," I say in a provocatively dreamy tone. "But he'd done some modelling. He was one of the most beautiful men in the world."

"He was a dweeb," Toby says.

"You sound envious."

Toby scoffs, "One of those guys who spent his whole life cruising on his looks. Nothing in him. Closest he probably ever came to real life was putting on a tool belt for a photo shoot."

I let out a laugh and say, "And I suppose you're fixing pipes in your house every day, are you?"

"How hard can it be?" Toby says through a smile I can hear in his tone. "I wouldn't be afraid to try, you can be sure of that."

"Oh, I'm sure you would, honey."

There's another laugh, the humor fading a little.

"The thing I remember," he continues, "is how everyone at that party kept saying that you were the perfect couple. How attractive both of you were, how good you looked together. The belles of the ball. That party went from afternoon to the next morning, and that whole time all I kept hearing was what a 'perfect couple' you two made…

"And all I could think was that everyone was crazy. The

guy was...*nothing*. He was your average failed actor. All phony charisma and overbearing energy..." Toby leaves another pause. "But I think I get it now."

"You do?" I say, acting disinterested.

"Yeah. It was never about the guy. It was *you*... They didn't see *you* the same way I did."

This time the pause isn't so comfortable. This time I hold my breath, because for him to even hear it might be revealing too much. I no longer even feel like I'm in my own bed, in the comfort of my own house, the sense of vulnerability and danger too much.

"Toby..." I say, his name coming out like a sigh. "What are we doing?"

The moments before he replies are almost painful.

"To be honest with you, Maeve: I don't know... I don't know...but...what if—"

"No," I interrupt quickly. "No 'what ifs.' I don't like them."

"Why?"

"What ifs... They're the path to sadness, to missed opportunities, regrets, and emotional paralysis," I say, reciting my oft-thought ideas. "'What if I had rich parents and a great upbringing, *then* I'd be the person I want to be.' 'What if I hadn't dropped out of college,' 'what if I *had* dropped out of college.' 'What if I had a nicer nose, or bigger tits, or lost some weight...' No.

"I prefer what *is*. And what *is*, is that it's nearly three in the morning on a weekday and I need to get to sleep too much to listen to your late-night drunk ramblings."

After a perfectly timed pause, Toby says, "What if..." I let out a breathy laugh of dismay, and he continues, "I were to come to your house right now."

"I wouldn't let you in," I say.

"What if you did..."

There's another pause, and in this game of psychological poker I reveal a little too much. The phone mic may be picking up a little too much of my deepening breath, certainly on the rustle of the covers as I squirm a little in bed, brushing thighs at even the suggestion of his presence here, now, with me in nothing but panties in my bed.

"What if I came up to your bedroom..." he adds. "Found you in your bed..."

"In my clown suit?" I say, but my voice sounds too low and sensual for the joke, making it sound more like an invitation than a dismissal.

"In nothing but your panties..." Toby continues, his voice lower, fuller, firmer. Steamrolling over my joke as if nothing can stop his intent now. "Your body spread out, facedown... Skin cool in the breeze from your open window, head buried in the pillow... And you know I'm there, but you're pretending not to..."

There's no hiding my reaction in the silence now. My shaky sigh, the sound of my wet lips parting, the slow rustle of my hand reaching down between my thighs.

"Then how would I even know it's you?" I sigh into the phone, my hips grinding into the bed in a slow rhythm now.

"You'd know..." he growls, a heavy breath crackling through the phone. "By the way I touch you... Fingers trailing up the soles of your feet... Teeth on the back of your ankles, kissing my way up your calves... I'd taste every part of you... Find every little imperfection of your body and mark it..."

I let out a soft murmur, my breath slow and warm, my body vibrating now to the forceful timbre of his voice.

"And what else, Toby?" I whisper on short breath,

Chapter 12

touching myself and arching my back in slow, swinging rhythm. "What are you going to do to me?"

"Gonna pull your thighs apart and put my face in your ass..." he says through gritted teeth, and I hear on his hard breath that's he's holding himself too. "Gonna pull those panties aside... And pull your ass cheeks apart... And put my tongue inside you..."

I let out a quiet, involuntary squeal, something inside of me tightening in the most satisfying way.

"I wanna pull your perfect little ass over my face... I wanna bury myself in you, grind into you, press my tongue as far inside of you as you can take it... I wanna kiss your tight little pussy until it's wet... I wanna suck and drink the juice out of you..."

"Yeah?" I say, but it's only a half word, the other half another surrendering squeal.

"Yeah," he says heavily, and I can just about hear through my own dizzy pleasure that his voice is shaking as well to his own touch. The thought of him clutching his hard cock while he's telling me all this pushing me even further, making my own hand quicker, my own urge more impatient. "Tell me what you want."

"I want you to fuck me, Toby," I gasp, words as careless and instinctive as my breath now. "I want your big dick inside me..."

I hear his breath quicken, the sound of gritted teeth as he tries to hold back, to maintain control.

"You want me to show you how hard you get me, Maeve?"

"Yes..."

"You want me to lift your ass up so I can fuck that tight little pussy of yours?"

"Yes..."

"You want me to pull you hair... Smack your ass until it's red... Swing this long, hard, dick into you so deep you feel like you'll break?"

"Yes... *Yes, yes, yes...*" I repeat, the word like a mantra, my last connection with conscious thought as my body hums and rocks to the sound of his voice, to a touch that doesn't even feel like my own anymore.

"My hand on the back of your neck, pushing your face into the pillow... Fingers pinching your nipples, my teeth on your shoulder... I wanna see your ass cheeks shake, Maeve..."

"*Yessss...*"

My voice is a long gurgle now, my body moving in spasms. The momentum of my impending orgasm too big and overwhelming to stop, so that even as I try to hold back, to dwell in this sweet moment any longer, I can't help myself.

"Show me, Maeve," he commands, his voice hard with his own hunger. "I wanna hear how you moan... I wanna hear the sound of your beautiful body coming for me..."

I go silent for a whole two seconds, my body freezing, my breath stopped, as if it's all too much to feel, to react to. A beautiful few seconds that feel like I'm flying, and then... Release.

A long, swirling moan emanates from my lips like the sound of gathering wind through a tunnel, a climax that comes in multiple thudding beats of sensual warmth. Every part of my body tensing and then releasing each time, toes curling, shoulders hunching, torso tensioning... And then the most lovely feeling of lightness, as if all of life's burdens no longer exist. A glimpse of heaven.

After almost a minute of wallowing in this wonderful post-orgasmic bliss, I realize I dropped the phone onto the pillow beside me. It's faint glow the only light apart from a pale moon peeking through the shutters. I pick it up and see that Toby is still on the call.

"Are you there?" I say, my voice back to its typically composed state, just a hint of its prior softness.

"I'm here," Toby says, back in his normal tone—though his normal tone always sounds a little amused.

I hear his movements on the line, rustling and scratching.

"You really are a bastard, you know that?" I say through a smile.

He laughs.

"I couldn't help myself."

"Well," I say, "let's call that the last time. We've already dragged this on longer than we should have."

There's a long pause before Toby answers, and I can tell he's thinking about it—right after coming is probably the only time he *can* think about anything.

"Yeah..." he says, regretfully but honestly. "Maybe you're right..."

"Good night, Toby."

"Night."

13

TOBY

I always walk into work with my chin high and an approachable expression, but there's a little extra zest in me when I turn up on Tuesday morning with coffee and donuts for Sharon and myself. I'm a little late, having gone to see a friend who works for a record label with a car collection you could race a grand tour with. He ended up lending me a Porsche 911 with the option to buy.

"Good morning," I call in a cheerful tone as I step inside.

There's a couple browsing the cases, and Sharon's chatting with an older gentleman over the counter. In the corner of the shop there are another two guys and two girls standing stiffly, their clothes a little too formal for their nervous expressions.

"Morning, boss," Sharon says, letting the older man continue looking himself.

"This is for me," I say, plucking my coffee from the tray, then pushing the rest toward Sharon, "and these are for you."

"Donuts?" she says almost helplessly, as if she knows

she won't be able to resist. "I told you I'm not doing sugar right now. Gotta get back in shape."

"Ah, forget that," I say, waving it away. "Gain some weight, lose some weight... You still have a smile that knocks the guys out."

She laughs and bites dreamily into a maple glazed, then looks a little more intently at me as I round the counter sipping my coffee.

"*You're* in a good mood," she says. "I'm not going to ask why."

"I think you can guess," I say, winking at her. I glance across the shop at the awkward group in the corner then back at her. "What do they want?"

Sharon looks at me for a second as if to be sure I really asked that.

"The candidates for the backroom staff? You invited them all to have interviews today."

"Ah shit," I say snapping my fingers. "Yeah... Yeah, right."

"There are probably more coming—these ones are just those who turned up early."

"Right right," I say, suddenly moving double time, looking around as if to check whether I need anything. "I'll get to interviewing then. You can handle the shop, right?"

Sharon gives me a look as if amused I would even ask such a dumb question.

"Okay," I say, turning to the group. "Let's get started, shall we?"

They look at each other, a couple taking awkward steps then stopping, a strange kind of half dance, their sense of politeness fighting with their desire to show initiative.

"How about you first," I say, "girl with the blonde hair. Follow me."

Chapter 13

Sharon turns out to be right, as usual. There are more candidates that arrive. By the time I finish interviewing the first four, another five show up, then another seven. My inability to discriminate, my desire to give everyone a fair chance, means that I have every kind of person showing up to interview for the job. From a woman who worked seven years doing sales at a prestigious jewelry store in Dallas, to a guy whose only work experience was a summer spent as a parking lot attendant.

Still, Sharon was too shy to string more than two words together when I hired her, and God knows I had to start my own business because not a single company would risk hiring someone who looks and talks (and acts) like me, so I know more than anyone that a resume can lie better than a person.

I spend the whole morning talking jewelry with the candidates. Evaluating stones, polishing metals, schools of design, trends and fashions, managing stock... The back-room employee isn't going to be selling the things, but they're going to have to know how to treat it and judge it as good as I can if they want to work for me. And since there's nobody who knows as much as me about gems, I'm looking for someone who's keen and willing to learn, and who knows just how much they don't know. That means the girl from Dallas doesn't make the shortlist, but the parking lot attendant does.

Around lunchtime, I finish up an interview with only three people left. That's when Sharon pokes her head into my office to tell me Mia's in the shop.

"Hey!" I call as I step out onto the floor and approach her. She's carrying Alison in her arms and has a shoulder full of shopping bags. "What a nice surprise!"

"I was just doing a bit of shopping in the neighborhood and—"

"Do you mind?" I tell Mia as I pinch Alison's cheek. "I was talking to this little cutie here."

Mia laughs and I look around for Colin.

"You three," I say to the remaining candidates, "come back tomorrow."

They look at each other for a second before shuffling out.

"Oh, I didn't mean to interrupt anything," Mia says. "I just wanted to—"

"They're here for a job," I tell her, but I'm still smiling at Alison. "If they really want it they'll be back. You wanna grab some lunch?"

"I literally came to ask you that," Mia says.

"Hey, Sharon," I say, but by the time I turn to her she's already waving me away. I turn back to Mia. "Let's go. Hey, gimme Alison, and those bags. I've got something you'll love."

Mia looks at me suspiciously for a moment as I take my niece from her and I answer her suspicions by handing her the keys to the Porsche. My sister always had a thing for nice cars—specifically driving them. Don't ask me why, all I know is that her eyes light up when she sees the horse on the keys the way mine do when I see a woman in a summer dress.

I help Mia get Alison's car seat situated, and then we're off. I think the baby likes the car as much as her mommy does, because she spends half the drive cooing and the other half sleeping.

After a long drive Mia eventually, reluctantly, stops outside a terrace café where we take a couple of seats with a nice people-watching view of the street.

Chapter 13

"What a car..." She's still fawning after we sit down as she tends to Alison in her lap. "It's so well-balanced. The back end just sticks to the road; even when you can feel it going, it's completely under your control. And the transmission is so satisfying, those long gears..."

"All I know is, girls like it but it's still comfortable enough for them to sit in."

"I want one."

"Even after it took ten minutes to fit your stroller into the back?"

"Totally worth it."

We order a couple of sandwiches and cold drinks, and enjoy looking at Alison a while as she stares wide-eyed at the passing people.

"Actually," Mia starts, "I wanted to ask you how things went with Hazel."

"And here's me thinking you just wanted to spend a little quality time with your brother."

She smiles and thanks the waiter as the food is placed before us. A Cubano for me, and an avocado club for my sister. Meanwhile Alison just gets a bottle, poor thing.

"It's just that... I saw her at work—" Mia starts.

"I thought you weren't back at work yet?" I ask.

"I just dropped by to see some people, and check up on a few things before—anyway, it doesn't matter. The point is, I saw her, and... She didn't say much about what happened. I didn't pry, but I could tell she was really into you."

I shift a little in my seat and take a big bite of my sandwich so I can delay talking back. The layers of melty Swiss cheese, seasoned pork, yellow mustard, and crisp sour pickles have me groaning.

"Are you going to call her?" Mia asks.

I finish chewing, swallow, then shrug. "She's great. Really an awesome girl," I say.

My sister cocks a brow. "So you *are* going to call her?"

"How come you even tried to set me up? I mean, the last thing I need is help meeting women. You know that, Mia."

"Not women like Hazel. She's really sweet, and kind, and down-to-earth without being boring. You can't tell me you're meeting girls like her at any of your lavish mansion pool parties."

"Sure," I say, shrugging again, feeling a little defensive. "But...you don't think it could get potentially messy? Me dating someone you work with? Someone you clearly like as a friend? I'll be the first to admit I'm not an angel, Mia. What if things go bad? What if we date for three months then I decide it isn't going to work?

"Next thing you know, you're working with a girl who resents you for introducing her to your asshole brother. And you can't hang out with her anymore because I might show up to a dinner party and the whole vibe will be really weird. I don't have a good track record with women—not in that way. And the last thing I need is for you to be in the middle of one of my fuck-ups."

I have to take a long drink of my Coke and look away now, unable to believe I'm actually saying all this—and saying it to *Mia*.

I'm literally doing everything I just told her I want to avoid. Here I am pretending to be the bigger man when I'm guilty. When I've already put Mia in the middle of one of my potential fuck-ups. And now I'm lying to her about it.

"Oh!" Mia says suddenly, as if noticing something. She looks at Alison conspiratorially. "Oh, I get it... Yeah... I see." She smiles broadly and looks at me incredulously. I feel my heart start to beat weirdly. "You're doing it again."

Chapter 13

"What?"

"You're doing it again."

I grab a fry and try to act nonchalant. "I don't get it."

"There's someone else, isn't there?" Mia says. "You've found some other 'impossible' woman to become obsessed over."

My instinct is to deny it, but I've already lied to Mia enough—too much.

"Well...maybe something like that."

"Oh no, Toby..." Mia says, disappointed. "*Again?*"

I shrug helplessly, staring down at my sandwich and suddenly finding I have no appetite.

"What do you want me to say? It's who I am."

"So now that you've convinced yourself you're in love with some unattainable woman, you're going to pass up a wonderful girl who could *actually* make you happy?"

"No no," I say, wagging my finger quickly. "It's not love. I'm not in love with her."

Mia continues to smile and jogs Alison on her knee a little.

"Well that's something of an improvement over all the others, at least," she says. "At least you're not deluding yourself this time."

I can do nothing but grimace, shrug, and sip my drink, almost afraid if I say anything I'll be revealing too much, this whole conversation already a little too dangerous for me.

"But she's unobtainable, right?" Mia says, not letting up, having her fun.

"Something like that."

She shakes her head affectionately. "You always want exactly the thing you can't have."

I let out the same sigh I always respond to that same line with.

"It is what it is," I say, forcing myself to take another bite of my food and trying to think of how I can change the subject ASAP.

"You going to tell me about her at least?" Mia says.

I look back at her, and shift in my seat, suddenly feeling like it's too small, too uncomfortable. I stare out at the street for a while and pretend to think.

The thing is, I *always* tell Mia about them. The women I get obsessed with. I've bored her to tears over so many of them that it'll be weird if I don't say anything now—and the last thing I want is for this to get any weirder.

"Well...I mean...she's hot..."

"Of course."

"But, like...not just hot...*beautiful*. Like...even her imperfections are perfect. The way she *moves* is beautiful. Her voice is beautiful. The way she *thinks* even, and acts... It's as if there's not a single thing she can do or say that she doesn't make beautiful... And not even just beautiful... Something more than that... It's like she's got this *spirit*... Or this passion... I've never seen it before... To me it's as if she's more *alive* than any other person, any other *woman* that I've ever met.

"And it's strange because when we're talking...just engaging with each other, it's different somehow. Like there's this clarity between us. This weirdly strong sort of understanding... Anyone else...there's that element of bullshit. Always. But with *her*...even when it's an act, it's real... It's easy, but not like 'give in' easy, or 'low standards' easy... Like...'This feels right' easy... And I'm not just saying I can be myself around her... Or maybe... No... I feel like I'm my *best* self around her. I like who *I* am around her... And I think I can bring out the best in her, too... Shit... I dunno... I'm rambling..."

I look up from my sandwich to Mia to see if she bought it, but her smile's gone. Instead she's staring at me with a look of earnest tenderness I haven't seen since I gave her a Miata as a gift.

"What?" I say, after half a minute of her staring at me.

"That's the most convincing, genuine feeling you've ever conveyed about anyone."

I laugh at her incredulously, pick up my sandwich then put it down again, and laugh again.

"Shit, Mia. You know me. I'm just a fucking idiot when it comes to these things. Always chasing what I can't have so I can feel hard done-by. Gimme a week and I'll probably be onto the next chick."

"No, Toby," Mia says, her voice calm and sisterly. "I don't think you should. I think you might actually be in love this time."

I laugh again but I can't stop it from sounding forced and phony, so loud it draws looks from a couple of the other diners.

"Christ, Mia," I say, smiling and gesturing at Alison. "Can we talk about how beautiful and sweet and smart my niece is instead?"

"Is she married?" Mia asks, not letting up.

"No."

"In a relationship?"

"No... I don't know actually. Maybe. Perhaps."

"Does she like you back?"

"Yeah... Well... I don't know... In the same way, not that I... It's more like... There's a lot of ways to like someone..."

"So what is it holding you two apart?"

I try to force another laugh but this time it doesn't come

out, only a strange half-exasperated sigh. I pick up my sandwich, grimace at it, then put it down again.

"Damn, this sandwich is dry... I'm not even hungry." I check my watch and make a surprised face. "Shit, this has been a long lunch. Spent a long time in the Porsche... Sharon's gonna kill me. I'd best get back..." I stand up and grab my things. "You're okay to drive yourself back to the shop, right? I'll just call an Uber."

"Toby..." Mia says calmly, but I'm already leaning down to kiss Alison on the forehead, then do the same to Mia.

"I'll catch up with you later, all right?" I say, already heading down the steps. "Just drop the keys off with Sharon when you get back."

"Toby," Mia says, loud enough to hear, but still calm, since she knows I'm not going to stop.

"Let me know when you wanna do this again..." I shout back over my shoulder as I sprint across the road, away from Mia, away from what she said, away from the feeling that she might be right.

14

MAEVE

Men don't plan. That's their great weakness—and only occasionally a strength for them.

They *think* they plan. They tell themselves that they do. They might even tell you some version of a "plan." But the reality is that men have desires, not plans. And they lead their in-the-moment lives eternally heading in whatever direction they think their desires lie. Like dim headlights on a dark night, they'll follow the road—until the sun comes up and they realize they've been heading in circles.

Add to this the fact that men's desires can change with the wind, and there's rarely an excuse for a woman who knows what she's doing not to get the better of them. I think about this as I scan my wardrobe putting together an outfit for the art exhibition I agreed to meet Asher at. Nowhere is that inability to plan clearer than on a date. Even a sophisticated, smart, experienced lover like Asher will dress to make a great impression. And I'm sure he will—but impressions based on appearances are overrated. Better to end a weak story strongly than start a bad story well.

Now I'm standing in my walk-in closet, perusing my

large coat collection, thinking about how I want this evening to end. As friends? Or as lovers? A peck on the cheek and a distant ambiguity that'll test how much he's into me? A proper kiss and a goodbye that'll further the sexual tension between us? The cold hard truth is that a date with a suave, handsome guy like Asher would have left me in no doubt just a short while ago. I'd want to end the night fucking him.

It's all there in front of me, my clothes like a map that'll guide me through the evening. I could have him staring at my breasts every time I talk so that it doesn't matter what I say, or compel him into my ideas with dangling earrings that draw attention to my mouth. I could force him to play the gentleman by dressing like a lady, bring out his sillier side with something shockingly colorful, or wear a dress that will remind him we're all animals and simply wait until he starts acting like one.

I go for something conservative. A cream skirt and white blouse, a long Burberry trench—leaving all the attention on a pair of spectacular leather riding boots with a series of buckle fasteners down the sides. It's a quick decision, a rash decision. I tell myself it's a classic outfit that leaves open all possibilities. I tell myself it's not too boring for me, that I'm not trying to dampen my possibilities or downplay my sexuality. I tell myself a lot of things so that I don't have to deal with the nagging thoughts that threaten to emerge if I spend any more time thinking about it.

I'll live this evening like a man, in the moment, going with the flow, without a plan. That's it. That's what I'm doing. There's nothing else to it.

Asher insisted on picking me up, even though I prefer neutral territory for the first strike of the evening. I'm still finishing off my makeup when I hear his car pull up in my driveway. He's early. I like that. Some men think it's cocky to show up late, but real courage is a man who isn't afraid to show how eager he is.

He sends me a message to let me know he's waiting outside. A relaxed message, as if he'd be willing to wait all night if need be. I don't make him wait quite that long, and soon head outside. He steps out of the car as I approach, looking absurdly hot; certainly more than even my rather fond memory of him at dinner last week. His shoulder-length hair behind his ears, still a little wild, but sexy enough to work. His fresh shaven face only enhancing his manliness by revealing a jawline like a monument. Most striking of all is his outfit. A low neckline shirt beneath a black long coat, crimson pants, and worker boots. Most men attempting to make it work would look like a transplant from a nineties teen drama about a goth kid. But Asher looks like an incredibly sexy Byron-esque poet who would be as comfortable at an underground European dance club as he most assuredly will be at the art gallery.

"Wow," he says as I approach.

"Wow yourself." I smile back, instinctively reaching out to touch and appreciate the fabric of his coat. "I love this... I'd wear it myself."

"Maybe you will by the end of the evening," Asher says, with perfect tone and timing, so that I impulsively return his knowing gaze.

"Where did you say you worked again?" I ask as I walk around to the passenger side. He steps ahead of me to open the door.

"Here and there," he says, before he rounds the vehicle and gets in. "Movies mainly. And producing most of all. But I've done it all in my time." He starts the car and continues talking as he drives. "I've been behind the camera, in front of it..."

"A jack of all trades."

Asher laughs, and instantly reminds me of what a nice, caramel-rich laugh he has.

"Always passionate about what I do, though. And these days that's the only thing that matters."

I smile forward at the road. "I agree."

After about a minute of a deliciously tense silence, Asher says, "You know, I've got a confession to make..."

"Oh?"

"This artist we're going to see. Jane..."

"Jane Murdoch."

"Yeah... Thing is, I have no idea what she's about. Never seen her art before in my life. I mean, I've heard the hype—who hasn't. But as for the art..."

"She's European," I explain, "but she's spent the past decade in New York. She's done a fantastic job of treading the fine line between hot enough to command high prices, but never quite getting big enough to become passé. She gives great interviews, but not many, and very rarely. It doesn't hurt that she's photogenic, either.

"Part of the excitement is that she's left New York for L.A. She's *ours* now, a lot of people feel, and they're determined to treat her just as well as the elites on the East Coast did."

Asher glances from the road to me so I can see his smile.

"Impressive," he says. "You know your stuff."

"It can be deadly if you don't."

"But...what about the actual art?" he asks. "What's that like?"

I let out a flighty laugh. "Oh honey, if you think the art itself matters then you know less about that world than you let on."

Chapter 14

Asher laughs gently, then nods at the building ahead of us as he turns onto a side street.

"I'm sure you could teach me plenty. Here we are."

He parks and we walk toward the modernist building in downtown L.A. in which the exhibition will take place, the beautiful people and some glimpses of the paintings and installations visible through the glass fronts. We make idle chitchat about how well we know the area respectively as we walk.

I've never liked the term *chemistry*, but there's definitely a pleasant and slightly exciting feeling between us. Asher has a kind of presence that's both intriguingly enigmatic, but engagingly uplifting to be near. He's attentive without being impatient or overbearing. Charming but subtle with it. And more than anything else, irresistibly cool in everything he says or does.

The exhibition is already filled with people who would have been fashionably late were this not the biggest event of the month. Fabulously aloof people who are experts at making themselves look even more beautiful than they are. People who learn how to stand and to move from studying fashion magazines and art films, and who rarely allow anything but a stoic detachment to express itself on their faces. My kind of people, in other words.

Our moment of idle intimacy chatting on the way from the parking spot to the exhibition ends almost as soon as we enter. Asher and I are immediately besieged by greetings and invitations to join already-formed groups. Soon the only words Asher and I exchange are the names and professions of our respective friends as we go through the formalities of superficial pleasantries.

"*Maeve*! How lovely to see you! When was it last? That

fundraiser for the hospital? I love what you've done with your hair."

"I think it was the Clapham launch event wasn't it? Speaking of hair, I love that color on you—just perfect."

"Thanks. Hold on, I've got someone I *have* to introduce you to..."

Everyone I know—or rather, those who know me—isn't surprised to find me accompanied by a strikingly attractive and charismatic man. Interestingly, though, none of Asher's friends seem too surprised to find him with a confident and smart woman, either. I find it a little encouraging to know they don't expect him to be with an empty-headed model or a woman who can't hold her own.

"And who's this?"

"This is Maeve. She works in fashion."

"Really? The name sounds so familiar, though I'm sure I would have remembered you if I'd seen you around before."

"Glad you finally have a chance to put a face to the name."

After an hour the champagne glasses start appearing as if from nowhere, as well as hors d'oeuvres beautiful enough to be framed on the walls themselves. The crowd gets a little louder, a little looser (a few of them even breaking into smiles) and Asher and I get split up for a while as we mingle and move with old and new friends.

Eventually I find myself staring at a canvas beside May, a rather savvy, hard-nosed, but witty older woman with whom I worked at a fashion label years ago. I always saw a little of myself in her, or perhaps saw her in myself. Either way, we stand and study the crude painting of an antelope, dangling our champagne glasses delicately.

Chapter 14

Eventually, May says what we're both thinking, in her gravelly, almost androgynous voice. "It's terrible."

"This won't fly in Los Angeles," I say.

"I'm surprised they loved it in New York."

"It's enough to be strange there."

"Yes."

"But you also have to be beautiful here."

"Speaking of which," May says, turning her head slowly from the canvas to me, "where did you find that entrancing accessory you came with?"

I turn to look at May and smile. *Accessory* is another word for *man* in her language.

"I was set up with him on a blind date."

May laughs because she thinks it's a joke, and I smile because I know it isn't.

"How is he?" she asks, only insinuating the "in bed" part.

"I don't know," I say, turning back to the painting. "I'm still making up my mind."

"That's unlike you."

"I'm in a funny mood these days."

"Well, don't take too long to decide, or you may get beaten to the punch."

She says this looking behind us, and I turn to see what she's looking at. Asher is smiling politely—though looking not a little embarrassed—as he tries to extricate himself from several attractive young women with avant-garde clothes and ravenous eyes.

He manages to placate them just enough so that he can sidle away and come over. May disappears with the elegance of a woman who swims through parties like a fish.

"Hey," Asher says, his smile genuine now.

"Hello there," I say, feeling a champagne smile myself.

"I've been looking for you for the past fifteen minutes."

I bring my glass to my lips and eye him provocatively. "Do I not stand out enough?"

He watches me sip before speaking.

"Sure you do," he says. "That's why I got bored of everyone else here."

I flash him an appreciatively warm look then nod toward the canvas.

"What do you think?"

Asher looks at it and almost winces. He shrugs his eyebrows and scratches his temple.

"Honestly? Not for me."

"Same."

"Like you said: it's the singer and not the song, I guess."

I look at him without saying anything for a moment. For the first time feeling a surge of pure attraction to him. Not attraction with caveats, or nagging feelings in the back of my mind, but full, bodily and mental attraction. His delicate charm and forceful magnetism having worked their way all over me, into me. Soothing and brushing all my mental baggage away, causing me to forget everything in the face of his beguiling gaze. It's a hell of an effect. Almost dangerous.

With perfectly imperfect timing, my phone rings. I'm willing to leave it but Asher politely smiles and looks away as if releasing his spell to give me opportunity. I pull the phone from my bag and see who it is.

Toby.

"Don't mind me," Asher says, and I realize I've been staring at it for two whole rings. "Answer it."

"Do you mind?" I say.

He plucks the champagne glass from my fingers and smiles.

"I'll go get you another drink. Stay here though so I

don't lose you again," he says, winking at me as he turns and moves into the crowd.

I bring the phone to my ear.

"Yes?"

"Let's meet."

"I'm out."

"In an hour then. That'll give me time to get some oils— I wanna take a bath with you."

I try not to smile, to cling onto the part of me that thinks Toby is childish and incredibly arrogant to think I would want to drop everything and run to him for something as silly as a shared bath, but I can't help smirking a little. It takes a couple of seconds for me to suppress it and answer.

"No. I'm having a lovely evening."

"Where are you?"

"I'm on a date," I say, catching a glimpse of Asher's beautiful profile across the crowd.

Now Toby is the one who takes a little too long to answer. "With that Asher guy?" he says, his voice drained of its prior humor.

"With that Asher guy," I confirm.

Another pause. "Are you two..."

"Having a good time?" I say, feeling suddenly cruel. "Yeah. It's been great so far."

"Are you gonna..."

"Fuck?" I finish for him, turning the screw, suddenly thinking that this might be the only way to clean this mess up, to push Toby away, to be the bad guy, rip off the Band-Aid, to stop myself from my own reckless wants.

I watch Asher across the room, though in my mind I'm seeing Toby. And though the words taste bitter to say, I start to feel like they might be the medicine we need. The only cure.

"Yeah. I think I might, actually."

This time I can't tell if the pause is long, or if it just feels like forever.

"Okay..." he says, and I have to concentrate to swallow. "All right... Well uh... Guess I'll see you around then."

"Yeah," I say, having to push the words out with force now, and my voice still sounds weak. "See you around."

He hangs up, and I hold the phone to my ear for a moment longer before dropping my hand and then stuffing my cell into my coat pocket.

I feel a little dizzy now. The crowd a little overbearing, as if somebody turned the volume up a touch too loud. Looking around, the lack of anything but other bodies feels suffocating.

"Here you go," Asher says, and I spin around to face him. He's holding out a champagne glass. "I grabbed a few of these prawns too," he says, holding up the paper plate. "You eat shellfish, right? They're pretty great—better than the—"

"Actually," I interrupt, putting a hand to my forehead. "I think I'm gonna head home now."

"Something wrong?"

"No... I just... I can't stand another drink."

"Okay. I'll drive you."

"No...no. It's all right. I can call an Uber."

"Come on," he says earnestly. "At least let me make sure you get home safe. I'm only here for you, anyway."

I look up at him, and the tender compassion on his face makes my body feel like it's being torn from the inside by violent emotions I don't even understand.

I sigh, then shrug, and say, "Okay."

15

TOBY

"...*Boss!*"

"Huh?"

Sharon rarely raises her voice, so when I hear her shouting from the doorway of my office it snaps me back to reality violently, and I immediately realize she's probably been calling me for a while with no response if she's had to resort to that tone.

I had no idea that she was even here, that the shop was even open. Last thing I knew I was coming to the shop at three in the morning to be alone. I sat down at my desk in the backroom, cluttered with tools and gems and old paperwork.

In my hand is a giant Imperial topaz that I've been turning in the lamplight for hours. My favorite stone. I bought it in the first year I owned the shop, and it cost me enough that I could have built an entirely new one. That was even with the client selling it to me for a great price because she thought it was cursed. She'd said that since she'd acquired the stone it had brought too much excitement to her life—too much danger and adventure, too much romantic restlessness. I'd told her that sounded like a blessing rather than a curse to me.

I ended up removing it from the tacky necklace it had been set in, but never had the heart or the inspiration to set it into something else—maybe I just never really wanted to sell it—and instead would sometimes take the stone and stare into its fiery pink-red light, cut so well and with such color it seemed to be alive.

"The interviewees you sent away yesterday are here again," Sharon says, walking over to the blinds and opening them to reveal a daylight that shocks me.

"What time is it?"

"Just after nine. Are you all right? Should I get you an aspirin or a coffee?"

"Yeah, no... I'm fine."

"Heavy night?"

"Something like that. Listen, give me ten minutes, then send one of them in."

She nods as she makes for the door and leaves me alone with the piercing daylight and the dancing gem.

Sharon's not too worried about me, and knows better than to ask any more. This isn't the first time she's seen me moping—it's practically routine at this point. I'm just pining for another woman who's just out of reach again. Ignoring what is possible in order to feel bad about the impossible again. Wanting what I can't have again...

Except this is different. This is *Maeve*.

All those married actresses and models I used to enjoy feeling bad over, they seem ridiculous now. Like phony trial runs for the real thing. Momentary whims that you can't even understand—even feel a little embarrassed by—once the moment passes. Maybe all that chasing and self-pity was just a game I used to play, a comfortable role, my typecast in

Chapter 15

a city of actors. I used to throw the word *love* around all the time, trying to convince people, myself, that there was something melodramatic and glamorous about what I was doing. In reality, I was just terrified of the real thing, so I instead convinced myself I was really chasing it. The beauty of going after women I could never have was that I never had to put anything on the line. No chance of needing to commit, no worries about one woman for the rest of my life, no possibility of actually following through and letting it overwhelm me. I just never expected that eventually *it* would chase me.

Now...I can't even bring myself to think that four-letter word. I spent my whole life cheapening it and it's something I still can't afford. Now I'm doing the opposite: trying to tell myself Maeve isn't as magnificent as she is, trying to persuade myself that I'm not as fascinated by her as I am.

I'm the boy who cried wolf, and the real beast is finally here.

I can't even think about her properly. Any time I try to order my thoughts, they slip away from me and turn emotional, erotic, thrilling... Except as wonderful as they are, they're balanced by an equally affecting sourness. A sense of something deeply wrong that I don't know how to fix. The contradictions in my mind like walls closing in, crushing me between them. *She was never mine, so why do I feel like she's slipping away? It was always about sex, so why am I getting so emotional? We did this all before six years ago, so why is it so tough now? We fucked already, so why do I feel like we haven't even begun?*

The knock at the door breaks my thoughts, thankfully, and I try to get my head back in the present as I conduct the rest of the job interviews, doing my best to give the remaining candidates a fair shake and not let my mood get in the way.

Even compensating for my mood, none of the candidates really strike me as any better than the ones I saw yesterday. I find myself at lunchtime dismissing the last one and turning back to my desk.

I should get out on the floor with Sharon, or at least get some of the paperwork on my desk done, but instead I turn to my phone for something, anything, that can distract me even more fully.

Texts...missed calls...emails... I look at the ones from women, almost like I'm hoping any one of them is going to have the same effect on me Maeve does, but they all just seem tiresome and second-best.

She went on a date...and she fucked him...

The thought sticks into my gut like a knife, twisting the more I try to push it out of my mind. Just like a blow, it hurts. It makes my adrenaline pump. Makes me angry. Makes me want to react...

When I see Hazel's name pop up as a newly added contact in a chat app, I don't even think before calling her. A brief mental image of her midriff, her dark eyes and bronze skin, flashing through my mind, the closest I've come to feeling anything for any other woman so far. As I put the phone to my ear and listen to it ring, I remember her laugh, her sultry eyes, how infectiously fun she is, and start to think I might actually be able to fix this, to fix *myself*.

"*Hey,*" she answers. Somehow, she manages to cram so much positive energy and exuberant joy into even that single syllable. Her voice hitting a note like the beginning of a song, it's a greeting that feels like it could go anywhere, open to anything. Right now that's exactly what I need.

"Hey, Hazel... How are things?"

Chapter 15

She laughs, from nothing else other than sheer love for life, it seems.

"I'm good. About to go on my break at work, just thinking about what I'm having for lunch."

I know an opportunity when I see it. "Can I buy you lunch?"

Hazel's positivity manifests in a sense of pleasant surprise now.

"Uh, sure! I've only got an hour max, though."

"I'll come by and pick you up in the car. Thanks to my sister, I know a lot of good places near the hospital."

"Great! Is fifteen minutes okay for you?"

"Perfect."

She laughs and we hang up. I bounce out of my seat and throw on my shirt as I stride out of the backroom.

"Hey, Sharon, I'm just heading out for an hour or so, do you mind if—"

She waves me on almost as soon as I start the sentence, and my sudden burst of enthusiasm makes me feel just as grateful for her. I remind myself to give her a good raise soon, and carry on outside to my car.

It takes fifteen minutes to get to the hospital in good traffic—but the bad traffic's okay with a Porsche, since I can just take the long route. Still, I use every second of it to talk myself up.

Of *course* this is the solution. This was always the solution. A new woman. A different kind of woman. To think I nearly passed on someone as incredible as Hazel because of...*whatever* it is that's got me stuck on Maeve. I press the gas to overtake someone and the rising volume of the powerful engine sounds like my own increasing sense of purpose.

Once I've parked at the hospital, I get out and lean back

against the car, putting my shades on to stare toward the entrances as I wait for her. When she emerges I reach inside to honk the horn and draw her attention. She jumps, startled, her silvery purple hair swirling as she looks about. She sees me and laughs, taking her hand away from her chest as she walks toward me happily.

I'm a little disappointed to see that she wears scrubs, but amazed at how on her they look like a fashion statement. Something about the way she walks making their frumpy bagginess an intriguing mystery rather than looking like she's hiding something.

"Hey," she says, that tone again.

"Hey."

She reaches in for the cheek-kiss even more enthusiastically than I do, her big smile never leaving her face. I open the door for her and get inside myself.

"I should have gotten changed," she says, "but it would have taken so long, and I'm still too new to be taking long lunch breaks."

"You look great," I say. "With that hair, and that smile, you could draw looks in a bedsheet."

"It's nice to see you're just as corny in the daytime," she laughs.

"Speaking of which: What do you fancy? Mexican? A burger?"

"Oh, I don't care. I'm up for anything."

I turn to smile at her before revving the car out of the parking lot. "I thought you would be."

I take her to a nice old-fashioned diner, a place with an atmosphere as easygoing as she is, but still quiet enough to talk. We take a booth and order, then sip our Cokes as we wait for our food.

She's not afraid to look right at me, to show how much

she's enjoying this, and I realize how rare it is for me to be with a woman who doesn't dance around her own happiness. Nothing but her infectious enthusiasm, her openness to life. No tricks or gameplaying. No complications. Nothing like Maeve, where even the simplest conversation is a battleground, where she's only direct when she wants something, when she... *Damn, Toby. Enough thinking about Maeve. Hazel's right in front of you... Forget her...*

"You know, I've got to ask," Hazel says, pausing so that our burgers and fries can be placed in front of us. She plucks a fry and bites it before continuing, as if she's got all the time in the world. "How come it took so long for you to call me? And randomly in the middle of the day, too."

I take a moment of throwing ketchup on my fries before answering.

"Honestly?"

She nods eagerly.

"Because I'm an idiot," I answer.

She laughs again, smile as big as her cute cheeks. "And *I* thought you were just a 'busy guy.'"

"I am—but only because I like to be."

She turns to wrestling with her burger and I go to pick up mine but stop when something hits me. All those texts and messages I'd scanned earlier in the day... Not one from Hazel. And that wouldn't be strange except now I'm here, sitting with her, talking with her, and the last thing I'd describe her as is shy, or the kind of person who wouldn't make the first move.

"I should ask you the same thing," I say as I grab my own burger. "You had my number."

She's taking a big bite, burger covering half of her face, looking at me as she chews, but I still see it. It's small, but in a face as cheerful as hers even the slightest dark thought becomes as visible as the sky.

She turns her eyes down as she continues to chew, and I know I've found something—something more than just a happy-go-lucky girl who's up for anything.

"What?" I say, showing her that I picked up on it. "What is it?"

She takes her time finishing chewing and when she's done her expression is more reluctant than anything else.

"Honestly?" she says, mimicking me playfully. "I...kind of... God, how would I say it..."

"Say it," I urge her, genuinely compelled now.

She puts her burger down as if she needs to move her hands to find the words.

"It was a great night—and *you're* great. And maybe I'm just a little head-fried from a ton of bad dates that I won't bore you by telling you about..."

"Go on."

"But there were a few moments when I just...got this... weird...*vibe*."

"Weird vibe?"

She nods, her eyes looking almost deeply apologetic. "Between you and Maeve."

I slump back in my seat as if she just pounded me in the chest.

"Obviously I don't know anything about you two," she quickly continues, as if pleading for forgiveness, "and you have this kind of... This *way* of interacting with each other. I've just never seen it before. And how much can I really know based on one evening. I shouldn't have said anything—"

"No," I quickly interrupt. "I'm glad you did." I smile to let her know I'm not offended. Then I find myself chuckling a little and having to look outside. "That's actually pretty...perceptive."

There's a little pause where she looks at me intently, generously, the same way she probably looks at her patients, as if she's judging whether I'm okay, and whether she can continue speaking her mind.

"You really like her, don't you?"

Hazel says this simply, matter-of-factly, but if the last thing she said felt like a punch, this feels like she's just stripped me naked. Everything we've done up to this point, my whole self-enforced purpose, pep talk in the car, decisiveness in taking her to lunch, now feels like a bad act on my behalf—and she's just yanked me off the stage.

I've had my mouth open for ten seconds without saying anything.

"Yeah," I finally mutter. "I really do."

Hazel picks her burger back up as if the toughness of the conversation has passed.

"But I guess you can't do anything because of Mia, or something? You're worried about ruining her relationship with her best friend?"

She chews and looks at me, as nonchalant as if we were talking about the weather, and strangely, her calmness and easiness with the subject makes me feel like talking about it more than I ever have.

"Something like that," I say, twisting a napkin between my fingers. "We actually—"

I stop myself abruptly, suddenly afraid of how relaxed Hazel has made me.

"Don't worry," she says, pausing to swallow, "I won't say anything to Mia."

At this point, I'm not even surprised she read my thoughts.

"We actually slept together a couple of weeks ago. Again. The first time it happened was years ago, just a random thing, and we agreed not to do it again—for Mia's sake, and kind of for our own, in a way. My sister knows about the first time, but not the recent one."

"Mia's cool though," Hazel says, one hand putting fries into her mouth, the other picking up her coke. After she's done with her mouthful, she adds, "Why would you both be so worried that she'd take it wrongly? From what I know of her it seems like she'd understand."

"It's more than that..." I say, still staring at my food. "It's... You saw Maeve. What she's all about. She's sassy and independent and fashionable and a socialite and she lives for herself. She takes what she wants from men and then tosses them away. That's her whole identity. She's always been that way, and she loves it. Too much to do anything different. She's not the kind of woman who's going to have a 'long-term relationship'... A 'boyfriend'... Not a chance... As for anything more than that...marriage...kids... You'd have to be insane to think Maeve wants any of that..."

"But you do?"

"*Me*?" I blurt out instinctively. "No! Hell no! I'm a player too. I'm a romantic. I like to have fun. I like the chase and the thrill and the—"

I look up to see Hazel covering half her face with her burger again, but once again I can see in her eyes she doesn't believe me, she doesn't buy anything of what I'm saying, and it's so plainly earnest on her that I feel ridiculous for trying to kid her.

"Fuck," I say, trailing off. "I don't know... I don't know *what* I want."

"What about..." Hazel says, as nonchalantly as if she's playing *I Spy*, "a long-term relationship with Maeve?

Chapter 15

Marriage with her? Kids with her? What do you feel when you think about any of that?"

I'm glaring at my burger now, wishing I could grab it just for something to do, but never feeling less of an appetite. And I know that if I stop twisting the napkin and lift my hand from the table it'll probably be shaking.

"Fuck..." is all I can mumble.

After downing a few more fries, Hazel says, "I mean...I get it." I look up at her, my expression almost pleading for the mercy of some way out, of some easy answer. "You're afraid to tell her how you really feel."

"Now hold on—"

"Bad choice of words," she quickly interjects, smiling at me. "No man likes to be told he's afraid of anything. Let's call it...*cautious*...*wary*... You're *wary* of telling her that you want something more with her."

I stare at Hazel for a few seconds, and suddenly find myself laughing. Now I'm not just naked, I'm being dissected with anesthetic. I thought I'd seen every kind of woman there is, but the cute, happy, sexy girl with the psychological insight of some Victorian detective is a new one to me.

"Where the hell do they make women like you?" I ask appreciatively.

She laughs as she readies to put the last of her burger in her mouth.

"I'm not sure they do anymore."

I watch her finish her meal and then ask, "So what do I do?"

"That depends. Do you want to do the *right* thing, or the *easy* thing?"

I let out a heavy grunt. "None of my options look easy at the moment."

"Oh, that's not true. It's quite easy to just sit back, feel sorry for yourself, and have life grind you into dust."

It's weird to hear such words spoken with a cheery tone, and I can't help thinking she's speaking from experience.

"And I suppose the 'right' thing is to tell Maeve how I feel?"

"Uh-huh." Hazel nods, then looks at my burger ravenously. "Are you going to—"

I push the plate toward her. "Take it. But I feel like I owe you more than a burger."

She laughs and picks up the plate.

"I'm going to get it wrapped up to go—I'm always famished after work."

"I'll do it," I say, taking the plate from her while I get up and pull my wallet out.

She goes to the bathroom while I pay, and we reconvene just outside the diner where I hand her the bag and we walk across the lot to my car. I feel a strange lightness in my body that isn't the hunger, and notice how pretty the street looks in the high sun, how pretty Hazel's hair is as it catches the light.

Near my car I go to open the door for her but pause to turn and ask, "You really figured me out, huh? All in one afternoon."

She shrugs and smiles and says, "To be fair, it was sort of a tell when you came out of the bedroom a minute after her all smouldering, your eyes all *sexy* and focused."

I chuckle and pull open the door, but she pauses before entering to let out a deep sigh—as indicative of some deeper sadness as her laughter is of her attitude.

"Plus," she says wistfully, as if speaking a prayer, "I just knew you'd turn out to be too good to be true."

16

MAEVE

I'm not focused, interested, or distracted by anything other than my work when I head into the offices. Curt greetings as I make a beeline for my desk are all I give my colleagues. I have a mental checklist of goals for the day; virtually impossible goals. A week's worth of tasks that I'm determined not to leave my shift in any state other than completed.

Even though I always preferred working smart to working hard, being smart is starting to feel like hard work. I need order, structure, and to reduce my life down to a measurable set of targets. Everything else is messy, abstract, and unpredictable—and I've had a little too much of those things.

Just a little after lunch (which I eat with one hand while working at my desk) I've already knocked out more work than I have in the prior week combined. Among which are a completed deal with a distributor over the phone, my tone hard and uncompromising enough to make the call short. A detailed response to a promising but flawed proposal for a loyalty program. And the final stamp of approval on Harriet's merchandising plan.

At this rate, I might get off work just an hour late.

Then my office door bursts open like a SWAT raid, and the terrible twins storm inside making enough noise for an entire party.

"Oh my God!" Brent exclaims. "You're a genius, Maeve!"

"Did you know there were photos?"

"This launch is going to be *so* hot."

"If we act fast," Harriet adds.

"Oh yeah, absolutely. We need to strike while the iron's hot."

"This can only get hotter though."

"*So* true."

I look up and glare at them in a way that stops them in their tracks. Both of them are carrying open laptops, and when I give them the death gaze their smiles drop and they stiffen up as if they've found themselves in the principal's office.

"The two of you putting your heads together," I say slowly, "and you still didn't think to knock?"

Brent hangs his head, Harriet shrinks into her shoulders.

"Sorry," she says.

"Yeah. Sorry. We just didn't..."

"Just so excited..."

"About what?" I ask.

They look at each other for a second, mentally urging the other to say it, then Harriet takes the plunge.

"About you and Asher Kitt."

I drop my pen and lean back in my chair, devoting all of my attention to them now.

"What are you talking about?"

They share another glance, and this time it's Brent who

Chapter 16

steps forward, rounding my desk so he can place the laptop down in front of me and show the screen.

A cluttered gossip website with images of me and Asher arriving at the art exhibition, the two of us engaged in conversation, looking at each other with a focus that makes us look like a loved-up couple. Another picture of us in a group, both of us amused at something that someone else has said—again looking like a couple, our distinct fashion making us stand out. Then another, clearer picture of Asher alone, one of me alone, all at the exhibition.

"These just hit the web," Brent explains.

"For God's sake…" I groan, putting a hand to my face. "You can't even go to an exclusive event these days without some idiot posting everything… Whatever happened to living in the moment?"

Brent swaps a look with Harriet, and she steps forward to take the lead again.

"It's kind of good for us though?" she says, a statement as a question.

"Yeah," Brent adds. "Asher's really hot."

"In *both* senses of the word."

"Did you know he'd released a record?"

"He's associated with movie projects right now that are getting a lot of buzz."

"His brand is really cool…"

Harriet adds, "Cult."

"Right. Not too mainstream."

"Among the cool crowd, he's the coolest—if that makes sense."

"And now that you're a brand…"

"It's just really good optics."

I let out a deep sigh, all my previous energy and focus

gone. "We just went to an exhibition together," I say. "It's just a photo."

After a little pause, another shared look, Harriet bravely says, "You know how this works, Maeve... All it takes is a photo of two people to make the world fill in the rest."

If she wasn't right, I'd think she was overstepping the mark, telling me how this all "works." But she's right. Undeniably, objectively, absolutely right.

I glare at the images on the gossip website, and Harriet and Brent remain quiet, as if recognizing by my expression that I'm trying to think, and not wanting me to berate them again.

Part of the reason I'd decided to throw myself into work today was so that I didn't have to think about this, the date, Asher, *Toby*. For a day at least I wanted to take a vacation from being "Maeve: The event-attending, man-eating, trend-setting socialite, fashionista, and minor celebrity." Today I just wanted to be "Maeve: Senior Buyer and Director of Project Management and Merchandising at Harrold's."

The truth that I know too well, however—a truth I can't really get angry at Brent and Harriet for simply acknowledging—is that there's no such thing as separation in my life. There never was. I'd always mixed business and pleasure. Always understood the overlap between the person and what they do, between how they look and how they're perceived. I signed up for it, I embraced it, I was *good* at it, but now... I just want to be rid of it.

I lift my eyes to look at Harriet and Brent.

"You two think this is a good thing, then?"

"Absolutely," Harriet says.

Brent nods enthusiastically. "We couldn't *buy* this level of publicity."

I ask, "What exactly are they saying?"

"Well," Brent begins.

"There were a whole bunch of pieces written today about the exhibition."

"It was a big deal, apparently."

"Like, 'culture pages of national news sites' big deal."

"So there were loads of photos from the event posted on social media."

"And included in a lot of the articles."

"And they seem to *love* the photos of you and Asher."

I shrug. "Understandable."

"Absolutely."

"And then of course there's your little contingent of fans who are into it."

"And of course Asher's little 'contingent,'" Brent puts in.

"Generally really nice hype and excitement in those corners."

"I mean, a few bitchy comments."

"There always are."

"But it's just great, really great, publicity for you."

"And thus the launch."

They stop talking and I take my eyes from them. My gaze rests on the screen again and I have to shut it so I can think. As soon as I do, Brent takes it away as if the mere presence of the laptop might offend me.

"I hate to disappoint both of you," I say calmly. "But I'm likely not seeing Asher again."

Harriet looks at Brent, who shrugs, and then she says, "No problem. I mean... It would be good if you did."

"But it isn't an issue if you don't."

"Not at all."

"Photos last forever, and these ones have legs."

"Your profile has been 'raised' already by this."

"And unless you do something *really* embarrassing."

"Like, 'get drunk and storm a televised awards show in a clown costume' embarrassing..."

"Then this is nothing but good for us."

"Absolutely."

"Harriet and I have a *ton* of ideas for the publicity campaign running up to the launch."

"And this whole thing gives us *so* much momentum to work with."

"Right."

They stop again, looking at me expectantly.

"Momentum?" I say, skeptically. "Isn't the launch over six months away?"

They share a look that is this time conspiratorial.

"Brent and I have been working *really* hard at this."

"Yeah. Like day and night hard."

"We could launch it in three."

"*Three months?*" I exclaim. "I haven't even gotten my preliminary designs down."

"You should work on that, then."

They nod eagerly like puppies.

"It would actually be better to launch sooner," Brent says.

"We'd catch the seasonal changes," Harriet adds.

"Cheaper to stock our stores in advance."

"Better ad-rates, too."

"And especially now that we can work with all this recent attention."

"There's just *one* thing missing," Harriet says, her voice slowing cautiously.

I take a moment before asking, her tone worrying me a little.

"What thing?"

She doesn't even look at Brent now, but simply winces as she says, "The actual jewelry. Even if you had your designs ready to go, we still have to find a manufacturer. No supply chain, no sales."

"We sort of left it to you because... Well, you did say you wanted to handle that yourself."

"But if you're too busy, we have a few ideas for already-made designs you could approve that would have your name on them—"

"Stop right there," I say, raising a palm to interrupt Harriet. "If I said I'd handle it, I'll handle it. There's no chance I'm putting something out with my name and somebody else's taste. I'm not curating this collection, I'm designing it. From the ground up."

"We've gathered some catalogs already," Brent says, ignoring me.

"We were actually going to put together like a little 'report' today," Harriet says.

"So that you could go through and choose."

"Make it easy for you."

"Some of them are stunning."

"Though the best ones are smaller manufacturers."

"So there are issues around quantity, even if we want to go for a capsule collection that's limited release..."

I'm not even listening to them now, drifting off into my own thoughts. The plain, obvious fact is that good jewelry is hard to come by. Even harder when it's unique. Virtually impossible to find pieces that are well made, unique, affordable, and exclusive for me to put my name onto. All the reports and catalogs Brent and Harriet can make won't change the simple economics of fashion. And anything less than spectacular simply isn't an option—I'll torch the whole idea before I put my birth name on something ugly. All of which means I have only one option…

How ironic, I think to myself. There I was worrying that everything that had happened with Toby threatened my very self-identity, as a woman with utter self-control and composure. A woman who knows exactly what she wants, and even more exactly what she *doesn't*. A woman who could say no to any man, because none of them have anything she wants. And now Toby might be my only chance to *maintain* my self-identity as a woman of taste and excellence.

My jewelry line failing isn't an option. That means I need to work with him. Better to eat a little humble pie in front of Toby than the entire world. Whether that's the only thing he'll make me do is the question…or perhaps whether I'm opposed to doing it is.

"Excuse me," I say, picking up my phone and standing up, "I have to make a call."

"We can leave," Harriet says.

"No." I smile. "I'll need some fresh air for this one."

I take the elevator down and move through the lobby, my mind still churning over what exactly to say when I arrive out on the street, so that I pace a little before I make my call, high heels clicking purposefully on the sidewalk.

I hit dial, and Toby answers after the second ring.

"Maeve?" he says, and I hear the chatter of his shop quickly disappear as he moves somewhere quieter.

"You sound surprised to hear from me."

"Unless you're calling just to fuck with me then yeah, I am."

I laugh and say, "Oh sweetie, when have I ever been cruel?"

Now he laughs, but there's something different in it. A

little less enjoyment in our back-and-forth, a little more gentleness. I start to wonder if he's genuinely hurt by our call last night, but discard the thought as soon as it occurs.

The only thing I could hurt on Toby is his ego.

"Strange timing," he says. "That's all."

"How so?"

"I was just thinking...that we should talk."

I grimace as he says it, a hand to my face. I sigh heavily. Already this conversation is going the wrong way.

"Ugh...Toby..." I say, trying to find the right angle. "I need your help... Which means I need you—*us*—to be able to operate at least a little *normally*... As normal as we used to be, at least. But if you—*we*—can't...then it's fine. It doesn't matter. I'll just find another way."

"No, of course," he answers quickly. "I'll help you. What is it?"

"It's fine," I say, almost apologetic now. "Forget it. I don't want this to get messy again. And I definitely don't want you to feel like I'm...using or...manipulating you."

"Maeve," Toby says, his voice firm, no longer gentle. "You're my sister's best friend. I've known you for over six years. I might be a dumbass, but I still have priorities. If you need help, I'll help you. I'm...at least *trying* to do the right thing from now on."

There's something weighty about the way he says the last sentence, as if it's a smaller part of something bigger, and I'm not sure whether to take it as ominous or encouraging.

"Okay. Well. It's the jewelry line," I say. "The plan is to launch in three months now, and I haven't got a single piece in my collection. I need it to be great, Toby. And I'm sure you of all people know how hard it is to find—"

"Say no more. I'll fix that. *We'll* fix it. No problem."

The ease and confidence with which he says it assures me more than anything.

"Okay. Good. I'd be extremely grateful," I say, only realizing how insinuating it could sound once the words leave my lips.

"Tomorrow," he says. "Friday. Can you come to my shop after closing time—eight? I usually stay late on Fridays to do the bookkeeping. I could leave the stock out instead of securing it away so we can look through it, talk design and logistics."

"That...sounds perfect actually."

"Tomorrow then," Toby confirms, conclusively, as if everything between us is forgotten now in lieu of his desire to help. "Don't worry, Maeve. I'll make sure you get the best."

I hesitate a moment before responding, and he hangs up, as if there's nothing more to say. Perhaps not. But I suddenly feel like there's a whole lot that could still happen.

17

TOBY

Nine p.m. I'm sitting in the backroom, in the dim glow of a standing lamp. All the jewelry cases are still laid out in front on the sales floor and the bright lights are on there, but the front windows have been emptied and the security grills are rolled down and locked, horizontal metal shutters blocking out the light from the street. I texted Maeve a couple of hours ago telling her to use the side entrance.

I sent Sharon home early, then did a rush job on the bookkeeping that I'll double-check on Monday. Did I tell Maeve eight or nine? Why would she take her time? She seemed pretty panicked about the whole thing on the phone.

I've spent the past hour in a state of agitation. Tension building up as slowly and as surely as the minute hand is moving on the big clock in the shop, which I check every minute. I've already laid out a bunch of pieces to show Maeve on cloths around the shop, pacing back and forth and changing a few of them up, sitting and jogging my knee for a few minutes before bouncing out of my chair to pace again. I'm feeling like a caged animal, a boxer before a fight, a last day on death row.

I'm not going to tell her. Not tonight, at least. Even though that bizarre talk with Hazel made it clear in my mind that I need to. It would be a dick move to tell her how I'm feeling just when she needs me most—when she needs me to be a friend (and only that). And I'm not interested in hearing what she thinks unless it's the truth, unless the playing field is fair. Besides, it's not like I'm in a rush to open myself up to be crushed anyway.

So not tonight, but I can still show her I care. I would have helped her out even before all of this began. I might be flaky, crude, irresponsible, sex-obsessed and as emotionally sophisticated as a pubescent boy—but I'm also generous. I've always liked helping people. I'd give anyone the shirt off my back. Maybe it's that I've always found the best things in life rarely last, so you may as well pass them around when you can.

Now that Maeve's given me the ideal opportunity to show off one of my best attributes, I'm not going to pass that up. I want her jewelry launch to be even more spectacular than she does. Just knowing how happy that would make her, how much it means to her. *Thinking* about her being happy...even if she ends up crushing me, I want that.

I jump out of my seat and do another lap around the shop, checking the clock, checking my watch. Then one more time. Then back into the backroom, where I slump down into the couch we squeezed in between the two large, cluttered desks.

It's not that she's a little late—we never made the time concrete. It's not the waiting. It's not even the fact that I'm not used to sitting around and doing nothing. It's that the more I'm here, alone, expecting her, the more chance there is for my mind to wander, and go places that can only cause trouble.

Three knocks at the door. Hard and fast. Almost impatient.

I'm on my feet and across the room like I just caught fire, pausing with my hand above the doorknob to take a breath, then opening it.

"You ready?" she asks.

I have to stop myself from smiling at the sight of her. It feels like forever since I have. Too long. Even the vivid, detailed, and vibrant way she's burned into my memory not quite capturing the experience of being near her, of seeing her for real.

She's dressed simply, and yet she's perfect. Tight black jeans, the rip on one knee revealing a glimpse of skin. A loose, striped, soft pink sweater than hangs over her shoulders and arms like a robe, making even the smallest movement seem like some graceful bird-dance. A small black purse and a pair of high-heeled sandals that reveal her pretty feet, her delicate ankles that I once had my teeth on...

"Yeah, I'm ready," I say, standing aside for her to enter. "I've been waiting."

She steps past, eyes revealing nothing but still painfully beautiful. I catch a wisp of her perfume as she passes and it stirs something deep and animal in me that I have to force back down.

I close the door as she steps carefully past the piles of boxes, glancing around the backroom.

"Thanks for doing this," she says, her keen, observant eyes scanning the cluttered desks, the worn couch, the cabinets lining the walls. "We'll compensate you, of course."

I glare at her so hard she notices and stops looking around to stare back, my offense written all over my face. It would be a bad enough suggestion if she were just a friend, but with all the other stuff, the idea of "compensating" me feels like a kick in the teeth. A way of distancing herself, a way of pretending I'm not doing her a personal favor. And there's the "we"—as if there's someone else with her right now, and she's not alone with me, as if it was never about just the two of us.

"If I was doing this for money, I wouldn't be doing it," I say firmly.

She picks up on my tone and smiles, looking away as if recalculating.

"I didn't mean it like that," she says. "I just wanted to show my appreciation somehow—and this is company business, so it'll come from Harrold's."

I decide to let it slide, but the distance it created between us remains. *So this is how we're gonna play it, huh...* I step past her into the shop.

"I've laid out some stuff you might be interested in," I say, now using the same tone I use for first-time business meetings, formal and calm. "We're not going to complete anything tonight, but if you give me an idea of what you like—stones, metals, designs—then I can sketch some stuff up for you later and then we can look at getting some samples."

She follows me into the shop, where I've stopped next to one of the cloths I've laid out. She's still clutching her purse like she's a casual shopper just dropping by, and the tension between us is a little uncomfortable, as if we both want to be elsewhere now.

I watch her eyes carefully take in the pieces, studying them as if reading them. She says nothing for a while, and my mind goes back to just a few weeks ago when she came into my shop looking for a gift. How animated and effusive she was back then, how easy and electrifying our relationship was, and how different it is now.

I take a step back so she can see the next layout. She says nothing, reveals nothing. I step back again so she can move to the next. Nothing.

"You don't like anything here?" I ask finally.

"They're beautiful."

"Then what's wrong?"

She frowns. "They're not *me*."

"What does that mean exactly?"

"It means that this jewelry is going to have my name attached. It has to represent the same things I do."

I let out a quick chuckle.

"Something with spikes then?" I quip. "Jewelry you could use as a weapon?"

Her eyes dart up toward me, that slight, composed smile. And suddenly that tension between us seems even more dangerous, but slightly more enjoyable. She steps away from the counter and moves around the shop, making her own route around the things I've laid out. I stand back and watch her. Trying not to think of the haughty grace of her body. Struggling not to get sucked in to her allure.

"Something like this might work," she says, finally taking off her purse and putting it on the counter to pick up a bracelet. I move beside her as she turns it in her fingers. It's a complex, Victorian-style gold bangle engraved with floral swirls, gypsy set stones all around. "Tell me about these gems."

"That's actually a pretty classic piece—blue zircons, Australian opals... It's the pearl that makes it work, though— the opaque whiteness bridging the metal and stones well but still allowing the colors to pop."

She glances at me, only for a second, but I can see she's impressed a little.

"How expensive would something like this be?"

"Expensive," I say. "Around five thousand, though I could discount it about twenty percent if the mood strikes. There are millions of dollars' worth of jewelry out here on the counters—but better to work from the top down. You find pieces you like and *I'll* find the closest substitutes for your budget."

She puts the bracelet down and moves away from the counter. I stand back and watch her look around some more. It's like a dance now, her moving like some bird between branches, me waiting for her to be still a moment before I come close again.

There's noise outside, cars and people, but faint through the slats of the security grills, so I've tuned it out. My focus on her, the only sound I hear is the soft knock of her heels against the carpeting of the shop.

"Oh," she exclaims, with uncharacteristic emotion, immediately darting toward one of the counters. "Now *this* is exciting..."

She picks up a chandelier earring of delicate but intricate design. Small diamonds but a lot of them, bristling light against a golden bezel frame that gleams like liquid. She holds it aloft and I see a glimpse of her expression—eyes wide and lips parted—that I'd only ever seen before when we...

She turns away to move toward the large mirror near the entrance of the shop and hold the earrings up beside her face there.

"Dim the lights," she says.

"What?"

"The lights," she says, not taking her eyes from the

mirror. "They're too bright. Jewelry always looks good in the bright light of a shop, but who actually wears it in such conditions? I want people to *love* my jewelry, not just *buy* it."

I smile as I move to the switches, not telling her that I believe just the same, that I never buy a piece I haven't seen in the natural light of day, that the shaded standing lamps I have in the shop aren't just for show, aren't just for their antique aesthetic.

I turn off the ceiling lights until there's just one in the far corner of the shop lending a dim glow, the light from the backroom seeping in from the other corner. We're almost in pitch-black for a few moments until I turn on a standing lamp.

Now the shop is dark, the light low, warm, and soft. A different place. One with shadows and secrets. The jewelry glimmers in the dark as if we've invited spirits into this place. I look over at Maeve and see that her eyes shine now, slivers catching her blonde hair, the curves of her body revealing and hiding themselves with an erotic power that turns me dumb and simple.

I take the other earring and step up behind her in the mirror where she's still holding the other against her face. The smell of her perfume, her body, more powerful than a drug. I hold it up to the other side of her face.

"Put them on," I say. Her eyes flick toward me, then back to herself as she puts one in, then takes the other from me to put in—her fingers brushing against mine faintly, yet it turns my insides volcanic.

In this moment I'm gone. Lost. Forgetting anything but the sight of her, beautiful in the dark. The two of us going through pieces so she can choose a range feels like something from another life, something I read in a book—and the new reality, the only one I understand, that makes sense, is her standing in front of me becoming as beautiful as a person can possibly be, for no other reason than beauty itself.

"These are wonderful...perfect... I'd maybe make them a little shorter, but otherwise, I'd love something just like this..." she whispers, but the words are like a foreign language to me, incapable of penetrating my heightened senses, my mind incapable of deciphering words now, only processing how magnificent she is.

When she spins away, back to the shop, to the other pieces, it's almost painful, wrenching me from my brief glimpse of heaven. The dance going on, but getting more intense.

In the dim light now, moving between the shadows, she looks majestic. Wide eyes, those sparkling earrings, her blonde hair like a glowing halo, a small stud on the strap of her high heels catching the light as she takes an elegant step. It's the kind of magic you're lucky to find in art, but transcendent when you find it in real life.

She lifts a festoon necklace set with white and yellow diamonds, holding it aloft in her equally delicate and beautiful fingers.

"Tell me about this."

"I can tell you that you pick the most interesting, expensive pieces," I reply with a smile. "But I expected that."

She looks at me from across the darkness, flashing light into me.

She carries the necklace back to where I'm standing by the mirror and stands before me—no sense of being too close now. We both look at her in the mirror as she holds the necklace up against her chest, turning this way and that so it sparkles. I reach around and take the necklace from her, my eyes on hers in the mirror.

"A piece like this is designed with everything in consideration," I say, as I hold the necklace to the side, away from her. "To draw the eye, accents around the collarbones, to swing the gaze out from the center. Weighted to rest perfectly against the neck, the body. Jewels cut and set to play the light against flesh, to make fair tones fairer and dark tones glisten. You have to see it against skin."

I said it like a challenge. Like a command. Like a provocation. All my original intentions for what was meant to happen tonight gone, as if the dark makes the rules not count anymore. She stares back at me in the mirror, pupils wide in the dark, eyes narrowed with the focus of this moment. Gazes as direct as territorial animals. But only for a few seconds. Enough time for her to come up with the idea, before acting without hesitation.

In a single, swift, neat movement, she takes the bottom of her pink sweater and lifts it up, over her head—experience and the loose collar allowing her not to catch those earrings as she removes it. Underneath she has on nothing but a black bra, thin straps. Then, her eyes never leaving mine in the mirror, she tosses the sweater aside onto one of the counters. She stiffens her neck, raises her chin regally. A tiny gesture that in the intimacy of the moment is a command to put the necklace on her.

I'm gentle with it. Slow. Partly because it feels like the slightest misstep or mistake could spoil this strange, fragile moment. Partly because I want to savor even the touch of her hair as I brush it slightly, the feel of her skin beneath my fingers as I set the clasp, each wisp of contact between us like some small-portioned delicacy.

She finally pulls her eyes from mine and looks at

herself, turning her chin to the sides, then her shoulders to give herself—and incidentally me—the best view. She brings her fingers to her neck to trace the chain and I feel like she's torturing me now. Her warm skin so close, outlined in light and shadow, necklace shimmering like it's part of her, brought out from within.

"You could do something like this for me?" she asks in a soft whisper.

"I could do anything for you," I reply.

She looks at me once more, face blank, eyes hard, but she lets slip something. Her lips part, so slightly only someone who looks at her as intensely as I do would notice. A gesture so nonchalant only somebody who knows her as well as I do would be able to decipher it.

Without thinking, without taking my eyes from her in the mirror, I bring my fingers to her back and slowly unclasp her bra. As slow as I can, I slide the straps from her shoulders, brushing my fingers against her breasts as I ease it down, peel it away from her, and let it drop to the floor.

She says nothing, but her eyes watch mine as I study every contour of her body, every line and shape in her skin, the half-light revealing more than it hides. A moment so loaded it feels like we've stepped out of reality, out of all the silly things we cared about ten minutes ago. Our history, her jewelry line, past mistakes... The people involved in all those things aren't here anymore. She looks like another person, and I feel like one.

"Stay here," I tell her firmly.

I have a strong idea of what she likes now—and it makes so much sense I should have just guessed. Baroque. Fine. Complicated. Things that intimidate with their extravagance, but force you still to be drawn into them. Jewelry like a labyrinth for the eye.

I take a collar necklace from its cloth, something more modern but still feminine. An inch-wide band of bluish-white pearls set into silver shaped into lashing waves. Then I return to her.

She's standing still, her composure utterly perfect. Half-naked and vulnerable—and yet in no way submissive. Her chin too high, her eyes too beautiful. As I stand behind her, wrapping the collar necklace around her neck, I wonder which of us is really in charge. Me, telling her to stand still so I can dress her. Or Maeve, who is allowing me to worship her.

I latch the collar and it's a little tight, her breath stopping a moment, though she barely shows it. I realize neither of us is in charge anymore. We're both slaves to something bigger that's happening between us.

Her lips are parted still, and I notice her breath stutters a little. I don't know if it's the collar or the tension between us. She turns her eyes to study it on herself, then brings those fingers to her neck to touch it. I see in her eyes a fire alight, the fire she always has, but it's pure and raging now.

"*Yes*," she whispers. Her voice so sensual and forceful it sounds like she's casting a spell, speaking an arcane word. A voice almost not hers, and yet unmistakably her.

I take a moment to appreciate her in the mirror, breath held, then move away to the counters. I bring back a bracelet of big marquise-shaped emeralds and small rubies in a stark pattern that resembles bramble thorns. I put it on her left wrist, handling the delicate part so I can appreciate how perfect she is even here, my thumb brushing over her pulse, feeling it like a distant drum in the dark. She brings her forearm to her chest to see it in the mirror, squeezing her breasts together a little. Her eyes narrow and the stillness on her face seems more like serenity.

Again, I pull myself away, but only to return with an enameled bangle of twisting snakes, their heads yellow and purple, for her right bicep. She doesn't move except to shift slightly and make it easier, now that this has become a private ritual that only we understand. Again I look at her, again I go and return with a long, thin chain from which numerous diamonds hang—small but refracting like spotlights—that I clasp around her waist, to drape against her beautiful hips. Another winding-patterned necklace of liquid silver. Rings of such spectacular, sculptural shape they seemed unable to be worn—until her—that I relish carefully putting on her long fingers. A clip in the shape of a butterfly for her hair, a necklace of multicolored sapphires so long it hangs to her navel.

Another bracelet, another bangle. And with each item she seems to grow, to straighten, as if rising to carry the weight of such beauty, to carry herself with even more elegance and poise, until she looks like a goddess. The goddess she always was. Timeless and profound, as eternal and unyielding as the diamonds themselves, an incarnation of something that precedes civilization itself.

Even with her queen-like stillness she shimmers in the dark, light dancing off her arms and her front, sparkling like magic, the shadows cast by her breasts, her chin, her sides, lending a mystique equally as intense as the extravagance of the jewels.

She gazes at herself in the mirror, turning slightly, each movement like some terrifyingly compelling dance. I stare at her reflection over her shoulder.

The words come without thinking, an impulsive whisper from somewhere deep inside, bypassing all thought, the only possible way I can express anything I feel, and yet still pathetically inadequate.

"You're the most perfect thing I'm ever going to see in my life."

There's the softening at the corner of her lips, the trace of the smile that only I ever look at her so intensely I can see. She raises her arms wide as if performing some black magic dance, embracing her final manifestation as goddess, the discovery of what she always knew. Then she raises her arms above her head, the twist in her waist, the lines of her body never anything but absolute exquisiteness.

Arms held high, she slowly reaches them back until her jeweled hands are in my hair, her forearms resting on my shoulders. Her back arches, chin so high she's leaning back now. I step toward her, press myself against her back, allow her weight to fall into me, my hands slow to come to her waist. It's an invitation to worship, to appreciate, to pay tribute.

"Don't just say something like that," she utters softly, sounding as majestic as she looks, "*show* me."

Wonder and awe make me slow as I move my hand from her waist to her hip, the other up to her breast, grazing against the jewels, gently tracing her body in the dark. Her shoulder blades lean further into my chest, her head tipping back against my shoulder. My deep breath on her neck. Cheek, nose, lips, grazing as gently as a breeze, as if she's too incredible to touch, a beauty too dangerous not to go slowly with.

She sighs, breath hard and short under the collar necklace, and I feel her breath move under my hands, under my lips at the back of her neck. Our bodies tuning in to each other, the dark and the jewelry accentuating every movement, every ripple of the experience.

I squeeze her breast a little firmer and she straightens up, backing her ass against my pants. I push my lips against her ear and she pulls away with a little hiss, teasing me even here, even this close. But I don't let her get away. Tongue against her ear, arms squeezing her a little closer, a hand reaching for the top of her jeans.

She writhes and sways and twists in my arms. Ass pushing into me, sliding up and down, lips moving close enough to taste her breath before pulling away, her hand in my hair pulling me toward her, then pushing me away. She's like a wave lapping up against me, pressing and pulling already, though the line gets higher each time, my hands get rougher each moment, my lust harder every second.

The jewelry clinks gently, her breaths shortened and stuttering by the collar, mine deep and suppressed, her heels on the floor as she sways and shifts her weight on and from me. A strange kind of music in the dark, like some forgotten mystical accompaniment to this strange ceremony.

I get the buttons of her jeans undone and she murmurs softly, chest vibrating under my palm, throat humming under my lips.

"Stay here," I whisper into her ear, and pull away slowly, trailing as I take my hands from her, as carefully as I put them on her.

Once I'm in the backroom I tear off my shirt, and tear apart my desk with the hurried impatience of an investigator, looking for a condom.

I take it back into the shop, where she's still looking at herself in the mirror, so transfixed she doesn't show that she notices me. She's still swaying to a rhythm only she can hear, her hand against her chest, turning herself to appreciate the jewelry—or rather, how she looks in it. A concentrated, fascinated expression on her face as if it's the first time she's seeing herself. As if, finally, she's seeing herself the way I see her.

Only when I move up behind her does she notice me, eyes flickering to my reflection as I appear over her shoulder. I tear open the condom packet and lower my pants to put it on, watching her all the while. I can see that she's started to sweat a little. Her body glistening like the jewelry, so that she seems even more a part of it, so that there's no separation, and once again it seems like some truer image of her, rather than an effect. A few strands of hair have fallen over her face, silvery blond streaks of light flashing across her eyes.

I toss the condom packet away and there's a loud click as she places a ringed hand on the glass, as if bracing herself. Back arched, ass toward me, eyes staring a challenge back at mine in the reflection. I lower myself behind her perfect body and pull her jeans down slowly, teasing myself now as I unveil her glorious ass and hold back from burying my face in it again. I do the same with her panties and then stand up behind her.

My cock between her thighs, she rolls her wet pussy back and forth over it as I press her into the mirror, bracelet thudding against the hard surface as her forearm goes against it. All the while watching her magnificent shape there. The sensation of her thighs over my cock feels so bracing and hot it almost stiffens me, my eyes closing as I groan at how good it feels.

When I open my eyes, I see her staring at me in the mirror, her back like a landscape before me, begging me to explore. I put my hand on her neck, jewels under my palm, sweaty skin under my fingers. I wind it around to her throat and pull her backwards, up toward me where she twists her chin for a few moments and we kiss. She tastes even more beautiful than she looks. Her wet tongue like honey, her hard lips like some exotic delicacy. It's a kiss that turns me ravenous, that sets me on fire, triggering every impulse for pleasure in my body, and loosening any ability to control myself.

As if sensing it, she pulls away before I get too manic, but I'm crazy enough for her now to do anything.

My one hand still on her neck, I grab a fistful of her ass with the other, so firm that the jeweled chain there scars my palm as I pull her back onto me, guiding her pussy until I can press my cock into its tightness.

In the mirror, I see her open her reddened lips wide in a stuttering gasp. I see her hard eyes soften into an expression of abandon. The sight of her only turns me on further, but I still hold it, pushing gently. The angle, my cock, her tightness, all compelling me not to rush, not to lose myself in how good it fucking feels to lick the sweat from her shoulder, smack her ass, take her breast in my hand. Even just watching her in the mirror, this feels special.

It's her who pushes further, one hand still on the mirror, the other going between her legs to touch herself as she pushes herself further onto me. I almost howl at how good it feels, how wet she is, how mesmerized I am by her face in the mirror. The unleashed eroticism in her eyes, the perfect images she creates. This being of light and dark, of gems and skin, flesh and diamond. This incredible woman becoming a goddess before me.

She sways and grinds over me as I fuck her now. Jewelry bouncing and scratching and swaying on skin. Its quiet jangling overwhelmed by our moans and heavy breaths. Our lust going from tentative, to thunderous, to achingly close. Maeve's moans get louder, faster, as she loses herself more, but I never take my eyes away from her reflection.

Fucking and pressing harder and faster as if wanting to press her up against that echo, as if wanting us to merge.

I reach for her neck again, grasping for something as if desperate to climb deeper inside of her, fingers going to that collar. She moans even louder, her breath stuttering in her throat even more, until I realize she's coming already, her pussy gushing over me, squeezing me one last time, but it's the look on her face that thrusts me over the edge. Lips pouted perfectly as she utters that glorious sound, eyes closing in helpless pleasure, chin quivering, head tilted so one earring is cast against her perfect cheek.

Even as I come I can't stop looking at her, can't break away from the spell the mirror's casting. My hands sculpt her sides one more time, one final inhalation of her perfume and sweat, one final shake of the heat between us. Even after the moment's gone, something lingers, as if coming only revealed something else underneath, a desire deeper than lust.

She fades a little, smiling and murmuring as she stands up and falls back against me again, her weight balancing between her heels and my chest. I put my arms around her and push the side of my face against hers.

Gazing at her hazy reflection in the steamed-up mirror, she smiles a little as she traces a finger across a red scratch on her breast. Several other red blemishes where the jewelry scraped and rubbed her warm, pliant skin.

"Your jewelry marked me," she says, with a dreamy humor.

I trace my own finger gently over the scratch and consider telling her that she's marked me too—although unlike a scratch, it shows no sign of healing.

But not right now. Everything is still too perfect to risk.

18

MAEVE

I only half wake up. Not opening my eyes. Turning my face into the pillow so that no light seeps through. Trying to relax so that I might slip into the dream again. Grasping at it as it tries to slip away into the depths of my unconscious again.

It's only when I fail—courtesy of a lifetime of getting up early to spend time over my outfit—that I roll onto my back and realize it wasn't a dream at all. The slight sting of the scratch in my breast is real. The sweetness of profound fatigue in my limbs is real. Toby really did dress me in millions of dollars' worth of diamonds and fuck me against a mirror.

I laugh in my bed, giggling in a way I never would in public. Perhaps remnants of the giddy joy still escaping my body, the looseness of an intense orgasm not eight hours ago allowing my composure to fail.

Remembering that it's Saturday, I wallow in bed a while, thinking of the night before. The childlike sense of play, the lavish extravagance of that much jewelry. His almost perverse pleasure in putting it on me, my easy acceptance of a role as totem. It was the sort of wild, eccentric, beautiful night that I imagined life would be full of when I was a young girl cutting photos from magazines and rewatching old Italian films. Until I found out the most wild and eccentric that most men get is a foot fetish. The most extravagant thing to happen most nights is somebody deciding to skinny-dip in the pool, and even then only with copious amounts of alcohol involved. I feel I'm often criticized for wanting more... And last night was certainly a lot.

More than that, it could only have happened with Toby, I realize. Despite all his faults, he's certainly spontaneous and playful enough to make something like that happen. His sense of romance—that he seemed to have cribbed from schoolboy fantasies and media advertisements—might be cloying and sentimental at most times, but last night... Something seemed to come together just right. For both of us. So that even as I'm here glowing the morning after, I want to know when we might get there again. Perhaps in a different way, under different circumstances, but *there*, where I felt that way, where he *made* me feel that way.

I'm in such a good mood I don't even check my phone once I get up, shower, and make myself breakfast. Now wanting to distract myself from the little echoes of giddy, sparkling pleasure that play across my skin as I mentally return to last night. I end up stirring my coffee for a full five minutes, smiling absently out of the window.

But there's only so long you can spend in your mind before you find all the bad things you left there. It's impossible to think of last night without thinking of Toby, and impossible to think of Toby without thinking of everything else. All the baggage and messiness. I start to wonder if he instigated last night as a riposte to what he presumed Asher and I had gotten up to. I begin to consider whether he's just

Chapter 18

using my jewelry line as an opportunity to get closer to me. Then I try to decide whether I even mind if he is...

Now, when my phone rings, vibrating across the counter as I eat my fruit salad, I'm glad for the distraction.

"Morning, Harriet," I answer.

"Hey, Maeve. I know it's Saturday but I wanted to ask you something."

"Go ahead."

"Well, it's maybe more of a suggestion—though it could be a question."

"Okay..."

"I mean, I kind of think it's just something worth considering?"

"It's a good thing you called me in the morning," I say, "because it sounds like this is going to take all day."

Harriet laughs away a little of her nerves. "It's about the launch—"

"What did I tell you about working on weekends?"

"It's not really something we worked on. Just something Brent and I were sort of talking about."

"Okay..." I repeat. "I'm starting to get more hyped for this idea than the launch itself."

Harriet laughs gently again.

"Well, we figured that the best sort of marketing would be pre-launch—build up so much hype that we have customers banging down the doors once the collection comes out."

"Go on..."

"We've got a real opportunity to actually create that kind of buzz. And then, imagine if it sells out? Then we *really* have that 'exclusive, hot, trending' feel. People will have to get on a waitlist while we manufacture a second run."

"Very good—but worth calling me for on a Saturday morning, sweetie?"

"The thing is, *if* we're going to really launch in three months, then we should really be going all out right *now*."

She trails off at the end, as if growing more cautious, preparing. I swallow a chunk of pineapple and speak.

"I get the impression this is where I come in?"

"I mean... *You* are really the best advertising we have, Maeve," Harriet says. "Even if Brent and I put together the most fantastic campaign—and we have, or, we're trying to, at least—even with that, *nothing* is better for the line than you building up your profile. A great picture of you on a fashion website is worth all the ads we could buy combined."

I almost choke on my coffee from my impulse to laugh. I cough it down and smile so wide Harriet can hear me.

"Oh honey, if you're asking me to throw myself about town in glamorous outfits, then I suppose I must."

Harriet shares my chuckle then continues more seriously.

"Sure. But...actually," she says, slowing a little again, "Brent and I thought it would be even better if..."

"Yes?"

"You *threw* a party."

I pause a moment, coffee still in my hand, about to take a sip. It's not a strange or bizarre idea—and perhaps that's what surprises me most of all.

"Hmm," I hum, to show Harriet I'm thinking about it.

"It's a great idea," Harriet snaps, immediately seizing on my interest, "because having people see you at this event or that opening is, like, cool and everything, but it just shows that you're popular. If you actually *threw* the event, and invited all the people you know—and I mean, you know *everyone*—then it would show you're actually a pretty big deal."

I laugh at this last bit.

"I hope you're not using 'a pretty big deal' in my marketing."

"Ha! No... Maybe we should... And also, we'll have that big launch party, but that's specifically for the jewelry—this is all about *you*—so it's almost more genuine."

"Nobody at an event is genuine, honey."

"Anyway, what do you think of the idea? Maybe you could wear a few sample pieces, too."

Nodding to myself, I say, "I think it's good. I used to throw parties all the time, but I stopped bothering with the fuss. Plus I hate not being able to leave early."

"We could help you arrange it. All you'd really have to do is invite every big name you know and then be there looking glamorous."

"Let's talk Monday."

"So you like the idea? It's on?"

"It's on."

"Awesome. See you Monday, Maeve."

I hang up and finish eating breakfast, feeling once again refreshed and back to my normal self. Back to my normal habit of thinking about the future so that I can forget the past.

Because I've never needed my self-defense mechanisms more than I do right now.

19

TOBY

I could have slept for days. The restlessness in the depths of my blood that's been there since I was a kid, that made me start a successful business alongside a reputation as a social animal, and also a sometimes insufferably hyperactive brother, is gone after that night in my shop with Maeve. It was a balm for my soul, like she's the antidote to me.

But however much I'd like to sleep in and wallow in this feeling, I can't. I had just enough time to pack the jewelry away, clean up, and lock down, but I worry I might have missed something. The last thing I want is for Sharon to show up and find evidence that I used the place to fuck someone. Not that it matters, and I doubt that she'd even mind—it's just a matter of simple respect. And who can respect a guy who uses his own business as a place to do that kind of thing?

Not that I'm not trying to think of how we could do it again...

So at five in the morning I'm driving back to the shop and, sure enough, finding sweaty handprints on the mirror that I'm almost reluctant to clean off. Reliving and rediscovering the whole night as I do so. Though the place seems entirely different in daylight, in full light, or maybe just because it was never *where*, but *who*.

The backroom also needs a little tidying, after my frantic search for a condom—the packet of which I almost miss nestled up at the bottom of one of the counters. I clean up everything as best I can, and then start checking over the accounts I rushed before Maeve had even shown up.

When Sharon arrives, we set up the shop and open. I watch her surreptitiously, in my periphery, trying to spot any signs that she notices something. Even if she did, she's so professional and focused she probably wouldn't reveal it. *I really do need to fix up that raise for her at some point...*

During a quiet moment, with only a few solitary people in the shop casually browsing, Sharon flicks through a sheet of papers and then brings them to me at the counter.

"Did you decide on who you want to hire?" she asks, her eyes scanning the resumes.

"Yeah actually," I say, reaching over to the sheets in her hand to find one, then pulling it out and placing it on top in front of her. "This guy. Nick."

"The parking lot attendant?" she says, looking curiously over his slim resume.

"Yep."

"Are you sure? This girl from Dallas has so much experience."

"No. Nick's our guy," I say, tapping the paper. "You give this guy a chance and he'll pay you back a thousand-fold. He just needs a little support."

"Hmm," she hums doubtfully.

"Hey, you were the same, don't you remember?" I say playfully. "Just an undergraduate who couldn't tell silver from stainless steel when I hired you."

Sharon laughs and rolls her eyes at me.

"As far as *I* remember I was the only person even applying for the job. And you weren't exactly such an attractive proposition yourself. Some random guy who talks fast and wears Hawaiian shirts, was up to his eyeballs in debt, spending every night out until four, who suddenly decided to start a jewelry business. I honestly thought it was all just a front for something illegal the first three months we worked together."

I smile and look back out over the shop, the browsers still looking interested in the pieces, uninterested in any help from us. I turn back to Sharon.

"How are things with you anyway?"

Still idly perusing the resumes, Sharon says, "I'm still decorating my new apartment. I'm seeing a guy who *might* just be long-term boyfriend material. And I'm getting very into imported teas. You?"

"Jesus Christ," I say. "Wish I could sum my life up in three sentences."

Sharon grins and flicks her eyes up at me. "I could probably do it in one for you."

"Don't," I say. "I like the illusion things are more interesting than they really are."

"Speaking of interesting..." Sharon says, her eyes now on the entrance.

I look over to see two guys step inside, one of them a vaguely familiar face. They're both wearing expensive shirts that would be appropriate for the office, but their collars are undone and one of them is in shades. He takes them off as he enters. They look like standard West Coast yuppies, all big money and bro-talk. Nothing wrong with that—but the last thing I'd call them is interesting.

I'm about to turn back to Sharon and ask what she

means when the guy who looks familiar sees me and smiles like I'm a long-lost brother.

"That's him," he tells his friend, smacking him on the shoulder. "That's the guy I told you about."

They make a beeline for me and when I turn to quiz Sharon I find that she's disappeared.

"Hey! How's it going?" the familiar guy says, opening his arms wide like he's about to embrace me over the counter. He offers his hand and I shake it.

I smile, all friendly, but when I reply, "Good, buddy. How about you?" he detects that I don't remember him.

"It's me, Greg Miller! You sold me a ring a few weeks back?"

"Oh right," I say, suddenly flooded with memories. "Yeah. The guy with the beautiful fiancée and the Mustang."

I'm remembering more than that, though. He's the guy who was here when Maeve popped in to buy a gift for her friend. When she looked so good our typical love-hate flirtations got a little too real. When I wrangled that invitation out of her to the party where it all began...

"Not my fiancée for long," Greg says, his smile big and genuine. "She said yes!"

"Congratulations, buddy."

"And that ring, with the rubies... You were *totally* right. Totally."

"She liked it?"

"She *loved* it," he almost shouts. "Seriously, I've never seen her so happy. She's like a different woman. Let me spend the whole weekend fishing. We haven't had a single argument since. And in the bedroom... Man, it's like when we first met. *Better*."

I give him a humble shrug. "Doesn't seem so expensive now, huh?"

"Best investment of my life," Greg says, shaking his head.

I laugh, and notice his friend looks a little less talkative, a little unsure, as if he doesn't know what he's doing there.

"So what can I help you with today?" I ask.

"Yeah," Greg says, turning and smacking his companion on the shoulder again. "My friend here needs your help."

"Matt," his friend says, offering his hand.

I take his hand and say, "Nice to meet you. Toby."

"He's planning on proposing to his girl soon," Greg explains to me, then turns to his friend. "Go on. Show him the pictures."

Reluctantly, as if his friend dragged him to a fortune teller rather than a jeweler's, Matt pulls out his phone, carefully brings up a picture and shows me.

Unlike Greg's soon-to-be, Matt's girlfriend looks like she'd struggle to enjoy a sunny day, let alone a fine piece of jewelry. Still, I play along, asking him a few questions and talking things through with him, eventually landing on a few options. All the while Matt hems and haws over the price, the look, his girlfriend's apparent dislike of anything too "fancy." Greg's enthusiasm is the only thing keeping me from letting Matt pick whatever gumball machine ring he'd pick otherwise.

After half an hour of grueling decision making, convincing, and doubt allaying, the guy eventually settles on a sleek piece with a princess cut diamond, and I hand him over to Sharon to finalize the sale and wrap it up. As she does, Matt starts talking to her with an enthusiasm he had none of when talking about his future wife.

Greg stays with me at the other end of the shop, casually hanging out at the counter as if we're at the bar.

"Hey," he says, leaning over, "so what's *your* deal? You married?"

"Far from it."

Greg chuckles. "A player? I'll bet all the ladies want to date a jeweler, right?"

"Most know I can't afford half the pieces I sell."

"I only ask because I know this woman that you'd—"

"Sorry, buddy," I interrupt quickly. "I'm not interested in getting set up."

"You gotta see her first," he says, already flicking through his phone. "She's my wife's cousin."

"Really, I appreciate the offer but—"

This time Greg interrupts me by putting the phone in front of my face, and it's the woman in the photo who stops my thoughts in their tracks. If his fiancée was a dime, her cousin is the whole dollar.

"She's something else, right?" Greg says with a smile, seeing how struck I am. He flicks through a few more photos, each one even more impressive than the last. "What do you think?"

His question resonates somehow. I'm thinking a lot of things. I'm thinking about how weird it is I feel almost guilty for looking at her, as if my loyalties are already taken. I'm thinking about why it is that gorgeous women like Hazel and this guy's cousin-in-law are being thrown at me and yet I can't muster up anything more than a keen look. I'm thinking about Maeve again—and then thinking about why every other beautiful woman just makes me think even harder about Maeve. I'm thinking a whole bunch, but all I end up saying is, "She's hot. But like I said, I'm not really interested."

"Seriously?"

"Seriously."

Greg looks at me like he's confused for a moment and I decide to give him a little more.

"I get you're trying to repay me for the help with the ring," I say, "and I appreciate the offer—your wife's cousin is a real knockout. But the thing is... I'm kinda... I got someone else on my mind these days."

"Oh, I see," Greg says, nodding. Then, in his newly friendly manner, says, "How's that going for you?"

I look at him and laugh.

"'How's that going for me...'" I repeat, as if thinking about that question for the first time. "To tell you the truth, buddy, I don't even know if it's going, or not at all."

"Does she know you're into her?"

I shrug and wince as if to say "doubt it."

"Then don't tell her," Greg says confidently. I frown at him and he continues. "You gave me advice, now I'll give you some—don't tell her. When things get all weird and uncertain, you gotta let the woman make the moves, give the signs, all that. Trust me, dude."

I look at him as if scrutinizing the source of the info rather than the info itself. Especially since he's telling me the opposite of what Hazel did, and I felt a lot of sense in what that other woman told me. I wouldn't really trust this guy with anything more than the keys to park my car—and even then, only if he wore the uniform.

But then again, this guy is about to marry a woman way out of his league, while the object of my desire went home with another man just this week. I might know how to get a woman into bed, but when it comes to anything more? I'm learning just how little I do know. And when it comes to

Maeve, I may as well be trying to decipher an ancient language.

"Anyway, dude," Greg says, snapping me out of a strange, staring mood that I didn't even realize I'd sunk into, "thanks a lot for the help. Maybe I'll come in again sometime—get something for myself."

"Any time. Catch you later. See ya, Matt. Good luck."

I give a slight wave to the two of them as they leave the shop, which is now a little busier, and then move into the backroom. On my desk I've laid out all the pieces I "discussed" with Maeve, with a brief plan to make some calls and check some prices and sketch out a few "inspired by" designs. But the second I sit down with the intention to start, I just end up losing myself in the memory all over again. Confused and excited and optimistic and concerned, without any real sense of what to do.

Tell her, don't tell her. Business one second, personal the next. Fucking one night, then the "agreement" the next. One minute she's heading home with Asher, the next she's coming here and pulling off her sweater at the slightest suggestion. Meanwhile I'm turning down hotties and even feeling guilty for looking at them, as if Maeve and I have been together for years.

Something's got to give. It's got to. I'm just starting to worry it might be my sanity before anything else.

20

MAEVE

I let Mia choose the restaurant this week. Back when we used to do our regular "Thursday sessions," part of the fun used to be the choice of place. I certainly enjoyed pulling humble, unassuming little Mia out to the hottest, most glamorous, and most exclusive places I could think of. And I'm sure she enjoyed dragging me to every relaxed, cheap dive bar and spicy-food-serving establishment equally. At some point we both agreed: the best food is rarely the most expensive, but there's more to a dining experience than just the food.

She decided to go easy on me tonight. Nothing too spicy, a relaxed Lebanese restaurant in Los Feliz, which I'm extremely glad about.

Because tonight I'm going to tell her.

I have to. I may not lead a life of many loyalties, but I keep the ones I have. The most precious one of all is my friendship with Mia. Since we've known each other, I've given her the rundown on every man in my life (and vice versa, though with Mia it tended to be more the absence of men in her life). And though I've rarely needed any guidance, Mia's opinion is perhaps the only one that matters to me.

More than that, everyone needs a venting board, and Mia has always been mine. Of course, it's a little more complicated than that considering this is about her brother, and the fact that he and I have been hiding things from everyone for so long—but all the more reason to bring some fresh air to the situation. In the end, the "forbidden" nature of my affair with Toby has certainly added a lot of spice, but it would be spicy enough without, and there's a point where danger turns from sexy to stupid.

I'm early—as I always am when meeting Mia—but she's even earlier. The restaurant is a simple, small place; tables crammed in close though there's a pleasant enough atmosphere as I step inside. Natural pale woodgrain and simple furniture. Pastel-colored artwork on white walls. A large exposed window to the kitchen. Smart, I think, to make this small place feel light and airy. Intriguing music and chatter fill the space, so that even with the tables being close there's a sense of privacy, as if this were the late stage of a dinner party with various groups splitting off rather than a public eatery.

The place is only a third full, but still, I'm so focused on finding a suitable empty table that I miss Mia's shock of red hair until she glances up and raises her arm like she's in class.

"Hey, sweetie," I say, touching her on the shoulder as I pass and take a seat on the other side of the small table. I angle myself sideways so I can stretch my crossed legs.

"Oh Maeve, you're gonna love this place. The food is truly incredible."

"It smells good."

"Would you let me order for you? There's some stuff on the menu I know you'd love."

"Go ahead, I'm happy to play guest."

As if she's been bursting to do it since she came, she quickly gestures at the waiter (who's been watching me since I stepped inside like I'm the first woman he's ever seen). She barrages the man with a list of things, and I only speak up to ask for a glass of red wine.

"So how are you?" I ask, once the waiter has departed with our order.

"Pretty good. Colin's mom is visiting us so we're making the most of having her babysit. He's out with the guys tonight."

I grin. "And my niece?"

"She's..." Mia starts and then sighs with a smile. "She's a constant joy—emphasis on 'constant.' Colin and I are sharing the duties pretty evenly, which means we both take turns losing an entire night's worth of sleep. Pretty tough when his new practice is really getting off the ground, and I'm still house hunting. Thank God for grandmas, right?"

"Actually," I say, "how long is your mother-in-law staying? I'm having a party this weekend. It would be wonderful if the two of you came. You should wear that sensational red dress of yours."

"Really? I thought you were done hosting parties?"

I shrug. "I was, but the jewelry launch is in a few months, and they want me to put myself out there a bit, get in the gossip magazines. Thus, I'm going to invite only the hottest, biggest, flashiest A-listers—you being the first."

Mia laughs.

"That sounds pretty exciting."

"Probably not," I say, glancing over to notice that the waiter's still looking at me. "The bigger the celebrity, the more boring. *But* the pictures will be good, and these days that's all that matters."

"You could ask Toby to come," Mia suggests. "He always livens things up."

I smile at her as our drinks arrive, along with the mezze platter.

"Since when did he ever need an invitation?"

We make small talk over the appetizers until the mains arrive. I interrogate Mia on her house hunting, on Colin's new practice, on life with baby Alison. It's always fun not to be the one answering the questions, and Mia has always been more open with me than I suspect she is with others.

When the entrees come, on multiple plates that cover almost every inch of the table, we stop talking and get down to the serious eating, communicating via murmurs and expressions that would be indecent anywhere else but the dinner table or the bedroom.

Only after half an hour of pigging out do we start to slow down, and devote a little more attention to our drinks.

"God this is good," Mia says as she takes another bit of manakish.

"Oh honey, I think I'm going to have to shop for an entire wardrobe a size bigger after this."

Mia laughs, and still can't resist chewing as she does so.

I wait for the waiter to come over and refill our wine glasses before talking again.

"So. Mia," I say, setting the tone by using her name—a rare occurrence. "There's something I wanted to tell you."

She puts her fork down and looks at me keenly. Before I can speak, however, she starts to smile, as if she knows something she shouldn't.

"What's that look for?" I ask blankly.

Chapter 20

Mia shrugs and pretends to focus on the food again, but she can't hide the smile. A terrible liar.

"Oh...nothing... This food, it's just..."

"Let's skip the dancing, sweetie," I say. "What is it?"

Mia looks up at me again, eyes full of mischief, and I can see she's considering another attempt to throw me off the scent, but she smartly gives in.

"I think I know what you want to tell me."

As if my gut wasn't feeling heavy enough, I suddenly feel my heart sinking into it like a stone. My blood suddenly goes cold and now *I'm* the one trying to hide my true emotions.

"Is that so?" I say nonchalantly.

Mia purses her smiling lips as if highly amused. She makes a playfully guilty face and then nods.

"Well go on then, tell me what's on my mind," I say, putting on my best performance of devil-may-care attitude even while my insides feel like a maelstrom of anxieties and falafel.

Mia hunches up her shoulders, fills her cheeks, as if she's blowing up with desire to talk about it but is struggling to contain it. I watch her wrestle internally, that big smile still on her face, until she inevitably breaks, and sure enough, when she does, it's like being barraged with how fast she's talking.

"Okay, well, I know I shouldn't be telling you any of this. It's really none of my business and I *definitely* don't want you to feel like I'm all 'in your business' or getting in the middle of things or like some sort of weird third party that you have to consider whenever you're doing whatever you're doing. But, I mean, it's not like you're some weird distant acquaintance who I can just hear stuff about and be completely detached about, do you know what I mean?

"It's us. It's you, Maeve, you're like a sister to me, so I just want you to know that whatever I know, or end up saying—and by the way, you know I'm just a bad liar, and you really ambushed me with this, I swear I didn't intend to tell you that I'd heard something—and I really did just overhear it, I wasn't 'digging' for info or poking my nose in. I really did just overhear—but all right, then I asked Colin about it and he told me—but we're married, right? And we're both new to marriage, I guess, so it's like, you talk about everything, right? Even as he was telling me I think he wasn't sure but regardless—"

"Honey, *honey*..." I interrupt, raising a palm to slow her down a little. "If you give yourself a heart attack before you get to the point I'll never forgive you."

"Okay, whew... Sorry," Mia says a little slower. She laughs gently, then paces herself a little before speaking again. "I overheard how great your date went with Asher." I roll my eyes and Mia takes it as invitation to explain herself rather than seeing it for the relief it actually is. "I wasn't listening, I swear. He was just in the other room and I guess he didn't know I'd come home since Alison was with me and she was so quiet for once. Anyway, the way he was talking, I kinda couldn't help but put two and two together."

"And surmise that Asher had swept me off my feet?"

"Yeah! I mean, I kinda asked Colin about it afterwards, and he told me Asher said you were incredible, the evening was incredible. That you had this really unique and strong connection."

"And then emailed over a full transcription perhaps?"

"*Maeve*," Mia laughs, too happy about it to accept my mockery. "Apparently the only thing that made Asher wonder a bit was that at the end of the night you didn't go home with him—"

"Jesus Christ..."

"But then *I* told Colin: that means it's really serious! 'Cause if Maeve was only half interested, she'd have had sex with him and forgotten him by breakfast. For her to *not* do anything, that's when you know she's hooked."

"And what do you think I'd do if I *really* didn't like him? Ask for a threesome?"

Mia freezes, as if she's finally hearing how silly she sounds, and her smile drops.

"Was I wrong? Did you actually not like him?"

I take a moment before answering, looking aside and shrugging.

"Asher's a lovely guy," I say sincerely. "How could any woman *not* like him? At least a little?"

"Great!"

"Hold on there, sweetie," I say, palm up again. "The thing is..."

I trail off at the end of the sentence, something I never do. I always know what I'm about to say before I say it, and there isn't a lot I'm afraid to say. But Mia's face stops me. She's looking at me so earnestly, so happy at the idea of me meeting a nice guy, of her having helped me meet a guy I like. I *want* to tell her about Toby. I *meant* to tell her about Toby. For my own sake just as much as hers. For the ability to vent about something. Simply to honor our friendship and the strange situation she's in—without even realizing it.

Yet her sweet face and her innocent excitement at the idea of me and Asher makes it impossible. I don't know how she'd take the fact that me and Toby have been fucking, but I'd wager certainly not as well as the idea of me and Asher hitting it off. Best-case scenario is that she just worries deeply for what will happen—and she's already got plenty to worry about.

Now, confronted with the moment I'd been certain of the second we arranged to meet, I realize that I shouldn't tell her. This mess is my own to sort out.

"The thing is..." I repeat. "It just doesn't fit with my image right now to be dating a guy."

"What?" Maeve says incredulously. She might be a bad liar, but she's still got something of a bullshit detector. "What do you mean?"

Fortunately, I'm good at bullshit. It's best when you wrap it up in a little truth.

"Who do you think is going to buy my jewelry? Who do you think will see themselves in me *as a brand*? Single, independent, sexually mature women. Women with careers and libidos and who are tired of having to play the same old game of 'fishing for a partner.' Except it's *more* than a brand to me. It *is* me.

"My philosophy has always been to enjoy myself, to take more than I give to men, and be beautiful for the sake of beauty itself—*not* in the hopes of reward. Now my philosophy has become a message, a symbol. How would it look if, at the launch of that 'symbol,' I'm shacking up with a guy who I already know is going to be a three-month affair at *most*?"

Mia sighs and leans back in her chair, finally a little deflated. She seems to think about it a bit, then shrugs as if getting the message.

"Well, I can't really say I'm that surprised."

I smile at her affectionately. "But you're disappointed."

"Mostly because Asher will be. I sort of feel bad after hearing how into you he was."

"Asher will be fine, honey," I say, waving it away and picking up a kafta as if to move the conversation on. "I'll invite him to the party and speak to him myself—I'm good at

Chapter 20

letting men down by building them up. And anyway, how ridiculous to feel sorry for a man like that. I took my eyes from him for ten seconds at the exhibition and he had the arty girls crowding him like he was handing out free Chanel."

Mia laughs and digs in to her manakish once again. I breathe a silent sigh of relief that we've moved the conversation on—even if I'm still in the same exact mess I was in before.

21

TOBY

Maeve's having a party. Apparently. And I'm not invited.

I only hear about it when one of Hollywood's most beautiful young actresses comes into the shop after hours for a private showing. Small talk about what we're doing this weekend until she mentions Maeve's name and my ears prick up. It's not a common name, less so just to refer to her by her first.

I call the director I sold the Ferrari to so I can ask him how it's running, and casually drop in her name. He confirms he's going, and asks if I am. I tell him I didn't get an invite and he laughs. A Lakers player who drops by the shop, a British musician I visit for the final payment on a ring he bought, even a woman with a reality show who calls me asking for a certain piece—they all say the same thing. A big event, and they've all been invited.

From the clientele, I'm guessing she's going for something that'll make the papers—probably it has to do with her jewelry line. I'm supposed to call her soon about the pieces, talk about potential designs, but it feels almost weird to call and talk business after what happened the last time we met.

Now that she's throwing a party everyone in town seems to have been invited to except for me, it feels even weirder.

Maybe it's her idea of a joke. I've got a reputation as the kind of guy who crashes parties. Or maybe she really doesn't want me there. Maybe it's the part of her life she's reserving for Asher. The bigger part. The part she shows the world. And maybe I'm just a dirty little secret for her that she can barely admit even to herself.

So here I am, lying in bed when I've been invited out to three different things, trying to resist the urge to look at her pictures online and jerk off to her. Going out of my mind with a problem I can't even bug my sister about like I usually do. Anyway, I know what she'd say. *You always want only what you can't have.* Maybe she'd add a little *your biggest problem is yourself.*

She's probably right about that, too. If I called Maeve up right now with the best intentions in the world—to talk business, or to sort out this whole mess—I'd probably just end up doing what we did on the phone last time... Last time...

My place is big, but it still feels claustrophobic. I need to blow off steam, but I don't want to deal with any other people right now. I think about a midnight run around the block, but instead just pace until I let myself fall back onto the couch and bring up pictures of Maeve.

And there she is. With Asher.

It shouldn't be a surprise. I *know* she went out with him days ago. I *know* Maeve is always having pictures taken whenever she goes out. I *know* she's becoming a minor celebrity. But knowing something and seeing it right there are two completely different things. I almost throw my phone against the wall, and raise it as if about to, but then succumb and just bring it back before me to glare at the two of them.

Chapter 21

There are more than a couple of pictures, and in all of them Maeve looks comfortable, confident, content. Asher too. She always looks like that, but something about looking like that with *him*, with another man, fills me with a sense of wrongness. I glare at the images, and they pull at something inside of me, as if they have some sort of occult power to reach inside my body and tear my insides to shreds. As close to physical pain as images can get, and yet so much worse.

I refuse to admit it to myself, and yet I can't help doing so—they look great together. It's painfully easy to imagine them getting along, building a connection, out and about in public while I've only been close to Maeve in secretive ways, always against the grain of the people around us. Suddenly the "forbidden" nature of me and Maeve doesn't seem so arousing, so sexy, so enticing. Compared to the images of her and Asher, it just seems shameful and tragic.

There are words around the pictures too. Articles, comments, captions. And though my thoughts are too chaotic and thunderous to focus on reading, my eyes skim over them and catch their awful gist. *A cool couple... So good together... He's perfect for her... Maeve and her gorgeous date...*

If there was any part of me still rational, any semblance of sense, I'd put the phone away and go for that run before I do something stupid, but this agony feels too true. As if the fact that it hurts makes it easier to believe. I think about calling Maeve and showing her my anger and jealousy, but I know she'd just remind me I have no right, that she didn't do anything wrong—however much it feels like that to me. My instinct is to speak to Mia, the sister who's always there for me, who I turn to whenever I feel this way, but even that avenue is locked away. I could...but it would only make all of this worse.

I flick through my phone looking for something, anything, that could distract me. A brief urge to call up any of the women in my contacts to fuck and forget, but none of them seem like enough, and I know I'd only remind myself even more of what I'm trying to forget. A petty desire to get my revenge bubbles under everything, as if I'd fuck another woman just so I could tell Maeve I did so, just to prove that I'm as cold and unyielding as she is... But I'm not. That's why this hurts in the first place.

The more I browse through my phone, through the unread messages and missed calls and gigantic contact list, the more this self-pitying grief spreads out to encompass every aspect of my life. All the famous and powerful names I know who'd drop everything if I asked them to, and not a single one I'd want to talk to about this. All the invitations to exclusive parties and underground gigs, all the comments about great nights in the past, all seem so empty and superficial right now. The hot women sending me nudes, asking if I'm free, letting me know they still think about me, all just reminding me of how little I really cared about anyone until now, about anyone other than her. The whole thing, my whole life, it's all nothing if I can't have her.

I'm about to break—and I don't even know what kind of break it's going to be—when I see one name that doesn't make me even more depressed. One name that still feels somewhat pure, somewhat accessible, somewhat like a path out of whatever you'd call this dark, oppressive mood I'm slipping further into. I press it and bring the phone to my ear.

"Hello?"

"Hazel," I say, my own voice sounding different, harder, tougher.

Chapter 21

"Toby?" she says, her voice groggy as if she was asleep. "It's two a.m. What is this? Is this a booty call?"

I smile, her joke opening a crack of light in my thoughts.

"More that I couldn't be bothered to find a crisis hotline number."

I hear the rustle as she sits up in bed, the swish of a water bottle, and the groaning sighs of someone waking up.

"Maeve again?"

"Maeve always," I reply, then suddenly feel guilty. "I'm sorry for waking you up. You probably had a long shift so I'll—"

"No, no," she interrupts quickly. "It's all right. It must be pretty bad if you called me of all people."

"Yeah... That's the funny thing about having a lot of friends. You end up with nobody you can *really* talk to."

She takes her time answering, her mind still in first gear. "So what's wrong? Did something happen?"

"You remember Asher? From the dinner party?"

"Of course."

"She went out with him again. Fucked him." The last two words come out like I'm spitting them. I can't help saying them with all the resentment and bile their meaning creates in me.

"Oh no..." Hazel coos sympathetically.

"And she's having a party this weekend—a big deal. She's invited everyone in town except me."

"Damn..."

"And we're supposed to be working together on this jewelry thing of hers. We even met for it the day after she went out with Asher and...well..."

My silence says it all.

"You ended up sleeping together?"

"Yeah," I say. "Except it was...well, it was amazing, but

we didn't really talk or anything. It was like...like it was just sex."

"I see..."

"Shit. I shouldn't be telling you all this."

"No, of course you should."

"I'm just kinda fucked up tonight."

"I can tell."

There's a long silence. The swish of her water bottle again. And yet the silence feels good somehow, as if just having her there makes it a little easier just to be.

Maybe it's the late hour. Maybe it's that I barely realized I've gone through a bottle of whiskey tonight. Maybe it's just Hazel, and the strangely comforting vibe she gives off, but I feel like I speak my mind as quickly as I think it.

"I want her, Hazel."

"Hmm."

"I don't even know why I want her. She gets me pissed. Frustrates me. Provokes me. Riles me up and always leaves me feeling like something is...not right. And I just want her."

"That's...life." The way she pauses before saying it makes me think she was going to use another word.

"If none of this was so messy, if we didn't have to do everything in secret, and could just be together—maybe we'd just date for a month and get it out of our systems."

Hazel takes her time before answering. "You think?" she says doubtfully.

"Don't you?"

"I mean... Haven't you known her for a long time?"

"About six years."

"What do I know? I'm just a single girl with a dating history as long and depressing as a Russian novel—but I sort

Chapter 21

of think people who get together after knowing each other a long time usually have pretty good chances."

"You think?"

"Yeah. Six years is a long time to know someone, for them to reveal all their quirks and flaws. If you knew her that long and it's only allowed your feelings to get stronger... I dunno."

I let the silence settle a little as I consider it.

"You think it's the same for her? The other way around?"

She sighs and says, "I don't know, Toby. I really don't. I wish I could tell you what she feels... The only thing I can say is that, from where I'm standing, you've got to make a move. You've got to tell her. I mean, you've got to at least *try*, right? Otherwise, you'll never know what could have been."

I feel like I can detect a little of her own pain in that last bit, as if she's talking to herself a little, trying to convince herself that she still needs to "try." I instantly feel a little selfish for unloading on her.

"Hazel," I say, after a long silence.

"Yeah?"

"How come you're still single?"

She laughs, and I once again find myself infected with her positivity.

"Toby, I still haven't figured that out for the past ten years of my dating life. I'm definitely not gonna be able to give you an answer before my shift in six hours."

I laugh and reluctantly realize I should probably let her get back to sleep.

"Fair enough," I say. "I guess we can save it for when I buy you the drink I owe you."

She laughs. "Deal. On one condition."

"What's that?"

"That when you do buy me the drink you owe me, you've at least told Maeve how you feel."

I smile. The silence goes on for long, but it doesn't feel like it with Hazel.

"Deal," I say. "Good night."

"Night."

She hangs up and I put the phone down, leaning my head back to settle into the feeling I'm left with. Not quite the end of all my problems, but the hope of a solution. A decision already made, but yet to be acted on.

I'm crashing that party.

22

MAEVE

It had to be the mansion.

A gala hall in the center of the city would have been more convenient, and probably resulted in a few more famous faces—but it would have been too "showbizy," too common. One of those modern architectural homes in the hills would have made for some striking photos and impressed the guests—but those open-plan, angular buildings feel too inhuman for a good atmosphere. For a few, brief moments I'd entertained something quirky, like a party in the desert, or in an abandoned warehouse, but though it would have gotten tongues wagging, this is a party with a purpose, and that purpose is to reflect on me. That's why it had to be the mansion.

The large estate is well-maintained but still feels somewhat lived in, despite the fact that the owner—a secretive tech billionaire I have fortunate access to—rarely stays there. The gigantic, detailed building isn't dissimilar to the mansions of England; though the resemblance isn't a gaudy pastiche, the building really is old enough to exhibit its colonial influences. Vibrant flowers line verdant green areas. A pool shaped like a half-moon forms the centerpiece of the rear, an oak-lined driveway as long as a side street leads to the large cherubic fountain that forms the centerpiece of the front.

Inside the place is even more impressive. Carpets as soft as the grass outside, beautiful artworks far newer—though not noticeably so—than the walls they hang upon. The acoustics are so good that a group of five people can feel like a hundred, and there are plenty of corners and rooms for people to tell secrets and enjoy moments of intimacy.

With the location settled on, just like one's shoes, the rest of the party falls into place. The catering is French, the cocktails classic, the decoration inspired by Fellini. For music in the lobby, I've booked a string quartet that I instruct to only play modern pop songs after ten-thirty (once everyone is reliably tipsy enough to not think it in poor taste). Outside, a versatile jazz band. And as an indulgence to Brent, a DJ and bar in a distant wing of the mansion where they can only be heard by the willing.

Harriet suggested we convert several of the large rooms on the first floor into "themed" areas, and I allowed her and Brent to go nuts. A cabaret room with some era-appropriate entertainment that I didn't have time to double-check and which I'm putting my faith in them to get right. A game room with poker and pool. And even one of those "puzzle" rooms people seem so fond of these days. Personally, I don't think they're exactly on-brand, but Harriet and Brent have earned the indulgence, and the mansion is large enough that those who aren't interested can easily ignore them.

For goodie bags the guests will be able to choose from either a carefully selected range of niche cosmetics and perfumery, or a designer scarf and bottle of malt whiskey. All the bags are emblazoned with my name in my own cursive—the logo for my brand, though since the jewelry line hasn't even been announced it seems more like an emptily egotistical gesture. It'll make sense eventually—as will the gigantic ice sculptures both inside and outside that have been cut into the shapes of various famous historical jewels.

At three in the afternoon, the estate is already buzzing and alive with just the employees.

"Sir?" I call out to a white-waistcoated waiter as I march through the foyer, "we need *two* people with champagne at the entrance at all times, yes? I don't want a single person to come in without being offered a glass, thank you so much darling... You there!" I stalk toward our head of security, whose shoulders are so broad he looks like an ape in a suit. "Do you have the list of photographers we're allowing in?"

"This is the list we were given," he says, pulling out a neatly folded piece of paper.

I scan the list of names.

"Oh no, not him," I say, pointing at one of them before drawing a line through it. "He took a downright malicious photo of a friend of mine last week—he's blacklisted."

The man nods and heads off.

"Where's the fireworks crew?" I call to the hurrying workers dashing in all directions around me.

At seven sharp, a sizable contingent of journalists and photographers (and a few overly eager attendees) have arrived, and we corral them around the pool and serve them drinks to the sound of the bands tuning up. I put on my pre-evening dress and heels to schmooze with them a little and get them onside in between my dashing about the estate to ensure all preparations are up to scratch.

By nine, the party's already in full swing, although I barely even noticed it since I've been doing nothing but managing it. Photographers are crowded at the front taking pictures of celebrities as they arrive, stepping out of their supercars to pose and smile their way inside. There's a throng of people around the pool making almost too much noise to hear the band. The vast dining hall is full of a surprising amount of people sitting down to take advantage of the dinner our caterers are laying out. Judging by the steady stream of people heading toward Harriet's cabaret room, it's a hit. And I'm in one of the lavish bedrooms hoping to get changed into my well-planned outfit quick enough that I'll actually have some pictures taken of me at my own party, still wondering where the hell my fireworks crew is.

There's a knock at the door.

"Go away!" I shout back. "This room is out of bounds!"

"It's me, Maeve!" Harriet calls back.

I wince as I squeeze myself into my little black dress.

"Well get in here then! What on Earth are you knocking for?"

Harriet opens the door just enough to sneak inside, looking like an absolute stunner with her hair up and her ruched cocktail dress.

"Get over here and help me with this, sweetie," I tell her and she quickly puts her clipboard down to help me zip up. "And leave the clipboard here—it ruins your outfit."

"Stay still," she says through a grimace, "I think I've got it."

With a final tug she pulls the zipper up, and the dress squeezes me into a satisfying, upright posture of dignified elegance. *And they wonder why I think so much about fashion...*

"One week is nowhere near long enough to plan a

party," I say, checking myself in the mirror before putting on my carefully laid out jewelry.

"Um. We have a problem," Harriet says.

"My biggest problem right now is being seen at my own party, honey."

"Do you know Melanie Powell and her family?"

"Unfortunately."

"Well they're filming the first season of their reality show and our security refused to let them in because they've got the cameras with them. There's a whole fuss at the front gate."

I smile in the mirror.

"That's not a problem at all," I say, looking at Harriet in the reflection. "Tell her that arguing petulantly with a security guard to get into a party she wasn't invited to is as close to 'reality' as her viewers are going to get from her." I turn to point at Harriet. "That's not a euphemism, honey. I want you to tell her I said those exact words."

Harriet winces. "She's pretty hot right now though. Are you sure you want to make her an enemy?"

I turn back to the mirror to put some fine touches on my makeup.

"I give it six months before her affair with her married producer gets out and she ends up dragging down everyone associated with her. Some enemies are better kept than reconciled with." I turn back to her. "Anything else before I get my first glass of champagne?"

Harriet faces me but her eyes flick to the clipboard on the bed, and she sidesteps slowly toward it as if not wanting to show that it's actually pretty important to her. I smile and sigh as if I get the message and she grabs her clipboard to read.

"Lars Lynch brought the entire cast of his latest movie and I let them all in—that's okay, right?"

"He's a sensational director. Of course."

"Also, Maria Neves is quite worried because she's got a blemish on her cheek and even though she's wearing her hair over it she's worried one of the photographers is going to release a photo of it."

"Tell her I have a grip like Stalin over what the photographers can release—but if some rando takes a photo and uploads it himself then she's on her own. Tell her to go to the DJ room, it's dark there."

"Okay." Harriet nods quickly and scribbles something onto her clipboard. "Oh, and what's your final decision on the outside lighting once it gets dark?"

"Leave the colored lights on the ice sculptures, one light on the outside bar, the pool lighting—and that's it. There will be enough light coming from the house, but I'd like it to be on the darker side."

"Got it," Harriet says, and carries on scribbling on her clipboard.

I step toward her suddenly and she looks up, aware I'm about to do something. I take the clipboard, tear off the top sheet, fold it, then wedge it carefully down into the bustline of her dress.

"Honey, I'd rather you get something wrong and look fabulous doing it," I explain.

Then I take the pen from her hands and toss it away.

"What if I need to write something down again?" she pleads.

"Ask the nearest handsome stranger," I say, gently turning her by the shoulder to come with me to the door. "Anyway, it's nine-thirty. No more planning. Now the party goes where it goes."

Harriet seems to relax a little and smiles.

"Actually, one more thing," she says. "Your friends are here. Mia and her husband."

"Wonderful," I say, as I open the door for her and she steps through.

"And also," she adds, with a big smile and a strange sense of mischief in her voice. "Asher."

"Asher..." I say, remembering there's still some work to do. "Very good. Okay, darling. Oh—listen, if you see the guy in charge of the fireworks crew, tell him I'm going to light a fire under his own ass if he doesn't come find me."

"Will do," Harriet says, then nods a farewell as she heads off to one of the theme rooms. I move toward the staircase, ready to descend into the crowd that's amassed in the vast hallway and let some steam off.

For the next hour, I'm in my element. The taste of champagne fizz on my lips, the sound of laughter and compliments in my ears, handsome and beautiful faces as far as I can see. My fingers on a cold glass, trailing numerous expensive suits and dresses as I pose for pictures and get close to old and new friends. My skin vibrating to the music, the crowd, the atmosphere. An uplifting thrum that seeps deep into my heart and makes me feel genuinely happy. The alcohol, the dusk, the attention, the energy, and most of all: the people making each moment more beautiful than the last.

I move through the party like the conversation and brief greetings and witty exchanges are a dance themselves, always leaving before anything even threatens to get stale, always seizing any opportunity to reconnect or allow a group of delightful strangers to distract me.

"Where on Earth did you get those ice sculptures? They're wonderful!"

"Call me Monday and I'll give you the number," I tell the woman whose face is familiar though she's had so much work done I can't think of the name.

"Are they anything to do with the rumors about you releasing some jewelry?" she leans in to ask.

"There are so many rumors about me even *I* don't know what to believe," I say as I glide from her to a handsome actor I almost slept with before he started getting a little clingy.

"Maeve," he says, face brightening up into a poster quality beauty, "great party. That cabaret room is something else."

"Don't tell me, sweetie. Go compliment my assistant. It was her idea. She's over there pretending to be a wallflower."

I give him a gentle shove in Harriet's direction as I spin away once again, intending to go and check on Brent's little "DJ room" but getting sidetracked by a chatty young pop singer who I'd met once. If I suspected the girl was infatuated with me before, I'm certain of it now, and find it both flattering and curious.

After another circuit of the party, another blur of introductions, exchanges, and even a brief dance that an extroverted, eccentric European artist seizes me for, I find May in a corner. She's with a group of people that nobody would notice, but happen to be the most influential people in the world of fashion and art.

May splits from the group to stop me and speak.

"Will your jewelry line be 'simple classical' then?" she asks.

"You know about it?"

May tilts her head and half closes her eyes. As if mildly insulted by the idea she wouldn't.

Chapter 22

"Intricate and baroque, actually," I say. "Think 'belle époque,' with a bit of a modern twist."

"That's somewhat against the grain."

"Beauty sometimes is. I want to make a statement."

"Difficult to do."

"The world's already full of people who do the easy thing."

She smiles at me, and I think I can detect a little pride in her protégé behind the well-practiced stoic expression.

"Some people are becoming very interested in you," she says, nodding behind her.

I glance over her shoulder at the group of people, who watch the party with eyes like elder hawks.

"The secret society of the stylish stiletto?" I quip.

May laughs—a brief, breathy, sighing laugh as close as she ever comes.

"Who are you working with on it?" she asks.

As soon as she asks the question, Toby comes to my mind, and for the first time this evening I feel a tinge of something negative, something less than smoothly pleasant, something more complicated than the thrill of the crowd. I'd spent the whole evening pushing him out of my mind, as if this whole party were nothing but a gigantic distraction from the messiness of my sober, waking life. I'd braced myself to see him here in case he decided to show up, and even practiced a few things I would say to navigate those choppy waters.

May's question brings to my mind all kinds of mixed feelings, but I show none of them, and instead smile demurely.

"I have my secret sources."

May winks at me and steps away, as skillful in the art of

timing as I am, and I squeeze her arm quickly as a farewell before turning to surf the rest of the crowd.

The party's gone from being energetic to raucous now. The photographers have been sent home. Inside and outside there are shouts and dancers, bodies so close they're bumping like it's a heavy metal concert but having too much fun to care. I slip through the crowd, returning looks with nods and waves, inside being too loud to hear anyone unless they're shouting. As I navigate the throng of well-tailored suits and shimmering dresses, I catch sight of a young couple, the man leading the girl away by the hand, both of them with excited looks on their faces. In another corner a group of drunk women are tossing champagne over an equally drunk man as he dances for them. Someone is being lifted onto someone else's shoulders. Everywhere you look there's some exuberant example of people letting go, enough to regard the party as at least something of a success. And it's not even midnight.

But May's reminded me of the cloud in this clear sky, and while I can just about push Toby out of my mind—especially since it seems he decided not to come—I'm also reminded that Harriet said Mia and Colin are here.

After what feels like fighting through a battlefield, albeit a very welcoming and happy one, I reach the large exit to the rear of the castle. It opens out to a high platform with steps running down either side, from which one can scan the partygoers around the pool, and the bar, and the various ice sculptures. Even the stone balustrade of the platform is packed with people—including a singer just about famous enough to make his necking session with another singer somewhat scandalous. I charm and nudge my way through a couple of men enjoying the view and look over the crowd myself, watching for Mia's distinctively red hair.

Chapter 22

My hopes aren't high of finding her—I'm starting to feel a little tipsy myself. The party and the fresh air only add to my sense of light, euphoric dizziness. Yet after only half a minute of looking I spot her, mainly because of what she's wearing. I smile more genuinely than I have all night and push my way back through the men, hurrying toward her as fast as it's possible to do while still looking elegant in heels.

Once I'm close enough for Colin to see me, he smiles, turning away from the couple they were talking to, and nudges Mia beside him. She looks over at me and suddenly opens her face wide in an excited look, then opens her arms to embrace me as I reach her.

"I'm so sorry, Maeve," she says when we pull apart, "Alison was being a little grumpy before we left and we didn't want to leave her with Colin's mom that way so we ended up being late. I'm so—"

"Oh, forget it, honey. I've been too busy fixing the party to enjoy it until now," I say, then step back to look at her stunning figure. "You wore the red dress? Very good."

"Of course!" Mia says.

She glances at Colin, and he can't hide the glimmer in his eye. I start to think that maybe the dress has more significance for Mia than just the fact that it's the most daring thing I helped her pick out for herself.

"This party's incredible," Colin says. "I think there are more people here than I've ever met in my life. Very 'Gatsby.'"

"I think I overdid it to be honest. You can't even move for all the people inside. I stepped on more Louboutins than carpet to walk outside just now."

"Whether you overdid it or not, I'm glad," Colin says. "We've been here an hour and three people have already asked to visit my practice. Who knew the rich and famous all needed good pediatricians this badly."

"Well you're *here*—that's as good a recommendation as you can get. You *will* stay a bit longer, won't you? We've got fireworks at midnight, although I think everyone here will be too intoxicated, aroused, or lively to even notice them."

"Sure," Mia says, looking at Colin as if to confirm it. "But we'll probably need to leave by one."

"Of course, honey. Don't let me keep you from Alison. I'm just glad I saw you."

"Asher's here too," Colin adds.

"Oh yes," Mia says. "He actually just left to look for you, but I don't think he had much hope he would after seeing how many people are here."

"Asher..." I say, hiding the slight heaviness in my light spirits. "Yes. Well, I *should* talk to him."

Colin says, "He went over by those ice sculptures, near the bar."

"I'll go look for him. You don't mind me leaving you?"

"Go!" Mia says, as Colin waves me away with a smile. "I can see you whenever, and clearly everyone here wishes they could do the same." As if to prove her point, Mia nods and I look in that direction to find an old coworker of mine waving frantically at me. I wave nonchalantly back, a regal smile, then turn to Mia one last time to hug her.

"Speak to you next week then, sweetie." I release her and grab Colin to do the same. "Give Alison a kiss from me."

A little reluctantly, I pull away and immerse myself once again in the crowd, the same routine of hellos and intros and brief conversations and silly jokes. But there's something detached in me now. My whole spirit no longer fully in the smiles and laughs I afford others. The weight of

Chapter 22

the recent past holding me back from being entirely in the present moment...

It's the impulse to put that negative stain in my mind to bed that makes me look for Asher's recognizably attractive face in the crowd. He's a lovely man. He'll understand when I tell him that I'm not really that interested. He'll probably play it off in a charming manner, making it easy for me even though he doesn't need to.

I just wish he was the only man I had to worry about...

23

TOBY

I've crashed parties all my life. In a way, it's the story of my life.

A young college dropout whose sister inherited all the brains, leaving him with nothing but audacity and an appetite for fine things. I would never have been happy with a regular job and only my weekends to play—I wanted more. More than a guy with my upbringing is allowed to want. More than it was realistic for someone like me to want.

I came to L.A. like half the people here: as a nobody. But even as an outsider, perhaps *especially* as an outsider, I knew how things worked. The high life doesn't hand out invitations—you're either born into it or you break into it. Mia's smart enough to run the country, but she still had to work her ass off just to get a stable doctor's position and a tiny apartment. Me, I learned one lesson early on, and ended up owning the best jewelry business in town: it's *who* you know.

A borrowed suit and the confidence to use side entrances got me into the bars and clubs only the richest could afford official entrance to. Arrogance and the ability to think fast got me backstage at gigs and events where I built up a phonebook that read like a who's who. A great gift got me into the garden party that got me first dibs on the premises of my shop. A few bribes, a few white lies, a few more side entrances and I could be in the right place at the right time, meet and persuade the right men and women to bankroll my whole idea of a jewelry shop.

I can't lie and say it was my plan all along. I'm not going to pretend it wasn't extremely fun, that I wasn't just living in the moment, that the thrill of living beyond my means, in places I would never have been allowed, charming people whom I would never meet otherwise wasn't incredibly exciting. But don't they always say to try to turn your passion into work?

Those are just old stories I tell for fun now. I haven't had to borrow a suit, pretend to be a bartender, or sneak through a kitchen in years. Now *I'm* being begged to attend rather than doing the begging. I made it. I live the lifestyle I dreamed of. No longer an outsider. That's the thing about crashing a party—once you're in, you can leave whenever you want.

Except...here I am getting dressed in my finest suit, about to gatecrash an event I was deliberately not invited to, an outsider all over again.

The thought makes me stop as I'm buttoning up my shirt in the mirror. I look at myself and realize something: that's exactly what Maeve makes me feel like, an outsider. Not to her party, or her world of fancy-ass fashion people, but to *her*. She'll tease me and intrigue me, draw me in and play the game with me—in her house, at the dinner party, in my shop—but the second I get too close, she gets scared and holds me off. Keeping her heart in a glass jar, there just to look pretty.

Just once I want her to let me in. To show me the real her, the raw her. Even if she decides to kick me out, I've got to smash that glass and truly touch her at least once. *Tonight.*

It's past eleven by the time I'm driving up the winding canyon roads that lead to the mansion. First rule of crashing a party: always show up late, when everybody's having too much fun to even care if they notice you. I can hear the place throbbing and pounding half a mile off. As if the large building is amplifying the noise inside. The air seeming electrified even around it.

I decide to avoid driving in through the front gates and park under a tree a little down the street, walking the rest of the way. There's security at the large front gates. They're big and mean and look like they were hired from the cast of a mob movie. I hang back while I figure out a routine to give them, but as I'm figuring out how to grease my way inside, I get lucky.

"*Toby?*"

The voice is calling me from the rear window of a Rolls Royce that's crept up beside me. I turn to it and see Dan Gibson, a financier I used to see around a few years back.

"Hey, Dan," I say, smiling as if I missed him as I step toward the car. I catch a glimpse of a beautiful woman in a gold dress beside him, though she seems uninterested in anything but her phone. "Since when do you show up to parties as late as I do?"

He laughs and gestures to the woman beside him.

"I was planning an early night after a business dinner, but my daughter insisted. What are you doing walking out there?"

"My car broke down a little back down the road."

"That Porsche? Those things never break down."

"Depends how you drive them."

Dan laughs, and his daughter huffs impatiently, as if I'm stealing precious seconds of the party from her.

"Hey," I say. "You wouldn't mind giving me a lift, would you? I know this place—the driveway's like a mile long."

Dan shoves open his door and gestures me inside happily.

"Thanks, Dan. You're a lifesaver."

"I wouldn't dare refuse with how much my wife loves your shop," he quips.

His daughter doesn't look so irritated now that she's seen me. Her huffing replaced by a bashful shyness as she crosses her legs and puts a lot of effort into looking nonchalant. I make small talk with Dan as we pass through the gates. Turns out he's in town looking to fund a television series. Business is the last thing on my mind though. I feel myself get a little edgy, heart a little quicker, as we coast smoothly through the driveway—catching glimpses of random stragglers from the party looking for quiet spots under the oaks.

Dan's daughter gets out almost before the car's stopped, a group of equally wealthy-looking girls waiting for her there with loud screams and open arms. I open the door and turn to Dan so I don't leave in such a hurry it seems rude.

"Listen," I say, "tell your wife to drop by next month. I've got some new stuff coming in that's perfect for her."

"I'm not sure I will," Dan says as he steps out of the car after me. "She's got so much jewelry, she used some of it to decorate the Christmas tree last year."

I laugh and pat him on the shoulder before leaving him to the girls and heading toward the mansion.

Chapter 23

There are people everywhere, too many for even the large estate to contain, so they spill out into groups. Couples darting about in the shadows around the building conspicuous but for the laughter and shouts they throw into the constant, exuberant hum of the music and chatter. I leap up stone steps where some are glamorously sprawled and sitting, looking as decadent as a painting of the fall of Rome.

Inside, the atmosphere is more like a nightclub than a luxurious event. The sweltering body heat of hundreds of people in an old mansion causing men to discard their twenty-thousand-dollar coats and unbutton their shirts. Women who would have spent four hours getting ready now so hot and sweaty their makeup is running, messing up their own hair as they dance and slink madly through the crowd. More people clutching champagne bottles than glasses, as much bare flesh on display as clothing.

I push through the kaleidoscopic orgy of colorful dresses and glistening skin, pretending not to hear anyone call my name, ignoring the hands grabbing for me as I'm shoved and shunted about. The air itself is intoxicating, from the smell of sweat and alcohol and perfume. The sound is dizzying, a constant euphoric frequency of voices and music that shakes the muscles and disorients the mind.

At another time, in another place, I would have loved this. An atmosphere so good it's as if everyone ceases to be individual. Where identities can be forgotten, and the typical structure of society, of thinking, don't make sense. A chaotic, concerted pursuit of absolute rapture. I would have let myself succumb to it, orienting myself in the crowd by a glimpse of elegant thigh or a female face induced to something bordering on the erotic by the music and the dancing.

But even if I wanted to, I couldn't let myself go. Like a stone in a pool, I'm too heavy, and I'm only immersing myself to find the bottom of this. The ecstasy around me only a distraction from my desires now, and no longer part of them.

I move through the crowd hard and focused, looking and thinking intensely. Maeve wouldn't be here. Not in this mass of dancers who are letting themselves go. Maeve doesn't do that—her inability to let go was maybe always her biggest problem.

Looking up, I see the balcony surrounding the main area, people coming and going and dancing and watching from up there. It looks like there are rooms, probably quieter places, probably places where the party has a more refined, composed tone. She could be in any of those, but I'll check later. I can see the flung-open rear doors now, the cool night air shimmering, and instincts compel me to search there first.

Pushing through, moving from the intense heat of the inside dancers to the cooler air outside, feels like coming up for air. I almost gasp it in, even though it still carries the fog of people and joy. I shove through the crowd to look out over the balustrade at the gathering there. It's less packed than inside, but only just.

The ice sculptures draw my eyes first. Glowing, colored, glittering ice sculptures in the shapes of various gems. I immediately connect them with Maeve—they're so clearly her idea—and I stare at them as if they're some kind of reflection of her. Imposing, attractive, impenetrable, *cold*. Things which seem clear, but only turn the light back on you.

I feel a strange stirring in my gut again, a surge of the impulse to find her, to tell her, to confront her. Somebody calls my name but I continue to search the mass of beautiful people for a hint of her, a clue, something to chase.

Chapter 23

Then I catch it—or at least, I think I do. For a split second, that blonde pixie cut appears in the crowd, near the ice sculptures by the bar, on the other side of the pool.

It could be anything, but hope alone is driving me now —hope alone is always what's driven me.

I shove my way back through the crowd on the landing and almost tumble down the steps.

Out here the people aren't dancing skin-to-skin, aren't entirely lost to the passions of their own bodies, so when I push through, knocking drinks out of people's hands, jolting them from their pleasant conversations, I leave a stream of grumbles and complaints that seem dissonant with the pleasantness of everything else at the party.

But I don't care. I need to find her, and I'm done taking the long route.

Shoving and forcing my way through, I only feel the intensity inside of me growing. Oblivious to the exclamations behind me, the sense of *rightness* too powerful to listen to anyone else. Wading through the crowd, toward something like a light, nothing else seems important.

I pause slightly when I see her twenty feet away, standing by one of the ice sculptures. Not just because I'm so close, not just because she looks as beautiful as ever, not just because actually seeing her only makes me one hundred times more certain that I *need* to do this—but because she's standing with Asher.

She's looking up affectionately at him, giving him a smile as warm as she knows how to. All the turbulence I felt nights ago, seeing those images of them, reading about how they're a "great couple" returns to my chest, mixing with my energy, turning it aggressive. When she reaches out and touches him on the arm, leaning forward, he laughs at something she says, and now my desire is painful, my intentions sharpening like a knife.

Six years I've known her, and even then, when we met we couldn't resist what we had between us. Six years of play-acting all the things that we actually felt. And now here's this guy—that she met only a couple weeks ago—who's taking a place I should be in. Who got to take her out and show the whole world. Who got to take her home when she should have been with me. And for no other reason than the fact that he was easier. More convenient. But it's not *right*.

I stalk toward her, hard with determination now.

"Hey, Maeve!" I call out confrontationally, taking her arm when I'm close and pulling her away. "I need to talk to you."

She looks at me with shock, and Asher instinctively steps between us, his hand on my forearm.

"Hey, buddy, easy there. Getting a little rough."

"Get out of here," I snarl at him, unable to hide the resentment in my voice. I turn back to Maeve. "Listen—"

"What on Earth are you doing here, Toby?" she exclaims, moving her shocked eyes to my hand on her arm.

"Calm the fuck down, dude," Asher says, getting more forceful as he shoves my shoulder, trying to pull me away from Maeve.

Instincts take over. I'm nothing but inflated, wounded pride now. Nothing but frustration and yearning. Emotions too big not to be sensitive, the moment too important not to seize. I'm barely thinking. The atmosphere too euphoric, Maeve too achingly beautiful, the situation too wrong. I'm just the need to take Maeve away, and everything in my way is an obstacle I won't allow—including Asher.

I swing at him. It catches him off guard, and sends him

flying into the ice sculpture. He grabs for it as he falls, but only manages to drag it down with him. The sound of a wine glass smashing can distract a room, but the sound of a six-foot ice sculpture hitting hard stone and shattering sounds like an apocalypse.

"*Toby!*" Maeve screams at me. Her voice, the sudden, strange quiet of the previously-cacophonic party, the spectacular sight of ice smashing into small pieces that each refract and catch the light, as if it were a real magical effect —it all gets through my heightened emotions for a second.

My blood thumps and my breath quickens, but I see a glimpse of what a scene I'm making, of what I've just done. A wave of regret, of the sudden realization that I've just done something I shouldn't.

Unfortunately, Asher doesn't know how I'm feeling. All Asher knows is that I just sucker punched him and sent him sprawling into cold, hard ice.

When he gets up, even the slipperiness of the ice crunching under his expensive shoes can't stop him. Everyone watching, a few men who know what's coming calling for him not to, and me standing there, stuck between wanting to apologize, and the suddenly understood fact that Asher isn't the type to take a hit and turn the other cheek.

He barrels into me with his head down, and if I didn't pull back he'd have had me on my ass in perfect position to be pummeled MMA style. It's only my reluctance to fight back that means instead, he bulldozes me a full five feet backwards until I crash into the tent-bar.

The wood counter breaks under the weight of my back, feeling like I'm being hit from behind by a freight train, head slamming so hard it feels like whiplash. Even as we crash into it, all I can think is that the sound of a thousand bottles of alcohol smashing is pretty similar to that of a seven-foot ice sculpture.

The two of us crash to the floor in a gigantic, cascading explosion of bottles and glass, the wood and cloth of the bar, the shrieks and shouts of the people around us. But in a fight you focus only on your opponent, and in the malaise Asher loses the upper hand, and I manage to shift his weight to the side.

We both scramble to our feet amongst the rubble of the bar, both of us drenched in champagne, Asher's face half bloody—the sting of a cut in my own cheek indicating I probably don't look that different.

He swings and I take the blow to the shoulder, then swings again and I manage to block it, delivering my own hit to his side. We're circling like boxers now; the cries for us to stop may as well be cheering us on. I'm tougher but he's faster, landing two on me for every time I touch him—though I can tell *my* punches hurt.

Then he catches me on the chin and a sound like an atomic bomb shakes my entire body. I see stars, exploding in different colors. Then I stagger back and realize it isn't me—the sky's filled with fireworks. I regain my senses just quick enough to block a few more blows, and suddenly find myself teetering on the edge of the pool.

There's no way I'm losing this fight. In my unthinking mind everything has mixed up into this singular moment, this sudden situation. My feelings for Maeve, my need to tell her, my desire for clarity, to bring everything out from the forbidden depths where they've existed too long. This man, Asher, my obstacle, my rival, as if the obstacles between us were given a human form. Something to defeat in the physical world as well as the emotional.

I'm fighting for *her*, I'm doing it for *us*. I'll beat this man

—whom I don't even really know well enough to properly hate—into a bloody pulp if that's what it takes to show her. I don't even know what he's fighting for, but it's clear even as we exchange blows poolside that his heart isn't in this as much as mine is. It's obvious he doesn't care as much as I do. I can only hope Maeve sees that.

I start raining punches on him, exerting all the strength I can muster. Bad tactics, bad strategy—don't waste your energy when fighting. But my energy isn't even my own anymore, it comes from something deeper, from a pit of emotion that's infinite. If it wasn't, I wouldn't even be here, doing this.

Asher blocks them as best he can, winding and stopping my punches like a pro, but I'm still pushing him back, threatening to break through.

Suddenly the pool is even closer to us, and the idea is impulsive. I stop hitting and instead reach out, grabbing his clothing and setting my feet to throw him in there, to mark the fight with some kind of victory.

He's quick though, and grabs me in turn, so that even as I throw him he pulls me with him, the two of us crashing into the water as fireworks explode. I take a lungful of water and start flailing, then hands grab me, and as much as I try to fight them off there are too many to stop myself from being dragged in some direction...

I'm pulled out of the pool spluttering and exhausted, as if my lungs had suddenly shriveled to the size of walnuts, not quite big enough to sustain me. The hands lift me to my feet and then leave me. Until one takes my elbow.

I look up and there she is. Scowling at me like she's thinking about throwing me back in the pool, and then she sets off, still holding me, and I oblige, all the resistance and tension and fight leaving my body now that she's the one touching me.

The crowd parts for her as she drags me like a naughty schoolchild through them, out of the party area, and into the dark trees far from the pool area. An unlit place so dark only the colored flashes of the distant fireworks illuminate her. And even there, even in that state, she looks even more magical than she ever has.

Eventually she lets go, tossing my arm away as if disgusted with it, walks two steps into the dark, composes herself, then turns that scowl back on me. She looks at me, panting and wet, as if I'm the most ridiculous thing she's ever seen. In her perfect black dress, looking like the kind of woman a man would dream about till death, I almost understand.

When she speaks, it's as if she has to wrench the words out of herself, as if words aren't enough.

"What...the fuck...are you doing, Toby?"

I take my time answering, still catching my breath, still gathering up the courage for this critical moment.

There's only one explanation I can give her, for this, for me, for everything.

"I'm in love with you, Maeve."

Her scowl turns into cold, blank surprise. As if I just socked a punch on her as well.

"No...you're not," she says.

"Yes, I am," I insist, stepping toward her so she can see the unreserved sincerity in my eyes as I say it. "I'm in love with you. And *you're* in love with me."

Maeve laughs. That same dismissive laugh that she uses to deflect everything—but I refuse to accept it now. I can hear the falsity in it, I know it too well not to notice that it's a little different, a little less confident than usual.

Chapter 23

"You crashed my party..." she says slowly. "Caused an absolute scene... Thousands of dollars' worth of destruction... Started a fight with a friend of mine... Made a fool of yourself...and me...so that you could *tell me how* I *feel*..."

"Well, God knows you're not going to say it," I reply. "You could spend the rest of your life ignoring what we have between us. But I can't. Not anymore."

"Toby, listen to me," she says, stepping towards me now. "This is not love—this is just *sex*. Okay?"

"Bullshit. You're better at lying to yourself than you are to me, Maeve."

She turns away from me and sighs, folding her arms and walking a few paces away, shaking her head as if exasperated.

"This is insane," she mutters to herself.

"Yeah, it is. Insane that you've started believing all your own hype. 'Maeve the socialite—so cool and distant and fashionable.' An 'icon.' Untouchable and invulnerable. Above everything. As if you don't get lonely at night. As if you don't ever feel the need for affection. As if you don't yearn deep down for somebody—for *me*—to get close to you."

"What the hell are you even talking about?" She turns to sneer at me, but her attempt at her typical sardonic tone falters, and I can hear the hot blood underneath it.

"I'm talking about all this *shit!*" I exclaim, gesturing behind me at the party, where the fireworks are still popping and crackling. "The parties and the dresses and the glamour and the photos in the magazines and the cult of personality and the fashion and the popular director you decide to pick up for a few months... Always jumping from one thing to another to convince yourself you're the kind of woman who doesn't need anything more."

"I *am* that woman," she snaps back at me, forcefully and loudly, so that there's no way I can deny it. Then she looks away angrily and shakes her head again.

"Sure," I say, stepping closer. I point at her. "But you're also *this* woman right here. A woman who can't even look me in the eye too long because she's afraid I'll see too much emotion in her. You're afraid, Maeve, and too proud to admit it. That's why you can go out and have the world see you with Asher—because you don't feel anything for him. But not with me..."

"And what, exactly, are *you*, Toby?" she says, turning to face me as if challenged now. She gestures at me. "What am I supposed to be looking at, huh? Tell me if I'm wrong—you are the expert, after all—but what I'm seeing is a man with bruises all over his face, drenched in alcohol, who's just been dragged out of a pool. You want to talk about egos? It takes something to beat a guy like that acting as if he has the moral high ground."

Maeve says nothing for a few moments. Beyond us, the last of the fireworks explodes, and leaves nothing but the distant hum of the party. The sudden quiet feels like the space between us closing in. The fireworks end, leaving a calm that we never even realized we were lacking.

"I love you, Maeve."

She turns to me quickly and replies, "Well I don't l—"

She stops herself and I smile. Then I laugh. Gently at first, and then a full laugh that causes her to look away again.

"You can't even *say* it... Because you know you *do*." I grin. "God, you're so full of shit, Maeve."

"*I'm* the one who is full of shit, am I?" she says, her eyes burning with a special kind of cruelty now. "Okay. Could you promise to answer me a question honestly then, sweetie?"

I open my arms out to the side and shrug as if it's easy. "Go ahead."

"How many times," Maeve begins, patient and slow, like she's about to twist a knife, "in the years I've known you, have you run to Mia and told her that you 'love' some random woman who was out of your reach?"

"That's different," I say, feeling like I'm failing to block one of Asher's punches.

"Off the top of my head," Maeve continues as if she didn't hear me, "there's the married Texan pop star... The Russian whose visa ran out... The older woman who'd been divorced twice and wasn't about to do so a third time... Wasn't there a lesbian in there somewhere?"

"Come on, Maeve, you know that's not the same."

"Oh, it's *never* the same," Maeve says sarcastically. "It's always *different this time*, isn't it, sweetie? Mia nailed you: you want only what you can't have. And since you figured out that you can't have me, *I'm* the one you want."

"It's different," I repeat.

"How?"

I step toward her to show my conviction.

"Because I *can* have you, Maeve. I can and I will. We belong together. It's just that out of the two of us, I'm the only one with the balls, with the honesty, to come out and say it. But sooner or later you'll have to face it."

"You'll be waiting forever, Toby."

"So be it."

There's another silence between us. Maeve paces on the grass, still shaking her head and sighing. I watch her, trying to figure out how to get through to someone who's spent their whole life not allowing people through.

Eventually she pauses and looks at me, all of her composure back, no sign of her prior weakness. I know that I won't get any further with her tonight.

"If that's all," she says, "then would you mind leaving my party now?"

I look at her and take a deep breath, knowing there's nothing more I can do. I nod and turn away, then stop. One last thing burning in my mind so bright I have to say it, to get rid of it, to exorcise its spirit.

"You know what?" I say. "I *hate* that I'm in love with you. You're so…frustrating and…*difficult*. Nothing is ever simple with you. You get me angry in a way I never get with anyone else. Under my skin…in my head…driving me crazy… I wish it was anyone else. Someone easier, simpler, more convenient…but it's you.

"And even though I absolutely fucking *hate* you… I *love you. That's* how I know this is real."

I don't wait for her response. I know she won't give me one.

I turn and start walking, heading back to the large building, the stinging in my cheek suddenly sharpening in a breeze so that I touch it and check the blood on my fingers.

It's a long walk back, but I'm numb to everything, including time. The party is past its peak, but it's still going strong. I avoid going through the building and instead take the long gravel path around it. There are still plenty of people there, drinking in small groups, moving between parts of the mansion, laughing and cheerful. I even hear a couple fucking in the bushes. Though I'm soaked and bloody, nobody seems to care—half the people here are soaked with sweat anyway, and I even catch sight of another guy nursing a fresh black eye.

I keep my hand to my face, partly to suppress the

Chapter 23

stinging pain of the cut, partly so that nobody recognizes me and tries to start up a conversation. The last thing I'm feeling is in the mood for company.

And yet after I've rounded the building, and I'm heading past the fountain, toward the long driveway that leads to the road, somebody calls out to me.

"Hey!"

It's a nonchalant, friendly shout, and the voice is familiar yet foreign enough to cause me to turn and look.

Asher's sitting there on the edge of the stone fountain, two blonde women tending to his own bruises like angelic nurses. When I turn and stop, he stands up and thanks them before walking toward me. The two women glare as if they're angry at me for taking him away, or ruining his beautiful face.

He peers at my face, my cut, then laughs good-naturedly.

"Is that all I did to you? A measly cut? I need to work on my form."

"Stings like a bitch though."

"Look at the size of this welt you gave me," he says, turning his head to show me. "Good thing I got long hair."

"Ah, it was a sucker punch. Once you were in the fight, I didn't land a single clean hit."

He laughs again and I laugh with him this time. The fight's drained from my body, and Asher's got a friendliness about him that it's hard to hate.

"You getting a cab?" he asks, nodding down the long driveway.

"No," I say, turning and starting to walk. "I parked a little down the road."

Asher laughs again as he walks beside me. "You crashed the party, huh?"

"I had to. Maeve didn't invite me."

We walk down the long, oak-lined driveway, nursing our bruises.

"You leaving?" I ask, once he's walked with me enough for me to realize he isn't turning back.

"Yeah... I'll call a cab from the road."

We walk on for a while longer, and I don't ask the obvious question, not wanting to hear the painful truth. Eventually, Asher is the one who brings it up.

"I don't wanna pry or anything... And I *think* I can pretty much get a rough idea of what happened..." he says. "But I'd just like to know—why the hell did you start a fight with me again?"

I turn to look at him as we walk, and with a mixture of humor and seriousness say, "Because I'm in love with your girlfriend."

Asher stops to look at me with intense confusion. I take one more step and stop myself, turning to look back at him.

"My girlfriend?"

"Yeah..." I say as Asher starts walking again. "Or whatever it is you two got going on. Fuck buddies...public relations thing...I dunno."

"I think there's some crossed wires here somewhere," Asher says confusedly. "Maeve and I went out once, technically. If you don't count the dinner date we were set up on, but—"

"Look, buddy," I say, stopping to face him, "you don't have to *explain* anything to me, or talk me down from a ledge or something... I'm the last person who can hate a guy for being into Maeve—Jesus Christ, that's my whole problem. I get it.

"As far as you're aware, you were set up with an incredible woman, you went out on a date, you fucked her, she invited you to a party—and then suddenly some guy comes along and hits you in the face. And that's about all you know of the situation. I get it. And I guess I should say I'm sorry, but I doubt it'll make the bruise hurt less."

I start walking again, but only take two steps before realizing Asher hasn't moved. I turn back again to look at him.

"We didn't sleep together," he says, then finally gets walking again.

"Oh really?" I reply sarcastically.

"Really. Don't get me wrong, I wanted to. She gave me all the signs too... And then as the night was winding down she said she wasn't feeling too good. I drove her home and that was it."

I look at him, searching for a sign he might be lying, covering for something, but he's not the type of guy, and this isn't really the kind of moment he'd lie in. The punches have already been thrown. He'd tell me if it happened.

After about a minute's walking, the gates of the entrance in view now, he laughs to himself and says, "You know what she was saying to me right before you rolled up and clocked me?"

"I don't—but it looked like you were both enjoying it."

"She was giving me the 'you're a nice guy *but*' conversation. 'I had a great time last week *but*...' 'I really like you *but*...' She didn't quite get to the 'but' part, but I could put the pieces together. Now I'm not saying she's into you, but she isn't into me, that's for damn sure—not that much, anyway."

"She's into me," I insist. "She's just into her whole lifestyle even more... I just can't seem to make her understand..."

"She's a tough woman."

"You're telling me..." I say as we near the gates.

After a few seconds, Asher says, "Don't give up though. I think you stand a chance."

I stop at the entrance to look at him, hope getting the better of me. "You think?"

Asher shrugs and nods.

"Yeah. I don't know why. Something in the way she acted toward you at dinner, and how she looked when you suddenly showed up tonight... Even the fact that she just suddenly left our date when it was going so well. I think you're under her skin."

We pass through the gates, nodding at the security there, and stop on the road.

"Hey, Asher," I say. "I've got a confession I got to make."

"Yeah?" he says, pressing his bruise and wincing.

"I should have passed that ball. You were right."

Asher laughs heartily, and smacks my shoulder. "At least you scored it."

"Luck."

He pulls out his phone and starts swiping it.

"You calling a cab?"

Nodding, he says, "It'll probably take them half an hour to get out here if I'm lucky."

"Fuck it then," I say, gesturing for him to follow me as I walk down the road to where I parked. "I'll give you a ride. Then we can call it even."

24

MAEVE

"What a success!"

"Even *I* didn't think it would be this big."

"Did you *see* the photos?"

"Oh! They're good enough to make a coffee table book!"

"With the ice sculptures and that house…"

"Amazing."

"And the trending for Maeve's name went through the roof."

"It *still* is."

"I saw—it's the goodie bags, right?"

"Among other things."

"I didn't even see half the stuff that people are saying happened at the party…"

"That's because you spent all night in that DJ room of yours!"

"Oh look who's talking! Every time I saw you, you were planted face-first in that actor."

"I was *not!*"

"Yes, you were! And I can see the layer of concealer on

your neck from here. Let me guess, you probably have so many hickeys it looks like you were mauled by a bear."

"Let's not get off topic."

"Of course."

"Point is, this was sensational."

"Right."

"We got what we set out to get."

"Much more."

"Attention for Maeve."

"And a sense of excitement around her name."

"Absolutely."

"So now..."

"Now we have to think about how we can *shape* it in the run-up to launch. Right, Maeve?"

"Maeve?"

"*Maeve?*"

The terrible twins have been bouncing off the walls during our Monday meeting so much that I've tuned out. Partly because I know they're too excited to say anything of importance, partly because the whole party feels less than important to me now. All but one part, at least.

You can't even say it... I can have you... I hate that I'm in love with you...

Those aren't the rules of the game. Toby knows that.

You don't put your emotions on the table like that. You don't bet on them. Life is easy when you put emotions aside. When you live for the senses rather than the heart. Toby knows that.

So what the hell was he doing?

"Are you okay, Maeve?"

"What?" I say, the strange tone in Harriet's voice snapping me to attention. "Yes, yes. The party was fabulous. The question is *now* what, isn't it?"

Chapter 24

Harriet and Brent start excitedly talking over each other again and I suddenly feel suffocated by them, by work, by the weight of my own inescapable thoughts.

I hold my palms up to stop them and immediately stand, gathering my phone and purse.

"Actually, I'd rather we did this tomorrow. I need to get some fresh air. Whatever you two decide, go ahead and do it. You can explain it to me later. But I'm sure it'll be fantastic. Go do your thing with my full blessing. Ciao."

I'm out of the room before they can answer—not that they would. With carte blanche they're probably already signing me up for a photo shoot in Russia, or arranging an appearance for me at a silver refinery.

Right now, however, I'm only worried about my own sanity. My mind feels like it's on uneven footing, unable to move forward properly. Something deeply unsettling at the core of my being. A sense of something very wrong.

After scrambling outside, the fresh air makes me feel less hot and flustered, but not really any better. I'm still reeling. Still feeling the aftershock, so that trying to assess the damage is impossible.

What the hell has Toby done?

He's potentially ruined a seven-year relationship with my best friend. Created a potential future of awkwardly avoiding each other at any event involving Mia. Let alone all the places and people we might share in common.

And then, of course, my jewelry line is now going to be a complete botch job. I have only three months to finalize it and there's no way Toby and I can work together now. I'll have to make all the contacts, the deals, and let alone the designs, from scratch. Three months meant that every week —every *day*—mattered. I might even have to push the whole thing back. All because he's such an *idiot*.

Because he's so fucking reckless and childish and impulsive and petulant and arrogant and selfish and brash and I l—

You can't even say it...

Absent-mindedly, driven only by the frustration of my thoughts, I find myself pacing toward my car, and then—without any idea what I'm doing or why—I get inside. Inexplicably, I feel both lost and trapped. Stuck and falling free. Aimless and yet unable to let things lie. There isn't a word for what I'm feeling.

Body still acting on its own, my mind lost among memories and abstractions, I find myself grabbing my phone and sending a text. To Mia. My only friend. The only person I can really turn to. My near-infinite phonebook seeming ridiculously pointless in this moment of crisis.

I ask her if she's free, and she texts back quickly to say she could spare a moment for coffee at a place near her apartment. I start driving, already feeling the pain of having to sit with her holding in this terrible secret. But I feel alone, and for once I'm not happy to feel that way—and Mia is the only person who I can comfortably feel alone with.

The café is a cutesy hipster place we've been to a few times for brunch. Vintage wallpaper on the walls. Plush, colorful couches and padded chairs. The tables a random mixture of metal garden tables and aged woodgrain, as if the furnishings of the place had been randomly picked from a street market. Which, maybe they have.

It's the kind of place that attracts all kinds of clientele, from businesspeople working alone on their laptops to trendy young men who sit by the window watching the girls go by. The kind of place where the staff are so relaxed and casual it's impossible to tell them from the customers.

Heading inside, I feel at odds with the place. A couple

Chapter 24

smiling at each other in the corner seem like alien beings to me. I'm so mired in my own heavy, complicated feelings that any sign of simple joy or people just getting along feels almost inconceivable to me. For the first time in a long time —perhaps ever—I'm self-conscious.

"Are you all right?" Mia says when I find her at a table by the window and wordlessly sit in front of her.

"Yes, of course," I say, unable to make it sound genuine.

"Are you sure? You look a little pale."

"Just trying a new look, sweetie," I say, fiddling with my purse so as not to look Mia in the eye.

Mia laughs gently. "I suppose that party took it out of you. I was only there for a couple of hours and felt exhausted afterwards."

"It was wonderful to see you there. And that dress of yours deserves longer than a couple of hours on show," I say, feeling like I'm only mimicking my typical voice.

I finally look up at Mia and notice that she's staring at me with a look of concern I find almost painful.

"Something's wrong, isn't it?" she asks.

"Most definitely," I reply, still struggling to play my part. "I'm wearing one of the shortest skirts it's acceptable to attend work in, and that waiter still hasn't run over to take my order." I raise a hand and draw the bearded waiter's attention, then call out, "Cappuccino, please?"

"Maeve..."

"And also, where the hell is Alison, Mia? It should be implied that when I want to see you, I'm presuming you come as a package deal."

"Maeve."

"God knows she's a better conversationalist than half the people I know."

"*Maeve...*"

I pause, grateful for the waiter bringing my coffee at this moment. I make eyes at him then look back at Mia, ready to pass comment on his attractiveness and the benefits of a man who knows how to serve you—but she's still looking at me, *through* me, in a way that makes me understand she won't be distracted.

"Have you spoken to Toby?" I ask as nonchalantly as possible.

"No," Mia says. "Colin called him yesterday to ask about soccer this week, but there was no answer."

"Asher?"

Mia shakes her head. "He told us to leave the party when we wanted—he planned to get a cab home. That was the last time we spoke. Why? Is this something to do with him?"

I smile almost sadly as I whip the froth into the coffee, not speaking for a few moments, relishing our friendship as it is now, before I change it entirely. Still unsure how, but fully understanding it could potentially be for the worst.

"Maeve?" Mia asks, gently insistent. "Whatever it is... Just say it."

I look at her and smile, wishing I was as ignorant of it all as she was, then I put my spoon down carefully.

"A while ago...Toby and I slept together."

"You mean six years ago?" Mia says. "I know that."

"No. I mean...a few weeks ago."

Mia's eyebrows almost shoot off her face.

"Uh...wh—how?" she stutters.

I almost laugh.

"How indeed... I'm not even sure myself. It just sort of happened. I suppose there's only so long you can jokingly flirt and mock one another before it becomes more than a joke."

Chapter 24

She screws up her face in thought. "Was this before or after the dinner party?"

"Before."

"So then..." Maeve's eyes flick around the table like she's trying to solve the Enigma code in her head.

"Yes," I say. "It was rather awkward. Especially since, when you all weren't looking, we ended up kissing a little."

Maeve leans back in her seat so suddenly it's as if I just punched her.

"Then..." I continue, "when I went to his shop to work with him on my jewelry line, we ended up... Well, you get the picture."

"I had no idea..." Mia gasps.

"You still don't," I reply. "I haven't told you the critical part yet."

"Okay. Go on..."

I take a slow sip of coffee to steady myself. I might not show it as much as Mia, but I'm as nervous saying it as she's going to be shocked to hear it.

"Toby showed up at my party on Saturday, got into a fistfight with Asher, wrecked the bar, and then told me that he...he, um—well, that he's in love with me."

Now Mia does nothing, freezing so still that if there weren't cars passing outside, I could almost believe that time had stopped. I watch her for a few seconds, not a twitch or a glimmer, and I'm almost compelled to remind her to breathe.

"Toby..." she mutters, so softly I'm reading her lips more than hearing her. "My brother...Toby...said he was in *love* with you?"

I nod, after a long pause in which life returns to Mia in parts—first the ability to breathe again, then the ability to move and look outside as she absorbs it all, and then finally the ability to look back at me and speak.

"And you?" she asks. "How do you...*feel*?"

I sigh and stare at my full cup of coffee. The million-dollar question.

"The problem, Mia, is that what I *feel* doesn't matter, and I'm fully aware of that. I always have been. I'm not a teenage girl, or even your average woman—as arrogant and as offensive as that sounds.

"I got where I am, everything I ever wanted, by putting my feelings aside. My career, my status, my lifestyle... I've always put my feelings aside to pursue all of them. Do you remember what I told you when you wore that red dress for the first time?"

Mia smiles through the surprise and the seriousness at the flicker of this simple, affectionate memory. She nods gently.

"Something about..." she begins. "Feelings being a 'choice'—so feel beautiful."

"That's it, honey." I smile back.

After another long while, Mia says, "But there's a difference there, Maeve. A difference between wearing a dress and being in love with someone. Some feelings are too big to choose."

I say nothing, my own talents failing me as I struggle to think of an answer. I pick up my coffee cup but feel queasy at the thought of sipping, so I simply put it down again.

"Do you..." Mia asks, "*love him too?*"

I look up at Mia, my face full of defiant humor, composure and repose, but when I open my mouth, nothing comes out. Me—the sassy bitch with a smart reply for everything, the unshakable, infallible, archetype of a confident woman...

And I can't think of anything to say even to my closest confidant.

My lack of answer is all the answer even a stranger would need, let alone Mia. Seconds after she sees that I can't bring myself to reply, her face relaxes into a look of sympathy, as if I've just confessed that I have a deadly affliction. In a way, I have.

She looks away, as if wanting to give me some space for a moment to gather my thoughts, and I'm grateful for that semblance of intuitive compassion, to have a friend who knows me well enough to know when I need some time to collect myself.

She sips her chai, nibbles her panini, and an age seems to pass. I watch the people pass by outside, and listen to the couple in the corner occasionally break out into secretive laughter, as if their jokes wouldn't make sense to anyone but them. Probably they wouldn't.

"It was never a question of feelings," I say, still looking out the window, the words coming out as soon as my thoughts can compile into some sort of sense. "It was a question of reality. I've never wanted a relationship—never wanted to feel 'dependent.' Perhaps I'm just too selfish, but I'm fine with that. And especially now that I'm supposed to be a 'celebrity' with a brand to uphold... A brand all about being an independent woman who plays the field... And then there was always the fact that he's your brother—"

"Oh Maeve, you know I wouldn't do or feel or get in the way of—"

"I know, I know," I interrupt. "But even so, even with you being a sweetheart... It's a complication. And there's the fact that..." I trail off and sigh, suddenly exhausted with thinking about it. "It's a different world, Mia. Entirely new.

And I'm not used to 'exploring.' It's so easy for me to do the things that are difficult for others—"

"Are you talking about being fabulous?" Mia says with a smile.

"Essentially," I reply, with only a little humor. "But *this*... Relationships that aren't purely transactional. Giving more than I take from men... It's new to me."

"You know, I always thought you and Toby were two of a kind, Maeve."

"Perhaps that's just as much reason *not* to do anything," I reply. "Don't they say opposites attract?"

"Well, they also say 'takes one to know one'—so I'm not sure how much wisdom you can glean from simple clichés."

I laugh gently, glad for the respite of treating it all lightly.

"Maeve..." she says softly. "I can't tell you what to do. I can just tell you that whatever happens, it's not going to change our friendship."

"I know."

"And also..." She takes a while before picking up where she left off, "Love is worth it. I mean, we're different, obviously. You have your fashion and your parties... I had my ambitions and my neat little safe life... And I still do. But of course, you have to give up a little bit... Colin did too... But it's *worth* it, Maeve. I've got a beautiful little girl now. A person, a partner, who I share everything with—including the weight of my own mind. All my own little issues. And he shares his. And it's... It's amazing."

"I just don't know if I'd feel the same..." I tell her, wrenching the thought from deep within me.

"Talking about clichés," Mia says, smiling a little. "There's that one about 'not knowing what you've got till it's gone.' And it's always used in a negative way...like 'losing' something. But for me...with Colin and Alison now... Honestly, it's like I never realized how lonely I was until I found him. Weird as that sounds."

"It doesn't sound weird to me, sweetie."

"Well, I'm not saying you'd feel the same or... I don't know..." Mia says, taking a sip of her chai as she sorts her own thoughts out. "I suppose all I can really tell you with confidence is that sometimes feelings matter. Sometimes they're the only thing that can guide you right. Sometimes everything else is just...a dead end."

I sigh heavily and we sit in silence a while. I try to figure out a way that's she's wrong, while also struggling to believe that she's right.

"Darling, I'll tell you something."

"Go on."

"If I had never met you, I would be totally surrounded by superficial friends who would tell me what I want to hear, rather than what I needed to hear. I'd be sitting across from someone right now who'd be telling me that 'of *course* I'm too fabulous to have a real boyfriend' and that I should just use him to get my jewelry done before having a month of casual sex to forget him. It would be so much more easy and convenient."

Mia laughs, then says, "If you'd never met me, you would never have met Toby, so perhaps."

I laugh with her.

"Oh, that ship has sailed, crashed, and sunk long ago."

Mia's phone pings on the table and she checks it quickly, wincing as she does so.

"Crap. I have to go. Colin's got to head off to meet a client and I was supposed to take Alison anyway. But if you need me to stay a little longer, I guess I could—"

"Go, go," I say before she can feel guilty. "I already

dragged you away on a whim, and I should probably check in at work myself. Thank you, sweetie."

Mia's already stood up and is throwing her purse over her shoulder.

"Oh, Maeve..." she says with a warm smile. "It would... I always... Ugh... Never mind. Whatever happens, you'll always be my friend."

"Likewise," I say, as she leans down to hug me. "Just do me one favor."

"What?"

"Don't tell Toby that I told you all of this... I mean, I wouldn't be surprised if he decided to tell you anyway but... Oh, anyway, you're a terrible liar, you'll probably let it slip—but if you can—"

"I promise," Mia says. "Well...I promise I'll try. You know that I'm terrible at—"

"Yes, yes, honey. We all know you're terrible at keeping secrets."

She smiles sweetly one more time, pats me on the shoulder, and then darts for the exit of the café quickly, bringing her phone to her ear as she does so. I watch her go, then glance at my coffee and wonder why the hell I even ordered it.

25

TOBY

Let's meet.

Only two words to the text message, but they change everything.

Only two words, but it's the name above them that makes them important.

Maeve.

I text back quickly. *Can you come by my shop today?*

Her reply is almost as quick. *Neutral territory. No houses. No drinks. No people.*

I stare at the message in confusion for what feels like a minute but is probably just seconds. I'm in the backroom at work, having ditched a customer and rushed back there the second I saw that I had a message from her.

I rack my brain trying to think of a place, as if I'm solving a riddle. Too desperate to grasp this small window of opportunity she's giving me to let my mind wander into the bigger questions just yet.

What does she want? Why a neutral place? What is she going to say?

I dismiss the first few places that come to mind. An

abandoned warehouse on the outskirts that there are sometimes large raves in. The top level of a sky-high parking lot that gives incredible views of the city and always struck me as a good location for a movie confrontation.

Eventually I settle on a spot up in the hills that an old friend used to visit to stargaze. A dirt path through the trees just about big enough to fit a car through, ending in a small cliff that looks over the dark edge of the city. I send Maeve the location and stare at my phone, immediately regretting it, wondering what she'll make of it.

She replies with one word—*nine*—and the smile on my face might as well be plastered on for as much as I can remove it.

For the rest of the day, I barely exist, all of my thoughts entirely on the future, tonight, and what will happen. Emotions stuck in the past, replaying everything that's happened recently, the events of the party.

By five I'm still smiling—it *has* to be good, right? She *has* to have come to her senses. Why would she ask to see me if she still wanted nothing to do with me?

By seven the doubts creep in. Why neutral territory? Does she think I'm going to make a scene? Maybe she thinks that because she's about to put the final nail in. And no drinks... As if she doesn't want to lose herself again...

By eight-thirty I'm just confused, uncertain, and anxious, watching the seconds tick, feeling like everything, good or bad, is on the table.

I get to the spot early, parking beneath an indigo blue sky and stepping out onto the dirt. I lean back on the car and gaze out at the view, arched by the trees overhead. The eucalyptus- and jasmine-scented air feels light but full of secrets. Perhaps that's just the adrenaline in my body.

After glancing back at the path for every sound that

might be her, one of them turns out to be right. Headlights blinding me as her SUV brushes the leaves of the tight road before parking, facing the view ten feet away from me.

She opens the door and gets out. High heels, a shiny pencil skirt in jade green, and a loose white blouse. Despite everything, the complexity of our relationship, my intense curiosity about what she wants, the regretful turn we've taken—I feel such a pure lust for her. A lust that goes beyond simple attraction, and borders on ambition. I'm starting to doubt it'll ever die.

I step toward her and we approach each other, stopping when we're close enough to see the light in each other's eyes even in the dusk. She looks serious, but no longer cruel. I wait for her to make the first move.

"How would this even work?" she says eventually, her voice as natural as our surroundings.

"Us?" I ask.

She nods.

"I guess it's a 'figure-it-out-as-you-go' deal," I say.

After a few more seconds, Maeve breaks her gaze from me and turns to the cliff's edge, walking toward it and stopping a few steps from it. A few more seconds go by and I follow her until I'm standing a little behind her.

"You're afraid?" I say.

"You're not?" she says over her shoulder.

"I guess that's one of the benefits of being a reckless idiot."

I can't see her face, but I know she's smiling at that.

"I guess..." I continue, "we *make* it work. We start trusting each other. Start giving a little. Start fighting *for* each other as much as we fight against each other."

I put my hands on her shoulders and feel them relax

under my fingers, her tension softening a little, Maeve's heart of glass cracking.

"Give a little..." she repeats softly, as my hands move down to her upper arms, down to her stomach so that I can embrace her, pull her back into me—like I did once before, except this time the fire is more than sexual, the feeling more than sensual. A connection deeper than skin-on-skin. "It feels like giving too much."

I press my chin against her hair, closing my eyes as I relish for the first time just being this close to her—not as part of some game, not as some ritual toward an end, but simply for the sake of it.

"But think about what you'd get," I whisper quietly, my mouth close to her ear so she can hear me loud enough. Her hands move over mine as they rest on her front, the two of us sinking together, falling closer, merging and fitting together so well as if it proves my point. "What we'd *both* get. We could be *amazing*, Maeve."

She spins in my arms, liquid and smooth and perfect, like the move to a dance. I don't take my arms from around her, while hers search out my waist. I put a hand to her hair and stroke it gently, and she closes her eyes as if trying to resist how good it feels to be this way, but failing.

"I don't think we'd ever stop fighting," she says. "I don't think I'll ever become that person."

"I wouldn't want you to be," I tell her honestly. "I'll fight you for the rest of my life if that's what it takes to keep you."

She smiles and opens her eyes finally, and there's a look in them that's entirely new. A softness, a vulnerability, and truth from deep within her. A look I don't even think she'd show the mirror.

And it's beautiful in a whole new way. An entirely new universe of her beauty. Something so real that it drives

Chapter 25

home the stakes, and shakes something in my own core. A face she'll only ever show me, a place she'll only ever take me. Beyond that cage she's kept around her heart her whole life.

Her lips part and it's an invitation only I can read, as big as a billboard. I move my lips to hers and when they touch—even this lightly—I feel the pain and frustration and agonized yearning for her that I've been walking around with for weeks rush out of me. Her kiss is like a cure for something in my soul, healing wounds I never even knew existed until now. Her kiss is like a confirmation of a future I'd worried would never come. I tighten my embrace, as if afraid she might slip away like smoke once again. I keep my kiss light as if to ensure I make the most of it in case she does.

Eventually she pulls away, slowly. Her hands on my chest where she was gently grabbing my shirt. We look at each other, close up, eyes reading something beyond words in one another's gaze.

A million wordless promises being made, every aspect of our souls on show.

"So..." I mutter softly, "where do we begin?"

She smiles, sultry and knowing, eyes flashing a little of their pride, a little of her typical character returning to her face. She pushes me gently away.

"Follow my car," she orders, as she turns and walks toward it. I watch her go, feeling like I'm full of fuel and she just lit a match. Knowing that she knows I'm looking at her, that I love looking at her when she turns her back on me. I let the sight of her stir me, turn me on, get me hot, and then when she's in her car I get into mine.

I follow her all the way back to her place, where it all began. Returning to the scene of a crime we only half finished, only now ready to steal everything we can from this place, this moment, each other.

She's already reached her house by the time I park behind her car. I get out just in time to catch a glimpse of her stepping inside. She leaves the door open, and something about pursuing her like this is already driving me wild. Only Maeve could understand the need for a man to hunt, and make a game of playing the hunted.

I get inside the house just in time to see her slip off to the side, where the stairs are. After shutting the door behind me I move through the house after her. At the bottom of the stairs I see her at the top, looking back at me as she pulls her heels off and tosses them aside. I glare up at her, take my own shoes off as if participating in some ritual, and start taking the steps as she moves away again.

She hasn't turned a light on, so her home is only lit by the moon and the streetlights outside, angular shadows cutting shapes across the landing. I pause there, looking about me to guess which room she went in, then see the light emerging from the open bedroom door. As if wanting to tease me further, or simply because she's impatient, her pencil skirt is tossed out of the door, to lay in the hallway like a sign, an invitation. I stop to step out of my own pants and approach the door, pulling off my shirt as I round the corner.

She's lying on the bed, in nothing but her panties and bra, arms above her head as if stretching out in the sun, though it's dark. The moonlight through the shutters casting strips of light that catch every sensual curve and erotic line of her body.

I hold back a moment to appreciate the view as she raises one knee elegantly, ankle over her calf, twisting a little as she languishes in the bed—only Maeve could move the way a dancer can even when she's lying down.

And beneath my hunter's lust, my carnal hunger, my infinitely hard desire, there's another thought, another *feeling*. Something that makes this more than just sex, more than just attraction, more than the basic physical pleasures of two human beings. It was there before with her, but it was half formed then, a crude version that pained as much as it pleasured. Now, seeing her writhe for me, stepping toward her in the dark, it comes to me in more than words, in a physical sensation like a slow-working drug.

She's mine...not just tonight...and not just her body...

Mia was wrong. Finally. I *have* her, and I want her— only her—more than ever.

I step around to the side of the bed and she rolls over, all perfect ass and a flash of her teeth as she bites her lip in the dark. I move back around to the other side as if I'm staking territory, and she rolls over again, her back arching off the bed as her whole body throbs and stretches and twists, utterly hypnotic in the dark. I'm not sure which of us is teasing who anymore, and I'm not sure I even care.

The twining of her legs is so spellbinding I don't even notice her reach out and grasp my boxers, pulling them down as she takes me in her hand. She looks up at me, sharp eyes catching moonlight as she watches my expression intently, studying how I clench my teeth, narrow my eyes, tighten my neck muscles, entirely under her control.

She caresses my cock like a weapon, perfect long fingers threatening to be too rough as they clutch and stroke, but never too much, never enough. It's the sight of her as much as the sensation, seeing her perfect face outlined in the slivers of light as she brushes it against her cheek, nuzzles it appreciatively. Then she extends her tongue and draws it firm and slow up the length, as if urging forth the volcanic heat inside of me. And as I'm still reeling, head spinning and breath heavy, she does it again, except this time her lips linger at the tip, slow and soft and warm and wet, and it feels too good for me to even look, my head thrown back by what she's doing.

But I don't want her like this. It's not enough. As good as it is, I need more. I need to feel her. To taste her. To press my whole body against hers. I grab her arms and lift her before throwing her back onto the bed. She lets out a quick shriek, a laugh like a broken champagne glass, but I'm serious about how much I want her.

I move over her, between her thighs, walking on my fists like an ape as I glare down at her twisting body. She arches her back and undoes her bra, and when I peel it from her like an unveiling, the sudden glimpse of her breasts in a glimmer of light is too much to resist. I dive into her and bite. She lets out a hiss, a moan, the music I like. Somehow she wriggles out of her panties as I taste her skin, and then she kicks them away so that we're both naked now—more naked than we've ever been. Nothing but flesh and sweat, nothing but my hardness and her wetness. No more games, no more teasing, no more emotions and thoughts between us, just two people wanting to mix themselves until they're one.

I kiss her and it feels closer than before, closer than with anyone else. Tongues whipping and thrashing, spit and sweat, my grunts and her moans a duet, two heats turning into a fire. My weight on top of her, squeezing everything I can against her, a hand in her hair, another on the thigh she wraps around me. A knot being tied as tight as we can, she squirms and pulls her lips away to gasp for air as her pussy finds my cock, and I press further, making her gasp again. I lick her neck, her chin, her ear, ravenous for every pore of her.

A little more, another gasp, nails in my back now, digging and pulling. A little more, another gasp that ends in a wonderful, curled-toe moan. She lifts her shoulder and I understand what she wants as if I'm in her head as much as her body now. We roll over onto my back, her hands moving to my chest, and she pushes herself up to sit on me, blue light on her torso making me feel like I'm in some other realm, something too stunning to exist in any reality I've ever experienced. Her body a place I want to go deeper into, a place I don't want to leave.

On top of me she dances a slow, primal dance. Hips swinging back and forth, shoulders swaying side to side, back arching like her whole body is nothing but a beating heart now. Her face moves in and out of the light. A hint of the perfect pout on her swollen lips. Eyes half closed in ecstasy. A hand pushing back her hair. Neck extended as she throws her head back.

I put my hands on her waist, grab at her breasts, reach fingers up across her neck until my fingers are in her mouth, before trailing her saliva down her sweaty body. It feels like she's burying me with her beauty, suffocating me under the flawlessness of her body, her moans, *her*...

Rolling me and squeezing me and pressing me and pulling me until it's taking every ounce of self-control I can still muster to hold back, until I'm gripping her ass cheeks like I'm holding on for my life. Until her back starts arching more tightly, more quickly, like she's snapping into place. Until her moans turn into long squeals of agonizing closeness. Until her nails are almost drawing blood from my chest, my shoulders, my neck.

Until she presses her hips once more into me with the

full force of her back, and stretches in front of me, tall and proud, breasts out, head back, and lets out a loud scream so good to hear I have to let myself go.

She leans forward onto me, clutching my shoulders as the heat continues to burn, as her hips still grind and swing to a rhythm she can't control, a softness emerging where we join as if we've finally done it—we've finally become one, for a few moments at least. I pull the back of her head to me, the other on her ass, and pull her close, tight, into me, still wanting every bit of her that I can get.

Seconds, minutes, maybe a whole hour later, we emerge dazed, stirring groggily from our position clenching each other tight. Pulling apart only just enough so that we can see each other. Maeve slides off me to lie on her side, head on the pillow, our arms still around each other. Her face is soft again, her eyes catching the light in the dark. We gaze at each other like we've got all the time in the world.

"I love you," I say, the words coming up from somewhere deep.

Maeve smirks, her face demure and dignified despite her nakedness, despite this moment, despite what we've just done.

"I still hate you," she quips, sassily.

"I love the way you hate me," I say.

She smiles, letting go of the feistiness for a moment, perhaps remembering that she doesn't need it anymore—not with me.

"Then maybe I'll hate you forever," she says, shuffling closer to me so that I can kiss her softly.

I pull away and notice how slowly she opens her eyes, as if now that she's letting go, she doesn't want to go back to reality. Then, her haughtiness fades, revealing the gentleness beneath it.

Chapter 25

"I love you," she says.

"Wow..." I whisper with a smile. "So you *can* say it."

She looks happy, as if she's just discovered something wonderful.

"I *love* you..." she repeats, smiling even more broadly. "I love *you*... I love you. *I love you...*"

Over and over she says it, as if making up for all the times she didn't, as if just learning how to say it, as if enjoying how it sounds on her lips, as if it's the only thing she wants to say.

"*I love you... I love you... I l—*"

I shut her up by seizing her lips with mine. A kiss to tell her I feel the same. A kiss to tell her that I know. A kiss to tell her that there's no rush.

After all—we've got the rest of our lives to enjoy saying it.

EPILOGUE
MAEVE

It's our biggest department store, and yet it's still not big enough. The entire mall has been converted into a gala hall this evening for the event. My name, in my own flamboyant cursive, is emblazoned on several banners and stands around the mall. I had to argue and work for days to get the lighting just the right amount of dark so that the ice sculptures—an ironic nod to the past—can look fabulous shining in their various colors.

The real dramatic flourish, however, is the velvet curtains draped from the balconies of the mall's three levels. A different color for each floor, gathered and tapered with gold tassels.

I was doubtful at first, but Harriet went to great lengths to show me an example, and that's all it took for me to insist upon her idea. Now the mall looks like some fantastical dream of a seventeenth-century castle. And perhaps more importantly, there are corners, places to hide from the crowd—essential for any event to really become something special. I presume I'll be spending the entire evening giving credit to Harriet—and perhaps the rest of my career worrying that everybody will be seeking to poach my burgeoning protégé from me soon.

After plenty of urging I also indulged Brent's idea of balloons in shiny silver, gold, and black; he's done so much good work these past three months to get us here, to the launch. His other grand idea was to have the waitresses wear pieces of my jewelry as they walked the event with drinks and hors d'oeuvres—that one he didn't need to convince me so much on.

It'll be a simple affair. The mall's closed for the evening so that industry people, a few celebrities, and everyone involved with my jewelry line can attend and drink and peruse the displays of the final product. Indeed, it feels more like the culmination of something than the beginning. The real launch is tomorrow, when the collection will finally be up for sale, and when we'll see if Brent and Harriet's prediction that it'll sell out within a week is prudence or hubris.

"I can't believe you managed to make something this good in just three months," somebody tells me as we stand by a table display sipping our drinks.

"What can I say?" I shrug happily. "It's ironic there's just one name on the brand, because the whole thing only made me aware of how much help I needed."

Saying it, I immediately think of Toby, and glance around the crowd for the fiftieth time tonight looking for him. For the past couple of months we've worked closely, intensely—as close and as intense as everything else between us—on the jewelry. At one point I was certain the collection would be no more than five pieces, and even two of those doubtful. Me agonizing over every detail, Toby creating dozens of designs for me to look over. Me asking for the impossible, Toby pulling out all the stops to make it happen.

In the end it's twelve pieces total, each one more than perfect, as if they're imbued with the passion and desire between us. It turns out we make a good team. Turbulent, but in the most productive way.

And now that the time has come to reap the rewards, I can't even find him. He was supposed to be here early, but it's past nine and he's somehow still missing in action. I curse him a little under my breath, and promise myself to scold him when I finally get my hands on him again. Instead, I notice another welcome face close to the entrance.

"Speaking of which... I'll speak to you later," I tell my companion as I pat her on the shoulder and move past her.

"Maeve!"

"Mia!" I call, as we embrace tightly before I push her away to appreciate her dress. "My God, where did you find that skirt? It's *perfect* on you."

I see Colin emerge from the crowd behind her, carrying Alison in his arms. The baby is wearing the star-spangled velour onesie I bought for her recently, and she looks like the perfect little angel. I immediately rush over to Colin.

"And a husband almost as perfect," I say, giving him a hug before nuzzling my nose against Alison's until she gurgles a little laugh. "How are you, sweetie?"

"I hope it's all right bringing Alison," Mia asks. "We couldn't find anyone to babysit and—"

"It's fine, honey," I say, waving her concern away. "It's all very 'family friendly' tonight."

"Is Toby around?" Colin asks.

"No," I say, a little taken aback. "I thought he might be arriving with you."

I look at both of them, and they look at each other, all of us mildly confused. Mia shrugs and turns to me.

"We haven't heard from him in a few days, actually."

I frown, only now realizing that I haven't heard from him in a few days either. Preparations for the launch keeping me so busy I'd not even noticed.

"Well," I sigh, "it was a fun affair while it lasted, but I suppose me killing him when I see him is as appropriate a way to end it as any."

Colin laughs and says, "I'm sure he has a good reason."

"Oh, I'm sure he'll write a whole book of excuses. Anyway, come with me, I want to introduce you to a few people..."

I lead them on a brief circuit of the growing party, getting them drinks and eventually stopping to form a little group with Harriet and Brent—who are both smitten with Alison more than anything else.

For a few moments, the conversation isn't centered on me, and I allow myself to settle into a comfortable silence, watching people I'm close to, people I love, interact and enjoy each other's company. The simple pleasure of real friends, of trust and comfort, of a child's smile. My jewelry, the event, my ego, all slipping away and being replaced by a warm softness in my soul. An openness to love. Still new enough to feel strange to me, still a little frightening, but it's a feeling that makes all others pale in comparison.

And yet the man who introduced me to it still hasn't shown up...

"Would you excuse me a second? I'm going to go look for Toby one more time before I have him assassinated."

I peel away from the group and make the rounds, careful not to miss a greeting, allowing myself to be slowed by the numerous congratulations and questions.

As I'm slipping past a curtain, I hear a strangely familiar, yet not quite placeable, man's voice call me.

"Hey there."

I turn to it and immediately smile.

"Asher..." I reply, surprised but pleasantly so. "How are you? I haven't seen you since—"

"The party?" He smiles.

"Yes." I smile. "Last thing I remember is you being dredged out of the pool."

He laughs and raises his glass. "Bruises heal, but a good story lasts forever."

"What are you doing here?"

"Toby invited me."

"Toby? You've spoken to him since—"

"Sure," Asher says with a broad smile. "I see him almost every week at soccer. We've formed a pretty good understanding on the field—when he isn't being greedy with the ball, of course."

"He never told me..."

"I imagine you've got better things to talk about," Asher says.

I smile and shrug. He's right. Three months with Toby and it still feels like a spontaneous, chaotic, hedonistic first date. We still live in the moment with each other, still fuck and fight like we're as much enemies as lovers—and I still love him more than anything.

"Have you seen him at all, sweetie?" I ask. "I've been looking for him all evening and he was supposed to arrive early..."

"I did actually," Asher says, looking upwards and gesturing with his glass to the third-floor balcony. "You know that outdoor terrace they have here? Up on the roof where the cafés are? I saw him going out there."

I frown at Asher, then up at where he's pointing, wondering why the hell Toby would be out there—but half the things Toby does make me wonder why the hell he's doing them.

"Thanks. I guess I'll go look for him then."

Asher nods and I flash him a warm smile before turning and making for the elevator. There are only a few party stragglers on the top floor, people who carried their drinks all the way up there for the view, or a little privacy. There's hardly anyone in the corner that leads outside to the terrace Asher mentioned. I almost wonder if he made a mistake somehow, if he meant somewhere different, but curiosity drives me on to the glass doors that lead outside.

Through the glass it's hard to see anything outside, but I catch a glimpse of something that looks like a figure, and when I push the door open, I immediately recognize him, even though his back is to me. He's wearing a suit I picked out for him, leaning over the railings that look out across the city lights. The cool night air feels still and stark compared to the warmth and bodies of the party inside. I step through and let the door close behind me, the sound of the event now nothing but a low, muffled hum.

"Toby," I say as I step toward him. "What are you doing out here?"

He turns to face me, the man I love, and when I'm close enough he puts his arms around my waist and pulls me into him like a storm. Kissing me like his life depends on it. Only letting me go once he's satisfied himself on my lips, though he continues to hold me close.

"I've been looking for you all night," I whisper, my hands fingering the buttons on his shirt.

"I've been waiting for you to find me all night."

"You've been... Why would you stay up here? What are you doing?"

He smiles, sighs, looks out at the city as if to refresh himself before looking back at me, something knowing and important in his eyes.

"*What am I doing?*" he repeats. "Exactly. I've got the most drop-dead gorgeous, talented, charismatic tiger of a woman... And she keeps throwing parties where hundreds of guys fawn and fight over her... And she's about to become a worldwide icon... And I'm here acting like she's all mine."

"I don't think they're quite courageous—or perhaps crazy—enough, to try like you did."

"Crazy..." he repeats again. "I'm definitely crazy for you, Maeve."

"Toby..." I say, simply for the joy of saying his name, pressing my face against his chest. Enjoying how I can be like this with him. Purely affectionate. Nothing but loving. He strokes my hair and I purr into him.

"How do you like your jewelry?" he asks.

"It's perfect," I say. "You worked a miracle for me."

"You haven't seen the best part yet."

I'm so confused by what he means I pull away to look into his eyes, but there's still a mystery in them, a secret he hasn't told yet.

"This," he says, reaching into his pocket, "was the last piece I made. Except it's not for sale. It's one of a kind. Like you."

I'm complete ice, frozen still as he brings the ring box up before me, in the close space between us, and opens it to reveal a ring set with a deep pink-orange gem so fiery and bold it seems more like a soul than a stone.

He says, "I know you might think this is too—"

"*Yes,*" I interrupt him quickly. I look from the stone up

to his eyes. "Toby. *Yes*." I reach up and place a hand against his face, as if just looking at him isn't enough. "You don't need to give me the pitch, warn me of the dangers, or tell me how you feel. I know what I want."

He presses his cheek back into my palm, turning slightly to kiss it. I peel it away and hold it out for him. Carefully, he takes the ring from the box and places it on me. I can't help holding out my hand to admire it, and the sherry pink glow of the gem against my skin is so perfect, it's hard not to believe it's always been there on my finger.

"It's an Imperial topaz," he says. "The stone of confidence...nobility...purpose. I've had this stone since I first started my shop. It's always been there, just waiting in the safe, and I never found the right project for it. Almost as if I *knew* it would be important, that something would happen eventually, where it would make sense..."

"'Every stone has a story,' right, darling? Isn't that what you say?"

He looks at my hand as he studies the ring on it, turning it gently.

"Funny thing..." he says. "The person I bought it from told me it was cursed."

I drop my smile and glare at him suddenly.

"*Cursed?*"

Toby laughs and puts his own hand on my face now.

"That's the thing, Maeve. That's what you made me realize..."

"What?"

He takes his time before answering, looking at me with so much of his soul in his eyes that I feel almost overwhelmed.

"That if you love someone enough, no matter what's

'meant' to happen, or who you are, or what's in your way... You've always got the power to change the story."

For once in my life, I can't think of anything to say. No witty retort, no sassy comeback.

The only response that makes sense, the only way to express this new kind of love, is to move my lips to his as he brings his to mine in a kiss that feels like it just might last forever.

Want to be informed when it goes live?
Sign up for my newsletter. You know how much I want to be in your box.

Want more Bad Boy romance?

Check out BS Boyfriend

She's the perfect fiancée... except for the perfect stranger part.

Being single wasn't a problem until it was... to my new boss.

So I picked the hottest girl out of the crowd, as though there was any chance she wasn't already promised to some other alpha jerk.

Turns out she was a unicorn.

Single, willing to play along, and oh so dedicated to her role as my wife-to-be. In dinners with the boss and even more so in the executive suite.

It's the most fun a guy can have at a work conference.

But what if I want to keep having fun?

What if she does too? It's just a flight away. So easy. But making it easy means wondering just what things could be like if we kept faking it.

Guess I forgot to ask her.

Get BS Boyfriend now, FREE in Kindle Unlimited

ALSO BY JD HAWKINS

Behaving Badly Series
Playing Doctor
Bad Boy Benefits
BS Boyfriend

Cocky Men Series
Cocky Chef
Flawless
All In

Bad Boys Series
Confessions of a Bad Boy
Love and Ink
Unprofessional
Temptation

Insatiable Series
Insatiable
Booty Call
The Bet

PAIGE PRESS

Paige Press is dedicated to bring you hot romances from amazing authors

Started by *Laurelin Paige*, her publishing company now features even more romance.

Sign up for our newsletter to get the latest news about our releases and receive a free book from one of our amazing authors:

Stella Gray
CD Reiss
Jenna Scott
Raven Jayne
JD Hawkins
Poppy Dunne

ABOUT THE AUTHOR

JD Hawkins writes erotic romance with modern-classic alpha males and strong, independent women. He currently lives with his wife in Los Angeles, CA. He loves to travel and has lived in many places, including New York City, India and Thailand. When he isn't writing, JD enjoys surfing, training in Mixed Martial Arts, reading and taking naps. He's always loved making up stories, especially ones inspired by real life.

Made in United States
North Haven, CT
04 August 2022